STUDIES IN ROMANCE LANGUAGES: 16

D1607823

THE BOOK OF COUNT LUCANOR AND PATRONIO

A Translation of Don Juan Manuel's
El Conde Lucanor

John E. Keller & L. Clark Keating

THE UNIVERSITY PRESS OF KENTUCKY

ISBN: 9780813152936

Library of Congress Catalog Card Number: 76-024342

Copyright © 1977 by The University Press of Kentucky

A statewide cooperative scholarly publishing agency
serving Berea College, Centre College of Kentucky,
Eastern Kentucky University, The Filson Club,
Georgetown College, Kentucky Historical Society,
Kentucky State University, Morehead State University,
Murray State University, Northern Kentucky University,
Transylvania University, University of Kentucky,
University of Louisville, and Western Kentucky University.

Editorial and Sales Offices: Lexington, Kentucky 40506

Contents

Translators' Introduction

Prince Don Juan Manuel's life reads like a historical novel.[1] Machiavelli might have used the prince as a model, since he drifted across the line dividing patriotism from treason. As a military strategist he was both bold and adroit. As a gentleman, sophisticated, polished, and educated quite probably beyond most of his contemporaries; as a sportsman and hunter; and as a paterfamilias par excellence, he could be matched with the great Renaissance gentlemen to come after him. And yet he also excelled in a quieter sphere. No Spaniard of his times surpassed him as scholar, thinker, and writer. Few read more widely or studied in as many diverse areas; no layman delved as deeply into philosophy and religion; and no one, layman or cleric, wrote more copiously. The list of his titles is as remarkable in its diversity as it is impressive in its length.

Now this is saying a great deal of a man living in a time when the cultural heritage of the "Alfonsine Renaissance of the thirteenth century" continued to blossom and to affect literary and cultural activity. Due to the wars and revolts, the plague, and the many dynastic woes that beset the country, some mistakenly assume that fourteenth-century Spain was an unproductive period when the nobility were roughnecked barons who cared little about books. No doubt many barons were of this ilk. But literary productivity proves that scholars did live in Spain and write in Spanish, and of course in Latin and Arabic, that cultural and human values continued, and that a reading public existed, especially among the nobility. Lyric poets of note like the Marqués de Santillana, who introduced the sonnet into Spain, flourished. Juan Ruiz wrote, contemporaneously with Don Juan Manuel, the greatest masterpiece of the Spanish Middle Ages.[2] Indeed, his *Libro de buen amor*, in the view of some of the best scholars, ranks with *La Celestina* and even *Don Quijote;* and from the impact of this book upon other writers, even into the fifteenth century, we are certain

1

that it was highly esteemed. Another significant author, a nobleman of consequence, was Pero López de Ayala whose *Rimado de Palacio* written in the *mester de clerecía* (fourteen-syllabled monorhymed quatrains) shows great erudition. His histories, the equal possibly of those of the Alfonsine period and of even better quality than Don Juan Manuel's *Crónica abreviada*, are noteworthy accomplishments. They treat the reigns of four Spanish monarchs—Peter the Cruel, Henry II, John I, and Henry III. López de Ayala even became the chancellor of Castile. He may be the author of the *Proverbios del sabio Salomón*. Pero López de Ayala was sixteen when Don Juan Manuel died, so his Spain was that of the great *cuentista*.

Important, too, was the Rabbi Sem Tob, who wrote in the first half of the century his *Proverbios morales*, the quintessence of wisdom concisely couched. Its aim was to persuade mankind to accept philosophically, and even joyfully, the reverses of life. Using the popular language of the Spanish people and drawing upon Eastern sources, particularly the Bible, the rabbi reached many people and was imitated by many, including the famous Marqués de Santillana. Menéndez Pidal considered the *Proverbios morales* to be the first occurrence in Spanish of gnomic literature. It was finished between 1355 and 1360, only a few years after Don Juan Manuel's death in 1348.

Someone, probably a monk, produced in the same period the *Libro de miseria de omne*, patterning it after the *Contemptu mundi* of Pope Innocent III. Along with biblical and profane considerations of the wretchedness and the defects of humankind, it contained hagiographical brief narratives. It is regarded as a valuable analysis of the social classes of the period, replete with pungent satire. Paralleling the purpose of the *Libro de miseria de omne* were two other didactic works which reveal the importance in the fourteenth century of philosophical appraisals of human life. Pedro de Veragüe composed a poetic *Doctrina de la discreción*, considered by many to be the oldest catechism in Spanish. And an unknown cleric wrote the *Revelación de un ermitaño*, which perpetuated the format and purpose of the thirteenth-century debates that did so much to develop the medieval drama.

Other valuable historical works were the *Crónicas* of Fernán Sánchez de Valladolid (1315-1359), a historian who wrote of the reigns of Alfonso X and Sancho IV, the oft-mentioned cousin and contemporary of Don Juan Manuel. There was also the *Poema de Alfonso Onceno*, a long epic-narrative poem about the wars of King Alfonso XI. And

2

considering epics, once so popular, the only surviving manuscript of the greatest epic Spain ever produced, the *Poema de Mío Cid*, was penned in 1307. While this remarkable document, a truly unique literary masterpiece, was composed much earlier, possibly around 1140, the fact that a certain Per Abbat copied it when he did proves that fourteenth-century people esteemed their epic heritage.[3] Of this period, too, was the well-known history of the Crusades called the *Gran conquista de Ultramar*, based upon French sources. The chapters which relate the legend of the Swan Knight contain one of the best and most attractive novelesque pieces of the Middle Ages.

One work of the period which was perhaps read assiduously as a guide for gentlemen from Don Juan Manuel's times through the seventeenth century—in courage, war, courtship, and manners—was *Amadís de Gaula*, Spain's most famous novel of chivalry. It is true that from the fourteenth century we have knowledge of this novel only from one mention of it made between 1345 and 1350 and from a fragment. But even these indicate that it existed in Don Juan Manuel's time, and its presence in the fourteenth century points to the respect that the gentry had for human values.

More consonant with the fiction of Don Juan Manuel's *Conde Lucanor* is the *Caballero Cifar*, to be viewed later. It is mentioned here as the first novel of chivalry and the first Byzantine romance in the Spanish language, since it dates from around 1300. Then, too, there was the translation of the Eastern novelesque work entitled *La doncella Teodor*, one of the first Spanish books in which a good woman is not only the protagonist, but the superior, in wit and courage, of men.

Men of the fourteenth century were familiar with the classic literature of Greece and Rome usually in the form of epitomes, florelegias, and commentaries prepared in the previous century at the behest of Alfonso X. But at least one work ultimately traceable to the ancient world was written in Don Juan Manuel's time. This was the *Crónica troyana*, not to be confused with the thirteenth-century *Historia troyana polimétrica*. Its origin is interesting, for it shows the close ties between French and Spanish letters. Its immediate source was the *Roman de Troie* of Benoît de Sainte-Maure. Some attribute it to Pero López de Ayala.

A work of great erudition for the times, and one worthy of the *studia* of Alfonso X, was *Los lucidarios*, attributed to the patronage of Sancho IV. It is a compendium of diverse knowledge that was to form a

3

bridge between medieval and Aristotelian philosophy and wisdom. Far more than a book of great philosophical and scientific truths, it was a source of specific instruction, allowing the student to acquaint himself with the rudiments of new scientific knowledge along with fundamental questions concerning theology placed beside the pagan parallels of Aristotle. The *Lucidarios* provides answers the good Christian in search of knowledge needed to know. With the dialectical approach—master and disciple talk as questions are asked and answered—the reader could prepare himself for the disputes which played so important a role in medieval education. This remarkable book reaffirms that Spanish letters were sophisticated.

Lastly, there was a work usually known as *El Corbacho* by Martínez de Toledo, archpriest of Talavera. Its varied and numerous sources reveal the author as the most cosmopolitan of men, insofar as literary backgrounds are concerned, in the fourteenth century.

Clearly, then, in that waning of the Middle Ages so artfully studied by Huizinga, fourteenth-century Spain was no barren wilderness of war and ignorance, but a place whose literary activity did much to lay the foundations of the Spanish Renaissance. An age that could produce writers like Juan Ruiz, Pero López de Ayala, and Don Juan Manuel had to be an age of culture.[4]

Don Juan Manuel lived, then, in a time of literary activity among many writers with whom he could converse and a reading public for which he could write. He knew his world thoroughly with all its complexities of races, religions, and cultures. Spain's classical past, as well as her Gothic heritage left its mark upon him; the quasi-oriental world of Spanish Islam and Spanish Jewry constantly impinged upon his thoughts, his writings, and his life. And the Church, which he respected and supported, was an ever-present guide and a balance against the secular world. Sophisticated, highly educated, trained in government, politics, warfare and its strategy, steeped in theology and philosophy, he was eminently qualified to gather and select the best materials and to write what some consider the best Spanish prose before Cervantes. His deep love of letters glows in his works. Comparing his prose with the best written before reveals the efforts he made to attain perfection and polish, to eradicate the vulgar, the unseemly, and the irrelevant. What he strove to produce was a *lenguaje culto* that could be understood and easily absorbed by his contemporaries, even by those who could not read but only listen to what was read to them.

4

He knew the worth of clarity, of a pure but not too rich vocabulary, of structure and grammar; and he was very well aware, indeed, of the value of catching and holding attention and of pleasing his audience.

Don Juan Manuel has been called vain and ambitious for literary fame. Perhaps he was. Certainly he made every effort to preserve all that he wrote, because he believed in his books and regarded them as contributions to posterity. He is quite frank when he writes that an excellent author should properly rejoice when he completes a fine book and realizes that it has gained success and esteem. His own writings reveal how distraught and even furious he became when someone knowingly, innocently, or carelessly marred his work. Since books had to be copied by hand, the danger of corrupting or damaging an author's lines lay in the hands of copyists. In his *Prologo General*, Don Juan illustrated in a delightful little anecdote what he feared and how he would react if he found his works warped or miscopied. The prince begins the prologue with an explanation of the pleasure a craftsman should take in a work well done and of the grief and annoyance he could rightly feel when he discovers that someone, deliberately or even innocently, does or says something through which the work will not be esteemed and praised as it should be. He goes on to prove the point by recounting something that happened to a knight in Perpignan in the days of the first King James of Mallorca:[5]

So it was, that a certain knight was a great troubadour and he composed fine songs and wondrously, and he wrote one exceptionally well and it had a fine melody. So delighted were folk with it that they would hear no song but that one, and the knight who had composed it was much gratified. Then one day as he rode along the street he heard a shoemaker singing that song so badly, both as to the words and the melody, that anyone who listened, if he had not heard it beforehand, considered it a poor piece and badly composed.

When the knight who had written it heard how that shoemaker was ruining his good work, he grieved and was vexed. Therefore he got off his horse and sat down near the shoemaker. The shoemaker took no notice of this and kept on singing, and the more he sang, the worse he garbled the knight's song. As the knight listened to his fine song so distorted by the coarseness of the shoemaker, he quietly took out some scissors and cut up all the shoes the man had made. And after he had done so he mounted and left.

When the shoemaker glanced at his shoes and when he saw that they had been cut to pieces, he realized that he had toiled for naught and he was in great distress. And so he went shrieking after the knight who had done it.

The knight said to him, "My friend, our lord the king is here and you know that he is a fine king and very just. Let's go to him and leave it to him to do what is right."

They agreed and as soon as they stood before the king, the shoemaker told him how the knight had cut all his shoes to pieces and had ruined him. And the king was wroth at this and asked the knight if it were true. The knight replied that it was, but that the king ought to hear why he had done it. So the king commanded him to say why, and the knight reminded him that he knew that the song he had written was very good and with a rare melody; and he told him how the shoemaker had distorted it, and asked the king to have the man sing it. And as soon as the king heard him sing it he saw the truth.

Then the knight said that because the shoemaker had ruined the fine work he had produced and that he had been greatly damaged thereby, he had destroyed the shoemaker's work. And the king and all who heard it were delighted and they enjoyed a good laugh over it. Then the king ordered the shoemaker to sing that song no more, thereby spoiling the knight's fine work, but he reimbursed the fellow for his loss and told the knight not to disturb him again.[6]

Don Juan Manuel's respect for letters, his near-modernity of approach and aim, and his escape in times of stress into the world of literature, are appealing. His esteem for his own writings, according to Valbuena Prat, seems the first evidence of a truly narcissistic feeling expressed in Spanish letters. One could argue with some reason, however, that Gonzalo de Berceo and Juan Ruiz were far from modest about their works.

Between Don Juan Manuel and his literary goals lay long years of ambitious and often Machiavellian efforts to make his and his family's future secure. How he found time for scholarly pursuits is difficult to understand. Perhaps his success is explained by his ability to escape from the active world of politics and warfare into the world of letters. In any event, some statement about his life should be given, if only to evince the duality of the prince's existence.

Born a prince royal on May 5, 1282, though not in direct line to rule, he was the son of Prince Manuel, brother of the Learned King Alfonso X, El Sabio, whose works greatly influenced Don Juan, even though he scorned that monarch's ability to rule. His mother was Doña Beatriz of Savoy, whose background and heritage opened to him still other doors to culture and learning. Don Juan Manuel was to become one of a long line of Spanish royalty who loved learning and aspired to cultivate it in the realm. Perhaps this trend had begun with his grandfather, Fernando III, known as El Santo. And his uncle, Alfonso X, of all medieval monarchs the most erudite and intellectual, had gone even further to sponsor learning in many areas—music, poetry, pictorial art, the sciences, law, history, and the art of fiction. Alfonso had also assembled a remarkable library which contributed much to Don Juan Manuel's education. The prince grew up, then, in an atmosphere of culture, and he profited by his opportunities. He studied much and acquired surprising knowledge in a wide variety of fields. And he wrote more books than any Spanish writer during or before his times. It is a pity that the Learned King died when Don Juan was only two years old, for had he lived, and if the child had matured under his tutelage, the prince might have accomplished still more.

King Alfonso's successor, his son Sancho IV, El Bravo, was far less interested in the arts and in culture. But apparently he was a good cousin to Don Juan Manuel, for he seems to have respected him and to have made certain that the lad was not overlooked, although he never saw him until he was twelve. The prince's rearing was at first undertaken by his mother, since his father died when he was two. Doña Beatriz proved a remarkable woman, gifted with courage and determination, and with a grasp of what the education of a prince should be. She showed her independence when she suckled the child herself, when it was common practice to entrust this duty to a wetnurse. When she died her son was eight years old; but the plans for his education she had begun went ahead uninterrupted, since she had provided him with the best of *ayos*, or guardians. These men, as Don Juan later wrote in chapter 67 of his *Libro de los estados*, followed the queen's directions closely. The child had learned to read by the time he was five. At that same age he had begun to study Latin, which he learned to read, to write, and even to speak exceptionally well for a layman. His training also embraced the study of the law, scripture, music, the arts, and history. Books, of course, were available in the vast Alfonsine compilations. Naturally, his *ayos* did not neglect such practical and necessary matters as horseback riding, military science, hunting, and the social graces.

It would be pleasant to turn aside and peruse Don Juan's delightful and informative comments about his youth and education in the *Libro de los estados:* of how, for example, he did not have to study on Sunday, but devoted his time to riding and to conversation with his friends and mentors; of how each day was carefully planned, with study generally scheduled for the morning and exercise and rest for the afternoon; and of how he spent Saturdays reviewing the week's work. Apparently the prince valued his training, because he recommended it strongly to teachers and guardians of all royal and noble children, adding that care should be exercised to prevent teachers from pampering their charges if the children were disinclined to work. He mentioned several times that he went to great lengths to provide for his own son's education.

When, in 1294, Don Juan Manuel was twelve, King Sancho sent him to Murcia, on the Moorish frontier, to represent the family and to learn the arts of warfare and government. Naturally, he was not sent into battle at this tender age, but he saw his pennon carried against the enemy and his troops return victorious; and he saw, also, the dead and the wounded. Thus he became familiar with war, whose very existence he came to hate, even in childhood.

Apparently Don Juan Manuel had not met his cousin the king and had never been presented at court. But in September of the same year his guardians presented him at last to his royal cousin in Valladolid. Soon thereafter he was obliged to entertain the king when the latter, seeking relief from the illness which would soon kill him, rested for a time in Don Juan Manuel's castle of Peñafiel. The cousins seem to have become friends, or at least to have recognized one another's worth. Certainly when the king lay dying in the rural village of Madrid, he sent for Don Juan Manuel and conversed with him lengthily and often in the presence of royal counselors. Sancho died reassured by his cousin that he would support Sancho's heir to the dynasty, a vow he was not always able to keep.

After the king's death, Castile again plunged into bitter civil war and chaos. A. Giménez Soler treats this strife in great detail. It is a moving but unpleasant story, and one best left to historians, save for the parts that touch closely the life of Don Juan Manuel. His trouble began with the succession of Fernando IV, whom many of the nobles refused to recognize as king. James II of Aragon supported the son of Alfonso X's eldest son, the dead Fernando de la Cerda, whose children Sancho had set aside and forced to flee for safety to Aragon. Since Don Juan Manuel supported Sancho's heir, James seized his holdings in Murcia, including the important city of Elche, one of Don Juan Manuel's most valued properties. The cost of patriotism, he learned, was high; the lesson was not wasted upon him.

When he was nineteen, Don Juan Manuel married the princess of Mallorca, Isabel; when she died in 1301, he saw the wisdom of winning the support of Aragon. To that end, he proposed marriage to the king's daughter Constanza, then a child of six and therefore not ready for wedlock. Until she reached the age of twelve, when she could be married, Don Juan agreed to house his betrothed in Alcalá de Villena. Meanwhile he regained King James's friendship, since part of the betrothal contract had been that James would support Don Juan against his enemies and restore his lands in Murcia. Fortunately, it was also agreed that in case of war between Aragon and Castile, Don Juan would not be called upon to fight his own people.

When Constanza was twelve in 1311, Don Juan married her. He was twenty-nine. If he had hoped to spend much time with his new bride, he was disappointed. In that same year the young Castilian king, Fernando IV, died, and again there was civil war. The successor to the throne, the child Alfonso XI, was quickly crowned; but he ruled under a regency—Queen María de Molina, his mother, Don Juan Manuel, his cousin, and Don Felipe, another relative. During this period Don Juan Manuel naturally played an active role in politics. Ambitious and ruthless, he longed to maintain his position, especially after the queen's death in 1321; but by then the boy Alfonso, probably influenced by other nobles, abolished the regency and removed Don Juan Manuel from power.

Clever politician that he was, Don Juan believed that he could regain some of his losses by offering the hand of his daughter Constanza, named after her mother, to the young King Alfonso XI. Indeed, at first it seemed that he would succeed, since actual betrothal was contracted. At the last minute, however, for reasons not clearly known, the king broke the contract and rejected Constanza.

It was after this that Don Juan Manuel made one of his greatest mistakes, revealing an inability to endure slights. Disillusioned and furious at the insult to his daughter, and therefore to his house, he deserted Castile and declared war upon his sovereign. He even committed a far more serious kind of treason: he sent a letter to the Moorish king of Granada seeking support and offering to join him in the intermittent war with Christian Spain. The letter fell into the hands of Alfonso XI and would have led to a complete and irreparable breach but for Don Juan's importance to Castile, which the king and his advisors fully recognized. A pact was made, therefore, which restored Don Juan to all his rights and privileges. More surprising still was the restoration of his governorship of Murcia.

Still vigorous at the age of thirty-nine, when the rupture between himself and the king occurred, Don Juan wanted additional heirs, since he had only two daughters, Constanza and Juana. His wife Constanza had died in 1327. He therefore married in the same year as his treason and its forgiveness (1329) the daughter of one of Spain's great families, Doña Blanca Núñez de Lara, and soon he had by her his beloved son and heir, Fernando, for whom much later he wrote the *Libro infinido*, or *Libro de los castigos*.

It has been noted that the six years from 1329 to 1335 marked the period of Don Juan's greatest literary activity. Recall that he not only deeply involved himself in the war with the Moors during these years, but also broke twice more with Alfonso XI, who on the first occasion in 1334 laid waste his lands, because Don Juan had failed to support him in the siege of Gibraltar. The second break came in 1335, when Don Juan was forty-three years old, brought about when he again deserted the realm in the belief that Alfonso had prevented his marriage to the daughter of the king of Portugal. On this occasion Alfonso besieged Peñafiel itself, but Don Juan had sagaciously quit the stronghold to flee to the safety of Valencia, under the sway of Aragon. From the safety of that city he eventually made peace with Alfonso and supported him when Spanish armies captured Algeciras at the Battle of Salado in 1337.

Soon thereafter Don Juan arranged the marriage of his son to the daughter of Ramón Berenguer, King James's youngest son. Don Juan was not to know, although the knowledge would have pleased him greatly, that his daughter, Doña Juana, would wed no less a personage than Enrique de Trastámara, later to rule as Enrique II (1369-1390), the grandfather of Isabella the Catholic.

For the next few years Don Juan spent most of his time in Murcia, where as a man in his fifties, with his children married, he could devote himself to ruling his estates and to writing. He died on June 13, 1348, at the age of sixty-six and was buried, according to his wishes, in the monastery of the Dominicans which he had established at his favorite castle at Peñafiel and where he had placed all his books for safekeeping.

Pride of authorship caused the prince to list his titles twice: in the general prologue to his complete works, and in the short prologue to *El Conde Lucanor*. José Manuel Blecua in his introduction to his edition of *El Conde Lucanor* (see bibliography) presents both lists in parallel columns, which we reproduce here.[7] The asterisks indicate those works which have survived.

Prologo General	*Conde Lucanor*
* *Libro de las armas*	* *Crónica abreviada*
* *Castigos y consejos a su hijo*	*Libro de los sabios*
* *Libro de los estados*	*Libro de la cavallería*
* *Libro del cavallero et del escu-*	* *Libro del infante*
dero	* *Libro del cavallero et . . .*
Libro de la cavallería	* *Libro del Conde [Lucanor]*
* *Crónica abreviada*	* *Libro de la caza*
Crónica complida	*Libro de los engennos*
Libro de los engennos	*Libro de los cantares*
* *Libro de la caza*	
Libro de las cantigas	
Reglas de trovar	

Some of these titles do not coincide from list to list: the *Libro de los estados* in the general prologue is listed in the prologue to *El Conde Lucanor* as *El libro del infante*. All of Don Juan Manuel's works are literary in the sense that they are carefully and artistically written with a conscious effort to present a clear and pleasing style. They include histories; political, military, or legalistic tracts; topics like falconry, chivalry, and even pietistic matters; and, most important to us, the collection of brief narratives known as *El Conde Lucanor*, or *Libro de Patronio*.

Since none of the works aside from the *El Conde Lucanor* contains brief narratives, this is not the place to describe them in detail. Even so, in the interest of giving the reader something like a concise account of the prince's literary activities, some brief and explanatory treatment is needed. The lost works, some of which would be more valuable to literary studies than some of the extant works, are these: the *Libro de los sabios*, whose content is not identifiable (it might have contained almost anything), is only mentioned by Don Juan Manuel once, and then in the prologue of *El Conde Lucanor;* the *Libro de cavallería*, extracts from which have been discovered, as Blecua reminds us in chapters 66 and 85 of the *Libro de los estados*, indicate that it was a book treating chivalry itself, and possibly was reminiscent of a similar book written in Catalan by Ramon Lull, a sage much admired by Don Juan Manuel; we know nothing definite about the *Crónica complida*, but since there is extant Don Juan's *Crónica abreviada*, the *Complida* was obviously a more extensive history; the *Libro de los engennos* must almost surely have been a treatise on siege weapons and other war machines; the *Libro de las cantigas*, also listed as the *Libro de los cantares*, must have been an anthology of poems, for poetry delighted Don Juan Manuel, and since he wrote another book which was almost certainly an *ars poetica*—that is, the *Reglas de trovar*—it is unlikely that the *Libro de las cantigas* would have been a second treatise on the art of versification. The extant books, most of which are not on literary subjects, are nonetheless valuable as studies of the times; and, even more important, they reveal a good deal about the author's life, since he had a penchant for placing himself in his various works (Blecua, p. 20).

Don Juan, apparently from early youth, was interested in the history of his people, which he could study in the really vast histories composed at the behest of his uncle, the Learned King. Blecua (pp. 20-21) happily quotes two passages that reveal the deep respect the prince had for his royal uncle's labors, remarking that Don Juan Manuel wrote in *El libro de la caza* that no one could calculate how much good Alfonso had accomplished in increasing knowledge and clarifying it. One can see why, then, that in the *Crónica abreviada* the prince followed the vast Alfonsine *Crónica general.*

Don Juan, apparently suffering from insomnia while he was in Seville in the year 1326, composed the *Libro del cavallero et del escudero*, as he wrote in his prologue. Some of it is original, but by his own admission he derived ideas for other parts from other authors, and perhaps the principal source was Ramon Lull's *Libre del orde de la cavaylería*. The book of Don Juan Manuel, like that of Lull's work, unfolds as an old knight discusses chivalry with a young squire. Lesser influences stem from the *Lucidario* and from Saint Isidore's *Etimologiae*.

The *Libro de los estados*, in which the word *estados* means "stations" in society rather than "states," treats also laws. It is sometimes referred to as the *Libro del infante*. Its first book deals with the *estados* of the laity, from emperors to peasants, while the second deals with the ecclesiastical hierarchy, from the sacristan to the pope. A novelesque frame carries the many arguments of this very lengthy treatise; this frame was derived from that of *Barlaam e Josafat*, in which a prince sees sights that make him fear for his soul. The lesson is that in all social stations or classes it is possible in the Christian faith to earn the right to go to heaven. Since the book contains much detail about the obligations of the stations to one another, and since Don Juan's personal observations are clearly his own and not quotations from other authors, the *Libro de los estados* is one of the most valuable works he produced.

Like most nobles of the century Don Juan Manuel was a great hunter. In the book on hunting, *El libro de la caza*, one reads that he talked with the great hunters and falcon-keepers of the time, as well as with such royal hunters as his uncle the king of Aragon. Anyone who cares to learn the intricacies of falconry—rearing and breeding, training, curing of ill falcons, places where they could be found and captured, and regions where hunting with these birds was best—can find it all and a great deal more in the lengthy *Libro de la caza*.

In the *Libro infinido*, or *Castigos a su fijo don Fernando*, the reader will find a remarkable guide for princes and one unique in many ways. Don Juan cited the famous *De regimini principum* of Egidio de Colonna, but he preferred to write in his own way using living experiences of his own and of people he knew. In the book he constantly counsels his son by name, thereby giving a most personal approach to the entire work, as his cousin King Sancho did when he caused to be written his *Castigos e documentos*.

The *Libro de las armas*, as Blecua says (p. 27), is a book like none other written by Don Juan or any other writer in the Middle Ages, either in form or in content. In it he exalts his own name and his own lineage—that is, his own particular branch of the family—as he explains why and how he and his line were privileged to have as their coat of arms wings and lions. He makes clear that he considered himself and his direct line, even exclusive of Alfonso X, whose father King Ferdinand III was Don Juan's grandfather, to be superior to all others. After all, he wrote, his father was the only one in the family to have received the paternal blessing as well as a family heirloom, the famous sword Lobera.

Though Don Juan Manuel may have been deceitful, though he is known to have executed—some say that he had murdered—certain of his enemies, though he was treasonable, he was nevertheless deeply religious. Like the ribald and at times almost sacrilegious archpriest of Hita, Don Juan respected his faith; like Juan Ruiz and nearly every Spaniard in the Middle Ages, and like many today, he revered the Blessed Virgin and sought her aid. It is not strange, then, that he composed a *Tractado de la Asunción de la Virgen*, sometimes titled *Tractado en que se prueba por razón que Sancta María está en cuerpo et alma en paraíso*. He wrote it for Brother Remón Masqueía, prior of the Dominicans in the monastery at Peñafiel. He argued with deep feeling in some of the most moving lines in all his works—indeed, as moving as any in tracts devoted to the Virgin—the many reasons for believing that she did go up to heaven in bodily form. The phraseology, the intent, and the depth of emotion displayed make this short piece distinct.

Versatile in the extreme, then, was Prince Don Juan Manuel as he wrote throughout a difficult era often torn by war. But like so many other writers who lived through periods of civil and military violence, he did not allow his interest in writing to flag.

Among his writings *El Conde Lucanor* is Don Juan Manuel's masterpiece, upon which his fame rests. It is a delightful collection of fifty-odd tales narrated in a style peculiar to its author and held together by an age-old framework stemming almost certainly from Eastern writings. In *El Conde Lucanor*, a count brings his problems to his counselor, Patronio, who suggests solutions through stories. Each tale teaches one or more moral lessons or truths, a didactic goal which does not preclude the pleasures to be derived from good fiction. Don Juan indicates both goals in his prologue, saying that he wrote the stories " . . . that all men should accomplish in this world such works as might be profitable to them, to their honor, and the good of their stations, and that they might be advanced thereby in their careers and be enabled to save their souls." So that the reader could enjoy himself as he learned, Don Juan wrote in an attractive way and chose interesting subjects. He felt that even unwelcome, stern, or hard lessons could be sweetened if he tucked them away in good stories, just as bitter medicine can be coated with sugar or honey. Writing with this dual purpose, he happily blended elements of interest, pleasure, and didacticism.

Such comments call attention to the need for some background on the genre of the brief narrative in Spain before Don Juan Manuel's time and until the close of the Middle Ages. Long before 1100 A.D. certain collections of brief narratives had been introduced into Spain by Moorish inhabitants and, to a lesser extent, by Jews who lived in the Peninsula. Written in Arabic and Hebrew, such books could not be read by many native-born Castilians, Leonese, and Aragonese; but even so they were important for bringing into the Iberian Peninsula a great variety of stories not before known there. Surely some went soon into oral Spanish and became part of the folklore of the Spaniards. Surely some also may have been written in Spanish, but not as early as the eighth or ninth centuries when, it is believed, the major collections were brought in from the Middle East. It was the *Disciplina Clericalis* (circa 1135) which first made certain of these stories familiar to the literate in a language educated Christians could read. Its author, the famous Jewish convert to Christianity, Moses Sephardi, had been baptized Petrus Alphonsus; but he was better known to his contemporaries in Aragon as Pedro Alfonso.[8] He was a scholar and scientist (he even served as physician to Henry I of England, circa 1100). But what had endeared him to the Church was his apostatizing of the Jewish faith and his famous tract entitled *Dialogi contra Judaeos*. It is not strange, then, that the *Disciplina Clericalis*, authored by such a distinguished personage, should gain fame from Iceland to Byzantium. Today some sixty-odd manuscripts of this small book are extant. In the Middle Ages there was scarcely a collection of tales in any language, Latin or vernacular, which did not owe a good deal to this Aragonese Jew. Don Juan Manuel seems to have been an assiduous reader of the *Disciplina*, since he utilized some of its better-known tales in the composition of his own *exemplos*. Indeed, quite probably he developed the format of presentation in his *Conde Lucanor* from that used by Pedro Alfonso in his work.

Pedro Alfonso's utilization of Arabic tales he himself mentions in his prologue, which incidentally makes quite clear his reasons for writing the *Disciplina Clericalis*, a book surely not what its title would indicate, since it is hardly a "Discipline of the clergyman," or even a "Guide for the secular clerk." In the prologue one reads, after some mention of the value of cleaving to God's will and the virtuous paths of life, that "I have observed that the temperament of man is delicate; it must be instructed by being led, as it were, little by little, so that it will not become bored. I am mindful also of its hardness, which must to some extent be softened and sweetened, so that it may retain what it learns with greater facility, remembering that, as it is forgetful, it needs many things to help it remember what it tends to forget. For this reason I have compiled this small volume, taking it in part from the parables and counsels of the philosophers, in part from the parables and counsels of the Arabs, from tales and poems, and finally, from animal-and-bird-fables...."[9] This line of thought is not far from that of Don Juan Manuel's in his own prologue.

The structure of the *Disciplina* is like that of many medieval works that followed it and of Eastern books that preceded it. In a very simple framework—a dying Arab relates to his son the various stories in the book—the content of the *Disciplina* is presented, just as in an equally simple framework Don Juan, through conversations between Count Lucanor and Patronio, presented the fifty-odd *exemplos*. It should be mentioned here, in order to complete a line of thought begun earlier, that Pedro Alfonso used several Eastern collections of stories as sources, but that he relied primarily upon two of them. One was the Arabic *Kalilah wa-Dimna* (translated from Persian into Arabic circa 750) which would appear in Spanish in 1251 as *Calila e Digna*. The Arabic original could have reached Spain shortly after 750, and only some four decades after the Islamic invasion. The other was an Arabic version of the *Book of Sindibad*, which would be translated into Castilian as *El libro de los engaños*.

It is strange that such a short book as the *Disciplina Clericalis* could have exercised the influence that it did. Its prologue is followed by a brief tract called *De Timore Dei* which, like similar tracts distributed throughout the work, is philosophical and filled with proverbs. In it the philosopher Enoch speaks. In the next section Socrates and certain nameless philosophers discuss hypocrisy. A third section urges the son to profit by the wise ways of the ant, the rooster, and the dog. The last remarks, on gratitude, lead to the theme of the first *exemplum* of the Half-friend, a tale, incidentally, refurbished and extended by Don Juan Manuel as *exemplo* 48. The stories, which are usually separated by brief observances, such as "On True Nobility" and "On Evil Women," number only thirty-four. Some of the *exempla* are of world-wide currency, in the East through *Kalilah wa-Dimna* and the *Book of Sindibad* and their oriental forebears; in the West primarily, or at least initially, through the *Disciplina Clericalis*. Others are from unknown sources, and not one is actually pious in the Christian sense of the word, although such tenets as those presented about "Riches," the "Receiving and Testing of Advice," and "On the Instability of Worldly Things" are the property of all of the great religious faiths. Versions of the *Disciplina Clericalis* eventually appeared in all the vernaculars, sometimes in verse (*Pierre Anfors* or *Castoiement d'un pere a son fils*), sometimes in prose (the *Libro de los exenplos por a.b.c.* of Clemente Sánchez de Vercial contains nearly all of Pedro Alfonso's stories). If there was a Spanish version before Clemente Sánchez's in the early fifteenth century, there is no evidence of it. The only version in English (presumably English versions once existed but have not survived the ages) is the translation of John E. Keller and Joseph R. Jones, *The Scholar's Guide* (Toronto: The Pontifical Institute of Mediaeval Studies, 1969).

Calila e Digna also served Don Juan Manuel well as he assembled his tales. Scholars today have good reason to believe that this Spanish translation of the Arabic *Kalilah wa-Dimna* was made at the behest of Alfonso X. The colophons of both manuscripts attribute the sponsorship to Alfonso. Moreover, a very interesting tradition for such sponsorship and patronage existed in the Spanish royal family of those times. Alfonso's brother, Prince Fadrique was, according to the introduction or prologue of *El libro de los engaños*, that book's sponsor; Alfonso's nephew and Don Juan Manuel's cousin, Sancho IV, El Bravo ("the Fierce"), is believed to have instigated the writing of *Castigos e documentos para bien vivir;* and, of course, Don Juan Manuel himself produced the collection of brief narratives par excellence. If Alfonso did indeed sponsor the *Calila e Digna* and if it was completed, as the colophon states, in 1251, then Alfonso caused it to be written when he was still a prince (he was coronated in 1252). *Calila e Digna*, then, would have been available to Don Juan Manuel in the royal library itself. And, in any event, Don Juan Manuel could have used the Arabic *Kalilah wa-Dimna* itself, since it is likely that he could read Arabic. Certainly he could have had it read to him in translation.

Calila e Digna is a masterpiece of the translator's art and is so close to the Arabic original that scholars can use it to fill in lacunae found in Arabic manuscripts of the period. *Calila* has a long and intriguing history. A good two-thirds of the Spanish work, like the Arabic, can be traced back to the Hindu *Panchatantra*, composed, it is believed, in Sanskrit circa the year 250 of our era.[10] *Calila* contains nearly all the stories from the original and includes, as its final third, a goodly collection of other tales taken from Persian and Arabic literatures. The bridge between the Arabic and Sanskrit versions of the *Panchatantra* was a sixth-century Pahlevi (Persian) version no longer extant. We do know that the Pahlevi rendition existed, for the name of its translator, a certain Abdullah ben al-Muqaffa, is attested. A convert to Islam from the faith of Zoroaster, he wrote the important Arabic translation circa 750. It was this version in Arabic that seems to have been carried to Spain, and it is from one of its manuscripts that Alfonso had the Spanish *Calila e Digna* translated.

Calila e Digna was written for the educated reader, for it had come from the erudite world of Islam; but for the erudite man it meant more than learning. It was also a book of recreation, even though it did not preserve the verve and lightheartedness of the *Panchatantra*—qualities the Hindu work owed to the sophistication of the times in which it was written, to an atmosphere of tolerance, and to a religion which, though extremely complex, was receptive to a much less serious philosophy of life than either Islam or Christianity. In the Sanskrit the lesson is similar, and sometimes identical, to the lesson preserved in the Arabic and Spanish versions, but there are divergences. The didacticism of the Sanskrit is markedly more tongue-in-cheek than in the other versions. Its dichotomy of purpose, didactic and recreational, is less evident. The dichotomy in the Arabic and in the Spanish is more firmly divided, but even so the mock-serious tone is far from absent. In Islamic culture, at the time of the translation of *Kalilah wa-Dimna* from its Persian form, the concept of *adab* was flowering. *Adab*, a literary philosophy of *belles lettres*, permitted the erudite to read and to talk about a wide range of subjects—some serious, some artistic, some recreational (polo, archery, and fencing), and some frankly scandalous and scurrilous. This mock-seriousness, which made it possible for the sophisticated to laugh at life and its seamier side while pretending to ponder the depths of philosophy and morality, had great appeal in the East; and quite naturally, it appealed to a sophisticated person like Alfonso. *Adab*, in concept if not in name, carried over into the Christian kingdom of Castile, and at the behest of Alfonso it was allowed to survive when *Kalilah wa-Dimna* was translated from Arabic into Spanish. It is hardly possible to believe that a worldly and urbane prince like Alfonso, in a court at which a deep and harmonious rapport existed with oriental culture, could have been so naive as to have excised all traces of *adab* from *Calila e Digna*.[11]

Calila e Digna followed the oriental pattern. It is made up of a lengthy introduction by Al-Muqaffa (which contains five brief narratives illustrating the translator's ideas) and eighteen chapters, all but two of which contain brief narratives of their own. Chapter 1 deals with the journey of a certain Bursöe, a Persian who traveled to India in search of herbs which would resuscitate the dead, and which turned out to be, allegorically speaking, books of wisdom, one of which was the Hindu version of *Calila*—that is, of course, the *Panchatantra*. Chapters 3 through 8 are, in fact, the chapters which reproduce the Hindu book; and these chapters, like the original, are very rich in brief narratives.

All of the chapters in *Calila e Digna* except 9, 10, 12, 14, and 15 contain interpolated stories. Chapters 3 and 4, which relate the story of the two jackals, Calila and Digna, provided Don Juan Manuel with the stories he used in *El Conde Lucanor*. These chapters, like all the longer chapters—and even the short ones in which interpolated tales are found—are framing stories, often novelesque in length, presentation, and plot complication. Each framing story can stand on its own merits, so that even if one chose to omit the interpolated tales, the overall plot structure would not be damaged. The personages or characters of the frame stories often tell stories themselves to enlighten other characters; and it is quite common for the characters in the interpolated story to relate stories of their own, and indeed, for characters in their stories to tell still other stories. The so-called Chinese box effect, so treasured in oriental literatures, particularly by the Hindus, is most evident in the Spanish version. Style in *Calila e Digna* varies from verbosity, especially when philosophical matters are under discussion, to a simple and lively presentation which is most attractive.

Calila e Digna, with its array of oriental tales, many not yet known in the West before the translation was made from the Arabic, brought a really vast repertory of stories which seems to have been quickly and gratefully accepted by Spaniards of the period. The host of new plots and motifs—about deceitful wives and light-handed rascals, novelesque adventures, and animal fables—together with an oriental vein of humor and turn of phrase, influenced deeply the entire unfolding of brief narratives in Spain not only in the thirteenth century, but also in the fourteenth, when Don Juan Manuel wrote, and in the fifteenth and later centuries. As might have been expected, some of the stories escaped from the realm of books to appear refurbished, and usually simplified and invigorated, in the realm of folklore. To this day tales exactly paralleling those found in *Calila e Digna* are to be heard from

19

folk in Spain and in Spanish America, including, of course, those parts of the United States where Spanish is still spoken as a native tongue.

The second book of brief narratives to appear in the thirteenth century was sponsored by the brother of King Alfonso, Prince Fadrique (in 1253), two years after the appearance of *Calila e Digna*. The origins of this book whose title is the *Libro de los engaños e asayamientos de las mugeres* (roughly translated as *The Book of Wiles of Women*), was probably of oriental provenience. Authorities differ as to its origin— India, Persia, the Moslem world, though some attribute it to Hebrew or Greek sources—but that it belongs to the genre made up of a framing story and interpolated tales no one denies.[12] Its purposes are purported to be didactic, but no one can seriously believe that is true, any more than Pedro Alfonso did when, with his tongue deep in his cheek, he pretended to believe in the didacticism of the several tales he borrowed from the Arabic or Hebrew versions of the *Book of Sindibad*. The framing story is of itself a wonderful piece of novelesque fiction, embodying the best elements of the motif known as "Potiphar's Wife," even though there is nothing Egyptian or scriptural in the Spanish version or in any of its immediate predecessors. The recreational, then, completely obviates the didactic. One could, therefore, deny any element of true didacticism. People read the book, in the East and in the West, purely for its ribald, bawdy, and otherwise recreational intent. The very frame story is humorous, if one looks beneath the surface. How could people read it otherwise? The only two moralizations ever voiced in the entire book may be summarized as admonishments against the machinations of deceitful people, primarily deceitful wives, and against acting in haste or without forethought. Mock-serious must be even Fadrique's statement in the introduction, where he is purported to say that the book was composed and translated to alert men against the wiles of women. Probably Prince Fadrique's book, like *Calila*, is in the literary tradition of *adab*. It definitely belongs to that lengthy list of books which delight in the hilarious Eastern antifeminism which the West was so quick to adopt and which is most familiar to educated people today in works like the *Decameron*, the *Heptameron* of Margarite of Navarre, and Straparola's *Nights*.

The sources of the *Libro de los engaños* (*Book of Sindibad*) are not as easy to trace as those of *Calila e Digna*. Some of its stories are identical in plot to some found in the *Panchatantra*, leading many to think that the original *Book of Sindibad* was of Hindu origin. Ben

Perry, whose studies of the *Sindibad*'s origin are most complete, attributes it to the Persians; on the other hand Maurice Epstein of Yeshiva University finds it of Hebrew provenience.[13] Versions appear in Syriac, in Arabic (the only surviving one is in the *Thousand Nights and a Night*), in Persian (several), in Greek, in Hebrew, and in the Castilian of Prince Fadrique. These versions are of the so-called Eastern branch. A Western branch, vastly different in that hardly any of the interpolated tales are the same as in the Eastern, is represented by the *Book of the Seven Sages of Rome*. The Arabic version was available in Spain from an early date. From it Pedro Alfonso drew at least three of his stories. The framing story contains some twenty-odd brief narratives varying in length from a few to several pages.[14] Don Juan Manuel, who never stooped to the scurrilous, did not use the *Book of Sindibad* or its Spanish rendition as the source for any of his *exemplos*.

Certainly known in the Alfonsine period and, of course, in that of Don Juan Manuel, was a book generally referred to as *Barlaam e Josafat*, which belongs to the famous group of books of Sanskrit origin. *Barlaam and Josaphat*, to use the English title, is a Christianization of the life of Gautama Buddha, or Siddharta, who flourished in the sixth century B.C. This very lengthy novelesque work contains only ten brief narratives or *exempla*, inserted to illustrate or point a moral lesson. In its original form in the Sanskrit *Jatakas*, the *Lalita Vistara*, and the *Buda Carita*, *Barlaam e Josafat*, belonged to the oriental genre of Hindu saints' lives. Its transmission to the West was long and complicated. Let it suffice to say that once the Buddhists of India had gathered the legends of their religious founder and couched them in a long and novelesque form, the book attracted the attention of other peoples and adapted itself remarkably well to a number of cultures and faiths far removed from Buddhism. The *Lalita Vistara* and the *Buda Carita*, the Persian, the Manichean, the Arabic, the Georgian, the Greek, and the Latin versions, and later all the versions in the vernaculars of the West, had the common aims of imparting moral lessons and strengthening the faiths of these cultures. As in the case of all such books, the element of interest had to be instilled—a simple matter here, since the Buddha's life was fascinating.[15]

The Spanish *Barlaam e Josafat* differs in origin from that of *Calila* and the *Libro de los engaños*, since the Spanish book stemmed not from an Arabic text but from a Latin one. Even the characters in the Spanish version differ, which has led some to believe that the Spanish translators did also have an Arabic text available. The Buddha's father, Suddhodana, becomes the Spanish Avenir, and the young man who was later to become the Buddha in the East was called Josaphat in the West, perhaps through a transformation of Bodhisatva, one of the names of the Buddha. The Buddhistic tale is dramatic in its conception and was successful in interesting those who heard it or read it. But it is in the West that the story reaches its greatest excellence, since under the influence of Christianity, the life of the Buddha is given greater dramatic appeal. Don Juan Manuel not only felt the power of the story of Barlaam and Josaphat, who were regarded already in his day as saints (in the Eastern Church they were canonized), but also used it as the frame story of his *Libro de los estados*, as well as using certain of its interpolated tales in the *Conde Lucanor. Barlaam e Josafat's* popularity was enormous in the Middle Ages; and its attraction would survive until well into the seventeenth century, when no less a dramatist than Lope de Vega wrote a successful drama entitled *Barlaam y Josafá*. It is not strange, then, that Don Juan Manuel utilized some of its *exempla* in his own writings.

Another work which might have been used by Don Juan Manuel as a source was the novel *Caballero Cifar*, to use the shortened title by which most people know it. Not essentially a collection of brief narratives, it nonetheless scatters many through its pages, and some are famous. The *Cifar* is chivalric in the presentation of the protagonist and his family, as well as in the deeds he and later his sons carry out; it harks back to the Byzantine romance in its depiction of piracy, the use of coincidence, the motif of the divided family and its subsequent reunion, the kidnapping and harrowing adventures. Reading it reminds one of Heliodorus and Xenophon of Ephesus, as well as of the *Life of St. Eustace* upon which its plot may be based. The first two parts treat the adventures of the Caballero Cifar and his wife and two children, all of whom become separated. The third part, devoted primarily to the instruction of Cifar's sons, is essentially a typical guide for princes, and as such it makes possible the insertion of moralized tales. The fourth part narrates the adventures of Cifar's younger son, Roboán. Whoever the author was, he was erudite in the lore of his times—Christian, Moslem, Celtic, or folkloristic. The strongly pious moral implications found throughout the *Cifar*—virtue, charity, and good works—may indicate priestly authorship; but patriotic and chivalresque elements might indicate that the author was a layman. There is strong emphasis

22

on the recreational, so that no matter how numerous or well-presented the moralizations are, this novel always entertains. The style of the *Cifar* is clear and readable, polished and uniform in grammar and syntax, all of which may be the result of standards set in the thirteenth century by Alfonso X. Several means of presenting the interpolated brief narratives are used. Some are integral parts of the framing story and are introduced as the characters act; others are told by characters whose adventures have little to do with the novelesque plot, suggesting the possibility that these characters were introduced for the very reason that someone was required to tell the stories; still other stories are straightforwardly related by the major characters who tell them for didactic reasons. Many of the tales are well known: the story of the "Half-friend," which appears in the *Disciplina Clericalis* and which would many years later be utilized by Don Juan Manuel, is one; Cifar's squire tells the well-known story of an ass that tried to ingratiate itself with its owner by fawning upon him like a lapdog; a third, a folktale, is told as though it happened to Cifar's squire, who is caught stealing turnips. The *Caballero Cifar*, set down most probably in Toledo, the center of Arabic studies, marks an important step in the brief narrative's development in Spanish.[16]

Fables from the Aesopic tradition are exemplified in Spanish by the *Libro de los gatos*, which was a near translation of the Latin work of an English cleric named Odo of Cheriton. We do not know when the translation was made into Spanish, but quite possibly it came about not long after Odo preached in Spain in the first quarter of the thirteenth century. The manuscript we possess dates from the fifteenth century. Don Juan Manuel might have had access to a Latin text from his own century or from the thirteenth; however, there is no proof that he ever used either the Latin or the Spanish translation as a source for any of the *exemplos* in the *Conde Lucanor*. Odo's work bore the title *Fabulae* or *Narrationes*.[17] Its value to Spanish literature lies in its introduction of stories not previously set down in Spanish. Odo and the Spanish translator included many of the most popular aspects of Western fable lore—oriental apologues, classical fables, bestiary material, tales from the cycle of Renart the Fox, and a few ecclesiastical *exempla*. As a cleric Odo wrote as one conscious of the evils and deceits of the world in all levels of ecclesiastical and lay society. The Spanish rendition preserves Odo's satirical remarks and even embroiders upon them. When one considers Odo's lively and popular subject matter, pointed and

23

relevant commentary, wry and bitter humor, and incisive penetration into the world's foibles and evils, one can imagine that his fables were well received. Odo, in the vein of those preachers who employed satire to teach and to entertain, realized how important humor was; and he was able to provoke laughter of a deep and wry variety. Humor to him was, then, not only a keen weapon against the human weaknesses he deplored, but also an attractive facet of narrative technique.

The *Libro de los gatos* does not always translate the *Narrationes*, for sometimes it enlarges upon the Latin work, especially in longer and more mordant moralizations. The Spanish author also managed to instill a purely Spanish quality, since he alludes more than Odo does to events, personages, institutions, and ideas which are purely Spanish. Readers of the *Libro* and those who heard it read aloud might well have delighted at the witty attacks upon the nobility, the aristocracy, and the members of the Church hierarchy. The language of the *Libro* is readable, easily comprehended, and filled with good dialogue and much wit. Rarely did the Spanish translator write awkwardly, and the reader is led to believe that he made an effort to write for the general public and not solely for the clergy.

The *Libro* contains fifty-eight divisions, most of which are made up of an *exemplum* and a moralization; however, since some sections offer more than one story, the entire corpus of tales in the *Libro* runs to sixty-five. The title has been the subject of much debate, for obviously the word *gato* cannot mean "cat." It must mean "story," though how this can be has not been determined to the satisfaction of scholars. Probably the best solution is that of J. M. Solá-Solé who derives *gato* from *cato* from Cato, a great storyteller of antiquity.[18]

The importance of the *Libro de los gatos* to studies in Spanish fictional motifs and to the development of the genre of the brief narrative in Castilian is large, since it proves that Peninsular literature of the Middle Ages had strong ties with traditional classical as well as ecclesiastical sources of Western literature and reveals that unsuspected areas of nonoriental fiction existed in Spanish from an early time.

All of the works discussed above can either be dated prior to *El Conde Lucanor* or can be considered its contemporaries, regardless of the date of the surviving manuscripts. Only three other prose works that contain brief narratives, aside from *El Conde Lucanor*, remain to be treated. One is the contemporary *Castigos e documentos para bien vivir*, written at the behest of Sancho IV, son of Alfonso X and cousin of Don Juan Manuel. A second is the *Arcipreste de Talavera*, more often referred to as *El Corbacho*, of Martínez de Toledo, archpriest of Talavera. The last is Clemente Sánchez de Vercial's *Libro de los exenplos por a.b.c.* of the first quarter of the fifteenth century.

The *Castigos e documentos*, identified early as a guide for princes, is just that, in that King Sancho, as though he were the actual author, speaks to his son Prince Fernando.[19] The influence of Egidio Colonna's *De regimine principum* is evident, but the *Castigos* contains many elements not found in Colonna. The brief narratives it contains are few; but they are well written and to the point, and they serve to lighten the overall heaviness of the Latin work's didactic goal. The *Disciplina Clericalis* was used by the author for at least one tale. Others stem from various ecclesiastical sources, and the influence of local legend and folklore cannot be overlooked. Even though the *Castigos* was written by or for Don Juan Manuel's cousin and quite probably might have been read by Don Juan, there is no proof that *El Conde Lucanor* felt its influence.

If other collections of brief narratives in prose existed in Spanish before Don Juan Manuel's death or afterwards until the time of Clemente Sánchez, they have not been found, save in sermons, most of which have never been edited for modern use.

El Corbacho is a long religious tract, a diatribe against sin purposely written in the hearty and pungent language of the man on the street.[20] Its three parts contain a total of sixty-two chapters, among which here and there are to be found brief narratives. The sources are far too numerous to mention, but they include many books, pious and secular, occidental and oriental, ancient and contemporary, Spanish and foreign to Spain. One should never forget that Martínez drew upon Boccaccio (especially upon that writer's *De casibus virorum illustrium*); Andreas Capellanus's *De amore;* Petrarch's *De remediis utriusque fortunae;* the *Dictorum factorum Romanorum;* the *Libro de buen amor* of Juan Ruiz, archpriest of Hita; the works of Saint Isidore, Saint Augustin, and Peter Lombard; and the Holy Bible. Martínez de Toledo was, then, the most cosmopolitan writer mentioned thus far. His brief narratives come from the *Disciplina Clericalis*, the *Book of Sindibad* (quite possibly from the *Libro de los engaños* or some Spanish version of it now lost), various of the works alluded to above, and his own personal experiences, probably even from the confessional, since he was a priest. His language is bawdy, popular, colloquial; and his presentation of stories on the wiles of women is the most obscene and randy in the repertory of medieval Spanish writing. Don Juan Manuel would have been horrified at the uninhibitedness of the archpriest of Talavera.

The last book of brief narratives in the Spanish Middle Ages is the fifteenth-century work of Clemente Sánchez alluded to above.[21] It is an alphabet of tales, a variety of book long out of vogue in other languages. And it is the most copious of all collections of Spanish prose brief narratives. Divided into 438 sections, some of which contain more than one *exemplum*, it actually numbers 548 brief narratives. There is no framing device save the alphabetical arrangement of the tales. The sources are numerous and many are cited. As was said earlier, virtually all of the stories of the *Disciplina Clericalis* are translated by Clemente Sánchez; many come from Valerius Maximus, others from Cato, Cicero, Livy, Vegetius, Seneca, Orosius, Josephus; and from the doctors of the Church come many, many more—Saint Isidore, Saint Augustin, the Venerable Bede, Peter of Cluny, Jerome, and Gregory, to name but a few. Folklore, and quite probably the personal experiences of Clemente Sánchez and of people he knew, abound in his *Libro*. Some of the best Spanish of the Middle Ages is found in the *Libro de los exenplos*. It brings into the Spanish language hosts of stories never before couched in it; its vocabulary is rich, its style comfortable; the variety of tales is unsurpassed. It is enduring proof of the wealth of materials at the disposition of educated people in the fifteenth century.

The wealth of brief narratives in verse, though far from being as great as that in prose, is nonetheless significant. However, no more than the briefest mention of the verse narratives can be given here. Berceo's *Milagros de Nuestra Señora* is composed of twenty-five miracles of the Virgin; the *Cantigas de Santa Maria* of Alfonso X contains more than 400 miracles of Our Lady. The *Libro de buen amor* of Juan Ruiz, archpriest of Hita, is contemporary with the *Conde Lucanor* and the most important of all works in medieval Spanish literature; it contains over fifty fables and other brief narratives from Aesopic, folkloristic, clerical, and Eastern traditions, some of which were utilized also by Don Juan Manuel.

Scholars have traced the sources of many of the stories in *El Conde Lucanor* and have revealed that originality of plot was not their author's forte. His freshness in other aspects, however, is apparent. Though he borrowed his basic plots, his narrative techniques were his own. Don Juan had the ability, then, to take a simple anecdote and rework it into a literary masterpiece filled with local color, contemporary philosophy, irony, pathos, realism, and other elements of good narrative technique. To be sure, not all the tales in the *Conde Lucanor* are literary gems, but the proportion of good stories is high. Few if any writers in Spanish before Don Juan's time were innovative enough or daring enough to personalize a folk motif by treating it as an event in the life of persons of whom readers had heard. In tale 33, for example, he deals with the folktale of a falcon and an eagle as though the falcon belonged to his own father. Sometimes he made the personality of a historical personage conform to his contemporary atmosphere. In tale 16 he characterized the tenth-century legendary hero Fernán González in a way attractive to his readers in the fourteenth century.

Don Juan's settings, too, are felicitously presented, apparently because he hoped that the correct background could serve to develop or present believable characters. Tale 35, about a young Moor who tamed a shrewish wife, is exceptionally well structured, with a setting calculated to reveal the protagonist in a striking way. Don Juan's style has appeared to some critics as burdened with long sentences and damaged by a propensity toward formality, heaviness, and complicated sentence structure; however, contrasted with the prose of Alfonso X, which undoubtedly influenced Don Juan Manuel, that style proves far more flexible.

Blecua (p. 34) goes so far as to relate that Don Juan Manuel's dialogues even anticipate the purity of Renaissance writing, save for a certain lack of humor and irony. But it can even be demonstrated that Don Juan exercised no little skill at being wryly humorous and ironical. The humor is low keyed, but it is present, nevertheless. In tale 32, with the motif of "the Emperor's new clothes," what better humorous touch could have been rendered than the description of the naked emperor who feared to admit he was naked? "And when the king was clothed as you have heard, he mounted his horse to ride through the city, but well it was for him that it was summer." And what could be more wryly humorous or ironic than the statement by the father of the shrewish daughter in tale 35 speaking to the father of the young man who wanted to marry her? "For God's sake, my friend, if I did a thing like that I would not be much of a friend, for your son is a good lad. . . . But so that you won't think I am saying this just to get out of doing you a favor, if you truly want me to, I will be delighted to let your son marry her—or anyone else who will take her out of my house."

Dialogue generally moves directly and gracefully and fits well into the mouths of Don Juan's characters. Moreover, the characters are Spaniards who speak in their own idioms and not in the Latinisms so often found in the *libro de buen amor* and in the works of Gonzalo de Berceo. Another element of Don Juan Manuel's art lies in his sense of propriety, which precluded unseemly words and avoided the scurrilous. And yet, he was not prudish, as is proved by his story about the old philosopher who had to answer the calls of nature and unknowingly wandered into the street of prostitutes.

His stories have such universal appeal that neither their medieval settings nor their roots in ideas and ideals of a bygone era destroy their charm. They are as pertinent now and their principles are as relevant and valid as in the fourteenth century.

SOURCES OF *EL CONDE LUCANOR*

It is always difficult to ascertain the exact sources of medieval stories. By the time Don Juan composed *El Conde Lucanor* hundreds of writers in medieval Latin, as well as in the vernaculars, had utilized many of the same tales, if not all of them, and so had Spanish Moors. If, for example, a story appeared in the *Gesta Romanorum*, in Caesar of Heisterbach, in Bromyard, in Etienne de Bourbon, or in Jacques de Vitry, to name only a few, that story could have reached fourteenth-century Spain in many streams, some faithful to the originals, some reworked, amplified, or curtailed.

Daniel Devoto (see bibliography) has catalogued nearly all of the books and articles devoted to Don Juan Manuel's sources. It would be repetitive for us to reproduce his long and detailed findings. Many scholars listed by him have attempted with varying success to trace the stories in *El Conde Lucanor* to their origins. In our remarks about Don Juan's sources we have been deliberately general. When, for example, we mention that Odo of Cheriton in his *Narrationes* included a version of a story later told by the Spanish prince, we do not assert that Don Juan Manuel ever read the *Narrationes;* rather we merely make it clear that the *Narrationes* was a possible source. When all is said and done both Odo and Don Juan Manuel, raconteurs par excellence, might have shared certain sources.

How did Don Juan Manuel come upon the stories he utilized for his own renditions? Surely the Dominicans could have provided him with many. No order was more assiduous in the use of *exempla*, and none was more ubiquitous. Devoted and industrious, the Dominicans wended over all of Europe, the Middle East, and North Africa; and many from foreign climes, especially from nearby North Africa, might have visited their brethren at Peñafiel.

Another source was certainly the vast Alfonsine archives assembled by Don Juan's uncle, the famous scholar and bibliophile, King Alfonso X, El Sabio. In that library were to be found such sources as the famous *Calila e Digna* and probably the *Libro de los engaños e asayamientos de las mugeres*. In the same archives could be read *Barlaam e Josafat*, many Spanish histories and chronicles, translations of Arabic histories, and epic poems and saints lives in several vernaculars as well as in Latin.

To the Spanish court in the time of the Learned King had come scholars, philosophers, astronomers—as well as astrologers—and poets and legists from as far away as Rome. Some had remained. Still others must have visited the Spanish court in Don Juan's own time when King Sancho IV ruled, and a patron of letters like Don Juan Manuel would have attracted learned visitors from a wide variety of places. Royal relatives from Italy, the Germanies, France, and England came and went; and Don Juan might have exchanged anecdotes with these people or with the jongleurs, scholars, musicians, and poets who came in their trains. Some of these visitors no doubt brought books from abroad with them.

In the kingdom of Granada, the last stronghold of the Moors, lived others who visited Christian Spain. Moreover, since Don Juan was a soldier and from time to time commanded the borders between Moorish and Christian domains, he had active commerce with the Moors, and at times, with those foreign Moslems who visited their kinsmen in Spain. Moorish professional storytellers, musicians, and poets came and went; Moorish captives languished in Don Juan's dungeons; and Arabic books must have been in his possession. Scholars believe that he spoke Arabic. It is not too much to believe that he read it.

And not to be forgotten is the wealth of folktales, both pious and secular, which flourished in every part of Spain—in the repertories of Christians, Jews, Moors, and natives of the lands beyond the Pyrenees who had settled in the Peninsula or who visited it on pilgrimages.

All of this and possibly more was at Don Juan Manuel's disposal.

Therefore, our remarks about the prince's sources can make no claim to be definitive or undisputable, although interested readers may find them useful. At least they should make manifest the richness of Don Juan Manuel's narrative repertoire.

After each tale the reader will find some brief commentary about its possible source or sources, together with an indication of the appropriate page or pages in Daniel Devoto's *Introducción al estudio de Don Juan Manuel y en particular de "El Conde Lucanor,"* in Reinaldo Ayerbe-Chaux's *El Conde Lucanor—materia tradicional y originalidad creadora*, in Stith Thompson's *Motif-Index of Folk Literature*, and in John E. Keller's *Motif-Index of Medieval Spanish Exempla* (see bibliography).

THE PRESENT TRANSLATION

We have not attempted a perfectly literal translation, for that would not have allowed us to render Don Juan's mid-fourteenth-century Spanish into our late twentieth-century English. We do not believe, even so, that lack of literalness can in any way lessen this translation's acceptability. A translation should, we believe, render the ideas and imagery of the original language into the second language with as few changes in meaning, concept, and thought as possible. We have taken very little liberty with the Spanish; but in the interest of euphony and to avoid monotony, we have sometimes translated the word *dixo* variously. When it seemed feasible, we have used the most modern and accepted parlance, for which we offer no apology at all; and we have, to enhance readability and convenience, broken up Don Juan Manuel's lengthy sentences into shorter and more easily digested units.

Couplets rhyming *a, a,* except in the cases of tales 1, 2, and 41 which are followed by quatrains rhyming *a,b,a,b,* are appended to Don Juan Manuel's brief narratives. These have been labeled as doggerel, perhaps with some cause. But why would a learned author, one who claimed to have composed an *ars poetica*, have included bad verse in a book of which he was obviously proud? Could Don Juan Manuel have couched his axiomatic verse statements in simple, terse, and down-to-earth lines in a deliberate effort to make them popular and easy to remember? Or did he perhaps choose an unpolished prosody for an outwardly quaint, but nonetheless cleverly concealed tongue-in-cheek rumor? Patronio's seriousness and his apparently unassailable didactic intent expressed in the moralizations of his examples might have been intentionally lessened, thereby giving the reader the option of serious acceptance of the moralizing aim or of a lighter kind of reading. One final question might be asked. Could Don Juan Manuel have actually believed that his verses were good? After all, some think that Cervantes esteemed the poems he included in *Don Quijote*.

Whether or not Don Juan Manuel did write good couplets and quatrains, we, as translators, have endeavored to render these short poetic pieces into English with the same spirit in which the prince wrote them in Castilian. If the verses in the original language are doggerel, then our renditions into English are also doggerel, just as they should be and for the same reasons as those which influenced Don Juan Manuel to compose the verses as he did.

Our hope and intent as translators is to make an important book of the past live in the present, keeping its historical perspective, but presenting it in a style pleasing to contemporary readers throughout the English-speaking world. We have made every effort, therefore, to make Don Juan Manuel speak as clearly and as naturally to our own times as he spoke to his, offering nothing in English that did not appear in essence in the original Castilian.

NOTES

1. The most complete study of Don Juan Manuel is Andrés Giménez Soler, *Don Juan Manuel. Bibliografía y estudio crítico* (Saragossa: Academia Española, 1932). Valuable and with an up-to-date bibliography is Henry Tracy Sturcken, *Don Juan Manuel* (New York: Twayne Publishers, Inc., 1974).

2. Editions of the *Libro de buen amor* are too numerous to list; even the list of translations into English is long. The best poetic translation is that of Elisha Kent Kane (Chapel Hill: University of North Carolina Press, 1968), which is a reprinting of the original translation made in 1933 and privately printed. The more recent printing contains an introduction by John E. Keller. The bilingual edition of Raymond S. Willis, *Juan Ruiz. Libro de buen amor* (Princeton: Princeton University Press, 1972) is the most reliable translation into prose. For information about all translations into English see John E. Keller, "The *Libro de buen amor* in English Translation," *Medieval Studies in Honor of Robert White Linker* (Madrid-Valencia: Artes Gráficas Soler, 1973), and Keller's more recent and therefore more inclusive "Traducciones del *Libro de buen amor* al inglés," *El arcipresté de Hita. El libro, el autor, la tierra, la epoca* (Barcelona: Edita S.E.R.E.S.A., 1973).

3. Few Old Spanish works have been translated, aside from the *Libro de buen amor* and the *Conde Lucanor*. There is no translation of the works of Pero López de Ayala, the *Libro de miseria de omne*, the *Doctrina de la discreción*, the *Revelación de un ermitaño*, the *Crónicas* of Fernán Sánchez de Valladolid,

the *Poema de Alfonso Onceno*, the *Gran conquista de Ultramar*, the *Doncella Teodor*, the *Crónica troyana*, Sem Tob, or the *Lucidarios*; however, several good translations have been made of the *Poema de Mío Cid*, the most recent of which is that of Lesley Byrd Simpson (Berkeley: University of California Press, 1959); *Amadís de Gaula* is in English at last, translated by Edwin B. Place and Herbert C. Behm as *Amadis of Gaul*, 2 vols. (Lexington, Kentucky: University Press of Kentucky, 1974 and 1975). A translation of the *Caballero Cifar* has been completed by Charles L. Nelson and it is scheduled for printing by the University Press of Kentucky.

4. Alan D. Deyermond in *A Literary History of Spain: the Middle Ages* (London and New York: Ernest Benn, Ltd. and Barnes and Noble, Inc., 1971), pp. 107-70, discusses the fourteenth-century contributions.

5. The translation comes from the edition of Pascual de Gayangos found in *Biblioteca de Autores Españoles*, 57 (Madrid: Real Academia Española, 1952), p. 233.

6. See bibliography for the best edition and the only complete translation.

7. José Manuel Blecua, *El Conde Lucanor o libro de los enxiemplos del Conde Lucanor et de Patronio* (Madrid: Editorial Castalia, 1971).

8. Alfons Hilka and Werner Sönderjelm, *Petri Alfonsi Disciplina Clericalis* (Heidelberg: Winter, 1911).

9. The only translation into English is that of Joseph R. Jones and John E. Keller, *The Scholar's Guide* (Toronto: The Pontifical Institute of Mediaeval Studies, 1969). The translated passage comes from p. 34.

10. The Hindu *Panchatantra* has been translated into English in complete form by Arthur W. Ryder, *The Panchatantra* (Chicago: University of Chicago Press, 1956) and was reprinted in 1958. A more abbreviated version in translation is that of C. H. Tawney in *The Ocean of Story*. This is the translation of Somadeva's rendition in the *Katha Sarit Sagara* (London: Clarke J. Sawyer, Ltd., 1928).

11. See Arthur Ryder, pp. 3-12; and John E. Keller, *El libro de Calila e Digna*, Edición Crítica (Madrid: Consejo Superior de Investigaciones Científicas, 1967), pp. xvi-xviii. The Spanish version of the Arabic *Kalilahwa-Dimna* has not been translated; however there is a translation from the Arabic, that of the Reverend Wyndham Knatchbull (Oxford: Oxford University Press, 1819).

12. For a comparison of the Eastern and the Western branches of the *Book of Sindibad* see Angel González Palencia, *Versiones castellanas del "Sendebar,"* (Madrid-Granada: Consejo Superior de Investigaciones Científicas, 1946), pp. xiii-xxvii; and for a listing of the two branches see pp. viii-x.

13. Ben Edwin Perry's study, "Origin of the *Book of Sindibad*," *Fabula* 3 (1959-60): 1-94, postulates a Persian source and supports it well; Morris Epstein in *Tales of Sendebar* (Philadelphia: Jewish Publication Society of America, 1957) believed that it was the Hebrews who gathered and disseminated the stories. The Hebrew *Mishle Sendebar* certainly existed then (Epstein edited it in his work cited) and might well have been the book that served as source for the other members of the family of manuscripts about Sindibad.

14. Domenico Comparetti, *Researches concerning the Book of Sindibad* (London: The Folklore Society, 1882) contains a complete translation into English. The other translation is that of John E. Keller, *The Book of the Wiles of Women* in *University of North Carolina Studies in the Romance Languages and Literatures*, 27 (Chapel Hill: University of North Carolina Press, 1956).

15. The most reliable edition to date is that of Friederich Lauchert, "La estoria del rey Anemur e de Iosaphat e de Barlaam," *Romanische Forschungen* 7

(1893): 33-402. The Georgian version, which may be the bridge between the Persian and the Greek, has been translated by D. M. Lang, *The Wisdom of Balahvar, a Christian Legend of the Buddha* (New York: Macmillan, 1957).

16. The best edition of the *Cifar* is that of Charles Philip Wagner, *El libro del Cauallero Zifar* (Ann Arbor: University of Michigan Press, 1929); an interesting and perceptive study is that of James F. Burke, *History and Vision: the Figural Structure of the "Libro del Cavallero Cifar"* (London: Tamesis, 1972).

17. See George Tyler Northup, *"El libro de los gatos,* a Text with Introduction and Notes," *Modern Philology* 5 (1908) and John Esten Keller, *El libro de los gatos,* Edición Crítica (Madrid: Consejo Superior de Investigaciones Científicas, 1958). The Latin text may best be read in Leopold Hervieux, *Les Fabulistes Latins: IV. Eudes de Cheriton et ses dérivées* (Paris: Librairie de Firmin-Didot, 1896).

18. J. M. Solá-Solé, "De nuevo sobre el *Libro de los gatos,*" *Kentucky Romance Quarterly* 19, no. 4 (1973): 471-83.

19. The best edition is that of Agapito Rey, *Castigos e documentos para bien vivir ordenado por el rey don Sancho IV* (Bloomington, Ind.: Indiana University Press, 1952). The older edition of Pascual de Gayangos in *Biblioteca de Autores Españoles* 51, is always available, since the *BAE* is kept in print.

20. A number of editions of *El Corbacho* can be studied. The most scholarly is that of J. González Muela, *Alfonso Martínez de Toledo. Arcipreste de Talavera o Corbacho* (Madrid: Editorial Castalia, 1970).

21. The *Biblioteca de Autores Españoles* 57, contains an edition of the truncated text which begins in the middle of the *c's*. A. Morel-Fatio, *"El libro de los exenplos por a.b.c."* in *Romania* 7 (1878): 481-526, presents the *exempla* missing from the truncated manuscript. John E. Keller, *Libro de los exenplos por a.b.c.* (Madrid; Consejo Superior de Investigaciones Científicas, 1961) presents the complete text of both manuscripts.

Don Juan Manuel's
Table of Contents

36

Don Juan Manuel's
Introduction & Prologue

INTRODUCTION

This book was written by Don Juan Manuel, son of the noble Prince Don Manuel, with the wish that all men should accomplish in this world such deeds as would be advantageous to their honor, their possessions, and their stations, and so that they would adhere to the career in which they could save their souls. And in it he sets down the most profitable tales which he knew concerning things that happened, so that men can do what has been mentioned above. And it would be a wonder if in this book there will not be found something which has happened to someone else.

And because Don Juan saw and knew that in copying books many errors occur, because letters resemble one another, and it is thought that one letter is another, and in writing the entire meaning is changed and by chance confused; and people who later on find it so written, blame the one who wrote the book; and because Don Juan was fearful of this, he beseeches people who read any book whatever which was copied from what he composed or wrote, that if they read an ill-couched word, they place not the blame on him, until they read the very copy which Don Juan wrote, which has been corrected in many places in his own hand. And the books which he has written up until now are as follows: *The Shortened Chronicle, The Book of the Sages, The Book of Chivalry, The Book of the Prince, The Book of the Knight and the Squire, The Book of the Count, The Book of Hunting, The Book of Siege Engines,* and *The Book of Songs.* And these books are in the monastery of the Preaching Friars that he founded at Peñafiel.

But after seeing the books that he wrote, let them not blame his intention for the failings they find in them, but let the blame rest upon his lack of wisdom, because he dared to involve himself in such matters.

For God knows that his intention was to have people who were not very educated nor very knowledgeable profit by what he had to say. And for this reason he wrote all his works in Spanish, and this is a certain proof that he wrote for laymen and not for those of great learning like himself. And at this point begins the prologue of *The Book of the Stories of Count Lucanor and Patronio*.

PROLOGUE

In the name of God, Amen. Among the many strange and wondrous things that Our Lord did, He thought it well to do an especially marvelous one, and it is this: that of all men who are in the world, no one is similar to another in countenance, for although all men have the same human features, their faces do not resemble each other. And since in so small a matter as the countenance there are great differences, it is less remarkable that there be differences in the wills and the minds of men. So it is that you will find no man is completely like another in will and intention. And I will furnish you some examples to enable you to understand this better. All those who wish and desire to serve the Lord desire but one thing, but they do not all serve Him in similar fashions, for some serve Him in one way and others in another. Similarly those who serve their masters all serve them, but they do not all do so in the same way. And those who plow, and raise animals, and joust, and hunt, and do all the other things, do indeed accomplish them, but they do not understand them nor do them in the same way. And so by this example, and many others too long to tell, you may understand that although all men are men, and all have wills and understanding, just as they resemble each other but little in their facial appearance, so they resemble each other but little in their intention and will. But they do resemble each other so much that they all use and desire and learn best those things that please them more than others. And because each man learns best what pleases him most, he who wishes to teach something to another ought to teach it to him in the way that he believes will be most pleasing to him who is to learn it.

And because many men do not catch subtle meanings, because they do not understand them well, they do not take pleasure in reading books, nor in learning what is written in them. And because they take no pleasure in this, they cannot learn nor be as knowledgeable as they ought to be. Therefore, I, Don Juan, son of the Prince Don Manuel,

Chief Administrator of the Frontier and the Kingdom of Murcia, wrote this book, composed with the most pleasing words I could find. And among the words I placed tales that would profit those who would hear them. And I did this in the fashion of doctors, who when they want to prepare a medicine that will minister to the liver, since naturally the liver likes sweet things, they mix with their medicine intended for the liver some sugar or honey or something sweet; and because of the pleasure that the liver gets from sweet things, as it takes them to itself, it takes along with them the medicine which is for its own good. And they do the same thing for any organ that needs medicine, for they give it with something that that organ naturally attracts to itself. And in this fashion, with God's help, this book will be written. And those who read it, if willingly they take pleasure in the profitable things which they will find therein, it will be well. And even those who do not understand it so well will not be able to avoid reading profitable things which are mingled there along with the charming and elegant words they will find in it. And even though they do not wish to read the profitable elements which they will find in it and may not desire them, they will be helped by them, just as the liver and the other aforesaid organs profit by the medicines which are mixed with the things they like.

And may God, Who is the Author and Maker of all good deeds, wish by His Grace and Holiness that those who read this book profit from it in God's service to the salvation of their souls and the good of their bodies, just as He knows that I, Don Juan, speak with this intention. And whatever they find therein that is not well said, let it not be blamed upon my intent, but rather on the weakness of my understanding. And if they find something well said or profitable, let them thank God for it, for He is the One through Whom all good sayings and deeds are spoken and done.

And since this prologue is finished, now I shall begin the presentation of the book in the manner of a great lord speaking to his adviser. And thus did Count Lucanor and his adviser Patronio talk together.

The Stories of
Count Lucanor & Patronio

1. What Happened to a King and His Favorite

It happened one time that Count Lucanor was talking privately to his counselor Patronio, and he said to him: "Patronio, as it happens, a great, powerful and much honored man, who claims to be a good friend of mine, told me a few days ago, that as a result of certain events, he is planning to leave the country never to return, and, because of his affection for me and his trust in me, he wants to leave me all his lands. Some he will sell to me, the rest he will leave in my hands. Now since this is his wish, and since this would be greatly to my advantage and honor, advise me as to what I must do."

"Sir Count Lucanor," said Patronio, "I do not think you really need my advice in this matter, but since such is your wish I will give you my opinion. First, then, I say that the man you believe to be your friend is talking that way solely in order to test your friendship. The case is much like that of a king and his favorite."

Count Lucanor asked him to tell him about it.

"Sir," said Patronio, "there was once a king who had a favorite in whom he put great trust, and since no one can enjoy good fortune without being envied by others, there were men close to the king who envied the favorite his good fortune and the esteem in which he was held by the king. They set out, therefore, to discredit the favorite with his master. But no matter what they said they never succeeded in getting the king to harm him, suspect him, or doubt his loyalty.

"When they could think of no other way to accomplish their purpose they finally succeeded in making the king believe that his favorite was plotting his death, that when he had killed him he would

43

also plot the death of his young son, and would then rule the country as his own. And although up to this time their plotting had been unsuccessful in planting doubts against the favorite in the king's mind, in his heart he was unable to resist certain misgivings. For if an evil deed is so awful that it cannot he hid, if carried out, no intelligent man will simply wait for proof. Therefore, as soon as the king had fallen into doubt and suspicion, he became most fearful. But he hesitated to take action against his favorite until he should know the truth.

"Those who were plotting the favorite's downfall told the king of a deceitful way of learning the truth of what they were saying. Then they told the king, deceitfully, as you shall hear, what to say to his favorite. And the king decided to take their advice.

"A few days later the king was talking to his favorite, and among the many things they talked about, he began to hint that he was growing weary of life in this world, and that nothing seemed to exist to any purpose. Then he said no more. A few days later, talking with his favorite again, he let him think that the conversation was turning to another topic, then he said again that his daily observation of the world and its ways made it seem less appealing to him. And he touched on this topic so frequently and on so many occasions that the favorite began to believe that the king took no pleasure in the honors of this world, or in its riches, its material possessions, or in any of the pleasure that the world affords.

"When the king saw that his words were having their effect on his favorite, he remarked one day that he was thinking of retiring from the world, of going to a country where he was not known, and of choosing some strange and distant place to do penance for his sins. In this fashion he thought God might bestow His grace upon him and admit him to the glory of heaven.

"When the favorite heard the king say this he marvelled greatly, and urged him not to carry out his plan. Among other things he said that he would do a great disservice to God, to desert the people of his kingdom whom he had maintained in peace and justice. If he were to leave, he added, there would be great troubles and strife among them, which God would look upon unfavorably, and the kingdom would be greatly harmed. And if he would not desist for the sake of his wife, the queen, and for the good of his very young son, it was plain that both his people and his possessions would be in great danger.

"To this the king replied that before carrying out his decision to leave the country he had thought of a way to provide for his wife and son and for his kingdom, and his plan was as follows: the favorite, he said, well knew that his king had reared him, had been good to him and had done him many kindnesses, and therefore he expected to find him loyal and willing to serve him well and properly. For these reasons he trusted him more than anyone else, and he thought it well to leave his wife and son in his power, handing over and entrusting to him control over the fortresses and strongholds of the kingdom, so that no one would be able to harm his son. And if he returned, some time later, he was sure that he would find everything accomplished as regards the matters left in the favorite's control; and, if perchance he should die, he was sure that the favorite would serve the queen, his wife, well, would rear his son, and would continue to guard the kingdom until such time as he could govern it. Thus he meant to leave him in charge of the entire household.

"When the favorite heard the king say that he would like to leave his son and his kingdom in his power, though he gave no outward sign of it, he was secretly pleased, believing that he would have all power and could act as he chose.

"Now the favorite had a slave at home who was a very learned man and a great philosopher. And everything that the king's favorite did, and the counsels that he gave, he managed with the advice of that slave. And so when the favorite left the king, he went to his slave and told him what the king had said, giving him to understand, with a show of satisfaction and joy, how good his fortune was, since the king desired to leave the entire kingdom in his hands.

"When the slave-philosopher heard from his master everything that had occurred between him and the king, and that the king seemed to wish his favorite to take charge of his son and of his kingdom, he knew that he had fallen into a trap, and so he began to upbraid him and to tell him that he was obviously in great danger, both as to his life and his possessions. For everything that the king had said was not said because he meant to carry out his plans, but because someone who wished his master ill had urged the king to say these things in order to test him. Then, if the king thought that he was pleased at the prospect, his life and his goods would certainly be in danger.

"When the king's favorite heard these arguments he was much upset, for he realized that things were as the slave had said. And when the slave saw his agitation, he showed him how to escape from the danger in which he found himself. This was the way: he had his hair and beard cut off that night; he put on a worn and patched garment such as is worn by wanderers who beg alms; he put on old shoes, studded with nails, took a staff, and stowed in the lining of his clothing a considerable sum of money. Before dawn he went to the king's door and told a gatekeeper whom he met to tell the king to arise so that they might set out before the people awoke; to tell him that he was waiting for him. And he begged him to tell this to the king in great secrecy.

"The gatekeeper was much astonished to see the favorite arrive thus dressed, so he went to the king and told him what the favorite had commanded. In his turn the king marveled greatly, and commanded the favorite to be brought in. And when he saw how he was dressed, he asked him why. The favorite told him that he knew that the king wished to go into exile. And since this was so, and since it was God's will that he should never be unaware of any good deed that the king did, and since he had had a share in all the king's honors and goods, it was altogether fitting for him to share in the suffering and exile that the king wished to endure. And since the king did not grieve over his wife, his son or his kingdom, which he was leaving behind, it was not right for him, the king's friend, to grieve over his own possessions. Therefore he would go with him and serve him in ways unknown to anyone, for he was even carrying sufficient provisions for them to live on. And since they were to leave, he urged him to leave before they were recognized.

"When the king heard what the favorite said, he thought that he was speaking in good faith and he thanked him heartily. Then he told him how he was to have been deceived, and that what he had told him was merely to test him.

"Thus was the favorite to have been tricked by unrighteous envy. But God protected him through the advice of the sage whom he held captive in his home.

"And you, Count Lucanor, must be careful not to be deceived by what you have been told by your friend, for surely what he said was simply to test you. You must, therefore make him think that your sole desire is his advantage and honor and that you have no desire to possess anything of his. For if friends are indifferent to such things, a friend cannot long endure."

The count thought himself well advised by his counselor, and he did as he was told and profited by it.

And Don Juan, thinking this a good story, had it included in this book, and wrote these verses to express the moral:

Be not deceived that any man will freely spare
What is his own, if harm alone will be his share.

and these verses also:

By friend's advice and pious deed,
Your troubles end, your will's achieved.

.   .   .

Don Juan Manuel used a story found in *Barlaam and Josaphat* which he could have read in Latin, Greek, Georgian Arabic or in one of the Romance Languages, Spanish included. The story was popular and was included by other medieval authors, Jacques de Voragine, for example in France, and in the fifteenth century in Spain by Clemente Sánchez de Vercial in his *Libro de los exenplos por a.b.c.* Devoto: pp. 357-60; Thompson-Keller: J. 152, J. 1634, H. 1556, and J. 810; Ayerbe-Chaux: pp. 2-7.

2. What Happened to a Good Man and His Son

Another time Count Lucanor happened to be talking to his adviser, and he told him that he was in great perplexity about something that he wanted to do. If he went ahead, many people would criticize him for it, while if he refrained others would object. So he told him what he had in mind and asked for his opinion.

"Sir Count," said Patronio, "I know you can find men to advise you better than I, and I know that the Lord has given you a good mind of your own, so I am sure that my advice will not count for much, but since you have asked for it, here is my opinion. Sir Count, I should like you to hear the story about a farmer and his son."

The count asked to hear the story, and Patronio began:

"Sir, once upon a time there was a good man and his son, and the boy, though young, was very intelligent. Now every time the father got ready to do something, because there are hindrances everywhere, the son would point out that things might turn out the opposite of what was intended. And in this fashion the boy kept his father from doing what had to be done for the good of the farm. For sometimes the more intelligent boys are the more likely they are to make mistakes. They know how to start something, but they cannot foresee how it will turn out. For this reason they go astray, unless someone can hold them back. Now the boy in question, by the very intelligence that kept him from doing anything, kept his father from doing his chores.

"The father and the son had been together a long time, and because his son had kept him from getting things done and because he was irritated by his comments, he decided to punish him and show him how to behave in the future. And this is what he decided to do.

"The man and his son were farmers and lived near a town. On a certain day the father told his son they ought to go and buy some things which they needed, and they decided to take along their donkey to carry the load back. As they were going to market they walked along the road leading the donkey, which carried nothing. On the way they met some men coming from the town where they were headed. And after they had spoken to them and had passed on, the men began to talk among themselves saying that it was not very sensible for a man and his son to walk, leading a donkey with an empty saddle.

"When the farmer heard this he asked the boy what he thought, and the boy said they were right. Since the animal had nothing to carry it was silly for them to walk. So the man told his son to ride. As they continued along the road they met some other men. And as they left them behind they heard them say that it was a great mistake for the man to walk since he was old and tired, while the boy, who was able-bodied, rode the donkey. So the father asked his son what he thought of this opinion, and the son agreed with it. Then the man ordered the son to get off the donkey and he got on.

"In a little while they met still other men who remarked that it was not very sensible to make a young and immature boy walk while his father, who was used to such things, rode the donkey.

"Again the good man asked his son what he thought, and the boy said they were right. Then he ordered his son to get on, and then there would be no one walking. While they were riding along, they encoun-

48

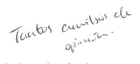

tered some other men who said that the donkey was so thin that it could barely keep to the road, and this being so it was foolish for two persons to ride him.

"The man asked for his son's opinion and he agreed that this was true. Then the father said this:

" 'Son, you well know that when we left the house we were both walking and the donkey had no load at all. And you told me that you approved. Then we met people on the road who said this was wrong. I told you to get on and I walked, and you agreed to that. Afterwards we met other men who objected, so you got off and I got on. You said that was better. And because some other persons disagreed I told you to climb on with me. You agreed that it was better for you not to walk while I rode. Now people are saying it's wrong for both of us to ride and you agree with them. Now since it has come to this I want you to tell me how we can keep people from criticizing us. We walked and they objected. I walked and you rode and they said that was wrong. I rode and you walked and that was wrong. Now we are both riding and they disapprove. Well, there is no way for us not to do one of these things, yet each one is said to be wrong. I did this to show you what happens on the farm. You can be sure there is no course of action that everyone will approve of, for if we attempt an improvement those who do not profit by it will complain. If an action seems bad, those who admire what is right will not approve of the harm you have done. For this reason, if you want to do what is best and most profitable for you, try to do what is right, or what will do you the most good. So long as you are doing no harm, do not stop because of what people say, for obviously most people simply speak their own mind without regard to what is good for you.'

"And you, Sir Count, as regards what you say you want to do, yet fear criticism, you must realize that you will be criticized even if you don't do it. You have asked for my advice. Here it is: before doing anything, look at all the possible advantages and disadvantages. Do not trust your own judgment, and avoid self-deception. Get advice from everyone whose opinions you respect and who is loyal and sensible. If you cannot find such a counselor do not rush into action but let a day and a night go by; that is, if the matter will permit of the passing of time. When it comes to things you have decided to do for your own advantage, my advice is never fail to do them for fear of what people may say."

And the count thought Patronio's advice good and he took it and profited from it.

And when Don Juan heard this story he ordered it written down in this book, and he had these verses written which contain in brief the lesson of the story:

Unasked advice will seldom do,
Your own best choice is made by you.

. . .

This fable is best known to English readers in translation from La Fontaine's *Le Meunier, son fils et l'âne.* Devoto, pp. 361-64. Loiseleur-Deslongechamps, *Essaise sur les fables indiennes,* pp. 174-75 (Devoto, p. 361), trace it to the version found in *The Forty Viziers,* as does Chauvin, II, p. 148 and II, pp. 139-40 as concerns *The Forty Viziers,* no. 138. Don Juan Manuel might have read it in the *Scala Coeli,* in Jacques de Vitry, and in one of the many Aesopic collections to which the tale had accrued. Thompson-Keller: J. 1041.2; Devoto: pp. 361-64; Ayerbe-Chaux: pp. 35-39.

3. How King Richard of England
Leapt into the Sea against the Moors

One day Count Lucanor took his adviser Patronio aside and spoke to him as follows: "Patronio, I have great confidence in your judgment, and I know that if there is any matter about which you are uninformed or unable to give advice, no one else can do so either. Therefore, I beg you to give me your best advice in the matter I am going to tell you about. You are well aware that I am no longer young, but from my childhood on I have been brought up to engage in war and to take great risks, sometimes against Christians and sometimes against Moors, and the rest of the time, against kings who are my lords and neighbors. And when I struggled against Christians I always tried to avoid war, but when I fought many persons who did not deserve it were badly injured,

50

and unavoidably so. And this is but one of the sins that I have committed against the Lord God. I also know that neither I nor any man can know for certain when he will die, and I am sure, in view of my age, that I cannot live much longer. I know that I must be judged by God who is a judge from whom I cannot escape, by words or otherwise, except according to the good or evil deeds that I have done. For this reason I know that if by my ill fortune I have been guilty of any crime which God must rightly hold against me, I am positive that I will not escape from the eternal torture of hell, and nothing in the world can save me. But if God by His grace should find in me enough goodness for me to be chosen the companion of His servants and reach heaven, I know that to this advantage, joy, and glory no other can be compared. Now since my salvation or my damnation can be achieved only through deeds, I beg you according to my estate, to consider and advise me how best to make amends to God for the sins that I have committed against him, so that I may deserve his grace."

"Sir Count Lucanor," said Patronio, "I am much pleased with what you have said, especially since you have asked me to advise you according to your status, for if you had said it in any other way I would have thought that you were trying to test me, as a king tested his favorite in the tale I told you the other day. But I am happy to learn that you wish to make amends before God for your faults, while keeping your position and your honor, for certainly, Count Lucanor, if you should leave your estate and join a monastic order or find some other means of renouncing the world, you could not prevent two things from happening. First, you would be misjudged by everyone. They would all say that you did so from lack of courage and because you were no longer willing to live among good people; and second, that it would be most remarkable if you could stand the harsh life of an order. And afterward if you were to leave the order or live in it without keeping its laws, you would do so to the discredit of your soul, and to the shame and affront of your body and your reputation. But since this is what you want to do, I should like you to hear how God showed a holy hermit what was to happen to him and to King Richard of England."

Count Lucanor asked him to tell about it.

"Sir Count Lucanor," said Patronio, "there was once a hermit, a man of good life, who did many good works and suffered greatly in order to win God's grace. For this reason God was gracious to him to the point of assuring him that he would obtain the glory of paradise. The hermit thanked God profusely, but with this assurance he asked God to please tell him who would be his companion in heaven. And although our Lord sent an angel to him several times to say that it was wrong to ask such a question, he persisted so that our Lord decided to reply. And He sent His angel to tell him that he would be with King Richard of England in heaven. This news did not much please the hermit, for he knew the king well, knew that he was a very warlike man, and that he had killed, robbed and disinherited many people. He had always observed that he lived a life the very opposite of his own, and he still seemed a long way from salvation. For this reason the hermit was in a bad humor. And when our Lord God saw this, He sent His angel to tell him not to complain nor to marvel at what he had been told, for certainly King Richard would do a greater service to God in a jump that he would take than the hermit had done with all his good works. And the hermit marvelled greatly at this and asked how it could be. The angel informed him that the king of England, the king of France and the king of Navarre had gone overseas. On the day they reached port, they were armed to capture the land, but they saw on the shore such a crowd of Moors that they doubted whether they would be able to land. At this the king of France sent word to the king of England to come to his ship so they could decide what to do. The king of England, who was on horseback when he heard this, told the envoy of the king of France to report as follows: that he well knew he was a sinner in the sight of the Lord, that he had done many bad deeds and had always begged for a chance to mend his ways and that now, praise God, he saw the chance that he had so long desired; for if he died there and then, he would have made amends before leaving the earth, and he would die in a state of penitence and his soul would certainly enjoy God's grace. If the Moors were defeated, God would be well served, and all would be right. As he said this, commending body and soul to God, he prayed for His mercy to save him, and making the sign of the cross, he ordered his men to come to his aid. Then giving his horse the spurs, he jumped into the sea toward the bank where the Moors were. And although they were near the port, the water was deep and the king and his horse were swallowed up, so that nothing of them could be seen; but God like a merciful Lord, and of great power, and in remembrance of the Gospel saying, that he does not desire the death of a sinner but rather that he should be converted and live, came to the aid of the king of England and saved him from death. And he gave him eternal life and he escaped the danger of the water. Then he went against the Moors. And when the English saw it they all jumped into the sea after him and attacked the Moors. And when the French saw it, they felt discredited and since they could not bear the thought, they all jumped into the sea against the Moors also. And when the latter saw them coming, and realized that they did not fear death, but were attacking them with a will, they did not dare to make a stand but deserted the seaport and ran away. And when the Christians reached the port, they killed as many Moors as they could lay their hands on, and distinguished themselves, and by so doing served the Lord well. And all this resulted from the jump taken by King Richard of England.

"When the hermit heard this story, he was greatly pleased, and understood that God was doing him a great favor by desiring him to be the companion in paradise of a man who had performed such a service to God, and such a saving deed for the Catholic faith.

"And you, Count Lucanor, if you wish to serve God and make amends for the evil deeds that you have done, see to it that before you leave your land you make amends for the wrongs you know you have done to those whom you have harmed. Do penance for your sins, and do not consider the world's useless pride, for all is vanity. Do not pay any attention, either, to those who say that you are already doing a great deal for the common good, for what they call the common good is an excuse to maintain a large company. They do not even look ahead to see whether they will be able to go on maintaining it. They fail to notice how many die and how many are left of those who claim to give attention only to this so-called common good, and whose real concern is as to how their establishments are staffed.

"And you say, Count Lucanor, that you wish to serve God and make amends for the evil that you have done, and that you do not wish to continue your present career, which is one of pride and vanity. But since God has placed you in a land where you can serve against the Moors, by sea and by land, do your utmost to see that what you leave behind is secure, and having done this, and having made amends to God for the sins you have committed, and being truly penitent, you may have due credit for all the good deeds you have done, and in this way you may leave everything else and remain in God's service to the end of your life. For I take this to be the best way for you to save your soul while keeping your estates and your honor. You must believe that because you are in God's service you will not die prematurely, nor live longer because you are on your own land. For if you die in God's service, living as I have described, you will be a martyr and a fortunate man, and although you do not die in battle, your good will and your good works will make you a martyr. And even those who wish to speak evil of you will not be able to, since everyone can see that you are not failing in anything that you should do as a knight, but that you wish to be a knight of God, and have stopped being a knight of the devil and of the world's pride, which is transitory.

"And now, Sir Count, I have given you my advice, as requested, as to how I think you can best save your soul according to your present estate. And your conduct in this will resemble that of King Richard of England in the leap and the good deed that he performed."

And Count Lucanor was very pleased with Patronio's advice and he asked God to guide him so that he might follow it as he wished in his heart.

And Don Juan, thinking this a good story, ordered it placed in this book and wrote these verses in which the story is summed up briefly. And the verses are as follows:

> *If you are in truth a knight,*
> *You'd rather take a leap in flight*
> *Than live within a convent's halls,*
> *Or be a prisoner held by walls.*

.　.　.

Much of the material about Richard the Lion-Hearted was available to Don Juan Manuel in a Latin or even in a Spanish version of the *Gran conquista de Ultramar*. However, the prince altered the historical account somewhat. The motif is not to be found in Thompson-Keller. Devoto: pp. 364-67; Ayerbe-Chaux: pp. 104-18.

4. What a Genoese Said to His Soul
When He Was about to Die

One day Count Lucanor was talking to Patronio, his adviser, and he told him that he had the following problem: "Patronio, praise be to God, my affairs are in order, I am at peace, and I have done my duty toward my neighbors and equals, perhaps more. Now there are persons who advise me to do something special, and I am much inclined to take their advice; but because of my confidence in you, I did not wish to start out until I had talked to you and asked for your counsel."

"Sir Count Lucanor," said Patronio, "in order for you to do what is most suitable, I should like you to hear what happened to a certain Genoese."

The count asked him to tell him what had happened, and Patronio replied:

"Sir Count, there was once a Genoese who was very rich, and very popular with his neighbors. Now the Genoese became very ill and when he realized that he could not escape death, he sent for his relatives and friends. And when all were with him, he sent for his wife and children. And he was seated in a room from which you could see both sea and land. He ordered all his treasures to be placed before him and his jewels, and when everything was there, be began to talk jokingly to his soul, in this manner.

" 'Soul, I see that you wish to leave me; I do not know why, for if you want a wife and children, you see them before you and ought to be satisfied. And if you want relatives and friends, here are a number of good and honorable ones. If you want great treasure of gold and silver and precious stones, and jewels, and cloth and merchandise you have so much here that you cannot need more. And if you want ships and galleys to make money for you, and bring you property and honor, you see them before you, for they are plainly visible upon the sea from this room of mine. And if you desire property and beautiful and delightful gardens, you see them from these windows. And if you want horses and mules and birds and dogs for hunting and sport, or clowns to amuse you and cheer you up or a good lodging with well-appointed beds and raised platforms and all the other things that are needful, it is all here; and since you have these possessions and are not yet satisfied and cannot stand your good fortune; and since you do not choose to remain but wish to go in search of you know not what, go in God's wrath, for it would be foolish to grieve for any misfortune that may come to you.'

"And you, Sir Count Lucanor, since, praise be to God, you are at peace and enjoying wealth and honor, I think you would be ill advised to seek adventures, and set out to accomplish what you have been advised to do. Perhaps your advisers say these things because they think that once you are involved in some activity you will be forced to do their bidding and follow their will, when you find yourself in a difficult situation, as they now obey you during peacetime. And perhaps they think that by getting you involved they will advance their own fortunes. But this will not be the case so long as you are honorably at ease, and so I tell you what the Genoese said to his soul; therefore, unless it is really necessary, you should not engage in any affair in which you take a total risk."

And the count was pleased with Patronio's advice, and he followed it, and profited from it.

And when Don Juan heard this story he thought it good. And he did not wish to write more verses, but set down a proverb of the old wives of Castile. And the proverb says:

> *Don't get up from where you sit,*
> *Unless there is some benefit.*

. . .

According to Herman Knust, the source was Bromyard's *Summum Praedicantium*, difficult to understand since Don Juan died before Bromyard finished his *Summum*, but Bromyard himself drew upon many sources, some of which might have been known by Don Juan Manuel. Other sources might have been Jacques de Vitry, number 170, Etienne de Bourbon, the *Recull d'exemplis* written in Catalan and the *Speculum Laicorum*. The story seems to be of Christian origin, although one cannot be certain, given the frequent utilization by the clergy of tales from Islamic and Buddhistic and Persian sources which could be adapted to Christian doctrines. Thompson-Keller: J. 321.4; Devoto: pp. 367-69; Ayerbe-Chaux: pp. 32-35.

5. What Happened to a Fox and a
Crow Who Had a Piece of Cheese in His Beak

On another occasion Count Lucanor was talking to Patronio, his adviser, and he said: "A man who claims to be my friend, has praised me heartily, giving me to understand that he looks upon me as a most honorable, powerful, and kindly man. And while he was flattering me in this way he presented me with a petition which, as far as I can see, will be to my advantage to grant."

And the count told Patronio the substance of the petition. And although the petition looked very advantageous, Patronio saw the trick which was hidden under the fine words. For this reason he said to the count:

"Sir Count, I think this man is trying to deceive you by making you think that your power and standing are greater than they are. And if you are to guard against the trick that he intends to play on you, I should like you to hear what happened to a crow and a fox."

The count inquired what had happened.

"Sir Count," said Patronio, "one time a crow found a large piece of cheese and he went up into a tree to eat it at his leisure and without fear of interruption. While the crow was thus busy, a fox passed by the foot of the tree, and when he saw the crow with the cheese, he began to scheme how to steal it. So he began to speak in this fashion:

" 'Sir Crow, I have long since heard of you and of your nobility and dignity, and although I have long been looking for you, it has not been God's will for us to meet until now. Now that I see you I perceive that there is even more good in you than they say. And so that you may see that I am not merely flattering you and in order to tell you of the dignity that I find in you, I will tell you also some ways in which folks find you less charming. Everyone knows that your feathers, eyes, beak, feet, and claws are all black. And because black things are not so agreeable as other colors, people say that as you are all black, this detracts from your distinction. But they do not know how mistaken they are in this, for although your feathers are black, so black and shining are they that they resemble the Indian black of the peacock's feathers, which is the most beautiful bird in the world. And although your eyes are black, they are prettier than any others, for the purpose of the eye is to see, and because everything black is easy to see, black eyes are best. Wherefore the eyes of the swan are most praised for she has the blackest eyes of any creature. Similarly your beak, claws and talons are stronger than those of any bird your size. You can also fly so fast that the wind cannot stop you however hard it blows. No other bird can do this as well as you. Therefore I maintain that with all your talents, God, who does everything properly, would not allow you to sing less well than any other bird. God has been kind enough to let me see you, and I know that there is even more good in you than I had ever heard. If I could but hear your song, I would think myself forever fortunate.'

"And, Sir Count Lucanor, the intention of the fox was to deceive the crow, who took his remarks for truth. Be assured that mortal deceits and tricks are ever spoken with deceitful truth.

"And when the crow saw in how many ways the fox praised him, and how truthfully he spoke (for the crow thought he spoke the truth in all respects), he thought he was his friend, and did not suspect him of putting on a show in order to deprive him of the cheese that he was holding in his beak, and because of the many good things that he had heard, and in answer to the flattering request, he opened his beak to sing. And when he did so the cheese fell to the ground, and the fox took it and ran away with it. Thus was the crow fooled, believing himself to possess more dignity and talent than was actually the case.

"And you, Count Lucanor, since God has been rather kind to you in every way, when you see a man who wants to make you think yourself more powerful and more distinguished than you really are, you should realize that he is trying to deceive you. Therefore, be warned against him, and be careful."

What Patronio said greatly pleased the count, so he spoke and acted as he was advised to do.

And because Don Juan heard that this was a good exemplary tale, he caused it to be written down in this book, and wrote these verses in which may be understood in abbreviated form the purpose of the story. And the verses are as follows:

> Who praises thee for virtues thou hast not,
> Would steal from thee what thou hast got.

. . .

Most probably Don Juan Manuel's source was a version of the fables of Phaedrus or of some collection of ultimate Aesopic origin, although it is believed that Aesop took the story from an Eastern source. Don Juan might also have come upon the story in Arabic letters or in folklore. It appears in Jacques de Vitry and in Frater Johannes Junior. Don Juan's contemporary Juan Ruiz, archpriest of Hita, also used it, couching it, of course, in *cuaderna vía;* and Clemente Sánchez de Vercial included it in his *Libro de los exenplos por a.b.c.* English readers probably read the story in versions based upon the fables of La Fontaine. Thompson-Keller: K. 334.1; Devoto: pp. 369-72; Ayerbe-Chaux: pp. 56-59.

6. How the Swallow Warned the Other Birds When She Saw Flax Being Sown

One day Count Lucanor was talking to Patronio, his adviser, and he said to him: "I am told that some of my neighbors who are more powerful than I are getting together to prepare tricks and stratagems to deceive me and do me great harm. And though I do not believe this, nor fear it, even so, because of the good intelligence that you have, I am asking whether you have any idea whether I ought to take action about this."

"Sir Count," said Patronio, "in order to do what I think you ought in this situation, I should like you to hear what happened to a swallow and some other birds."

The count asked what had occurred.

"Sir Count," said Patronio, "the swallow saw a man sowing flax, and she realized by her lively intelligence that if the flax were to grow, men would make nets and snares out of it to catch birds. So she went to the birds, brought them together, and told them that the man was sowing flax, and certainly that if the flax grew they would be greatly harmed. Her advice was that before the flax seed came up, they should go and uproot it, for things are easy to undo at first, but hard later on. But the birds made light of the matter and did nothing.

"The swallow kept on insisting until she saw that the birds were indifferent and did not value her advice at all. And by then the flax was already so tall that they could not uproot it either with their claws or their beaks. When the birds saw that the flax had grown and they could

59

no longer undo the damage that would follow, they were very sorry not to have taken the earlier advice. But repentance came when it could no longer do any good. Wherefore the swallow, when she saw the birds would not take action against the harm coming upon them, went to man and put herself in his power and won safety for herself and her descendants. Since then swallows live in man's domain and are safe. But the other birds, who refused to protect themselves, are caught every day in nets and snares.

"And you, Sir Count, if you wish to be protected against the harm that you say may come to you, take note, and prepare a remedy before the harm occurs, for it is not prudent to notice things after they happen. He is a wise man who, through signs and activity of every sort, understands the danger that may arise and takes counsel to keep it from happening."

And this pleased the count very much, and he took Patronio's advice and profited from it.

And because Don Juan thought the story good he had it placed in this book and wrote these verses:

> Be early warned of coming danger,
> And you to ills will be a stranger.

. . .

Aesopic in origin, insofar as is known, it was therefore available to Don Juan Manuel in many renditions—Latin, Spanish, Catalan, French, and even Arabic. It appeared in Bromyard, in de Vitry, in the *Romulus*, in Marie de France, in fact, in nearly every body of fables in Europe. Thompson-Keller: J. 621.1; Devoto: pp. 372-75; Ayerbe-Chaux: pp. 59-64.

7. What Happened to a Woman Named Truhana

On another occasion Count Lucanor was talking to Patronio, his adviser, in this manner: "Patronio, a man has explained a plan to me and has showed me how it may turn out. And I tell you that it has so many profitable aspects that if, God willing, it should succeed as this man says it will, it would be greatly to my advantage, for so many things may happen, one leading to another, that I might profit greatly."

He told Patronio how this could be, and as soon as Patronio heard the story he answered the count as follows: "Sir Count, I have always heard it said that it is good sense for a man to stick to a sure thing and not cling to vain hopes, for sometimes those who indulge in daydreams have happen to them what happened to a woman named Truhana."

The count asked what had happened.

"Sir Count," said Patronio, "there was once a woman named Truhana, who was rather poor than rich. One day she went to market, carrying a jar of honey on her head. And on the way, she began to think about selling the jar of honey and how then she would buy a clutch of eggs. From the eggs chickens would hatch; with the money from the chickens she would buy sheep; thus she went on making purchases from the profits each time until she was richer than any of her neighbors. With the wealth which she thought she had, she imagined that she would arrange marriages for her sons and daughters and go through the streets attended by her sons-in-law and grandchildren, and that they would say of her how lucky she was to have become so wealthy, in view of the poverty she once suffered.

"While she was thinking about all this she began to laugh from the pleasure she took in her good fortune. And while laughing she struck her forehead with her hand, and the honey jar fell into the street and smashed. Now when she saw the broken jug, she began to cry, realizing that she had lost everything that she had imagined if the jug had not broken. And because she wasted all her thoughts in daydreams, she finally accomplished nothing that she expected to accomplish.

"And you, Sir Count, if you hope that all you have been told and can imagine is true, think about and believe in only those things that are certain, avoiding the vain or dubious. And if you wish to take a chance, be careful and risk nothing important solely for a dubious profit."

And the count was pleased with what Patronio said, and he acted accordingly and profited thereby.

And because Don Juan liked this story, he had it placed in this book, and wrote these verses

Put your trust in concrete things,
And leave all vain imaginings.

.   .   .

Most probably the version of the story used by Don Juan Manuel was that found in *Calila e Digna*, texts of which were available in the library of King Alfonso X, who, it is believed by many, caused *Calila* to be translated from the Arabic *Kalilah wa-Dimna*, whose Indic source, the *Panchatantra*, is well known. The Buddhistic book and its Arabic descendants, as well as the lost Persian version, make the protagonist a man. But Don Juan was not the first to create a female protagonist, for de Vitry had done so earlier. Perhaps Don Juan utilized some popular version of Spanish vintage which had grown out of an Arabic folktale based upon the material in *Calila*. Thompson-Keller: J. 2061.1, J. 2061.2; Devoto: pp. 375-79.

8. What Happened to a Man
Whose Liver Had to be Washed

On another occasion Count Lucanor was talking to his adviser Patronio, and he said to him: "Patronio, although God has been good to me in many ways, I am now short of money, and though it pains me awfully to do so, I shall have to sell one of my properties. And as much as it grieves me, any other course of action would be equally upsetting. So I must do it if I am to get out of my bad situation and predicament. And while I am preparing to do this to my hurt, many people come to me and ask me to give them some of the funds which have cost me so dear. Now for the understanding that God gave you, I beg you to tell me what to do."

"Sir Count Lucanor," said Patronio, "I think that what is happening to you is like what happened to a man who was very ill."

The count asked him to tell him what had occurred.

"Sir Count," said Patronio, "a man was so very ill, that the physicians told him there was no way to cure him without making an opening in his side, taking out his liver and washing it with certain necessary medicines, since it was in a very bad condition. And while the man was suffering and the physician was holding his liver in his hand, another man who was present spoke up and asked him to give him the liver for his cat.

"And you, Sir Count Lucanor, if you wish to harm yourself by giving away money where it will be wasted, I say that you may do so if you like, but you shall never do it on my advice."

And the count liked what Patronio said and he acted upon it and it profited him.

And because Don Juan thought this a good story he ordered it written down in this book and composed the following verses:

From random gifts, you soon will learn,
A random ill may oft return.

.   .   .

No one has discovered the source of this story. Scholars have stated that it comes from the chapter "De Concordia" in the *Gesta Romanorum*. It does not. Devoto: pp. 378-79.

9. What Happened to Two Horses Which Were Thrown to the Lion

One day Count Lucanor was talking to Patronio, his adviser, in this fashion: "Patronio, for a long time I have had an enemy from whom I have taken some punishment, and he has suffered at my hands too, and because of the harm we have done each other and our mutual ill will, we are on bad terms. Now it happens that another man, more powerful than either of us, is beginning to do things that we are both afraid of and from which great harm may come to us both.

"And my enemy has therefore sent a message, urging that we cooperate to defend ourselves from this third party who is against us, for if we act together we will surely be able to defend ourselves, whereas if one of us neglects the other, it is plain that the man we are afraid of can destroy either of us easily. And if one of us is destroyed, the one who is left will be most vulnerable. And now I am in great perplexity about this: for on the one hand, I am afraid my enemy is trying to deceive me, and if once he had me in his power I would be afraid for my life; but if we put mutual trust in each other, he could not fail to trust me nor I him. The situation worries me.

"On the other hand, I am sure that if we are not friends as he suggests, great harm can come to us both in the way that I have described. Now through the great trust I have in you and in your judgment, I beg you to advise me in the matter."

"Count Lucanor," said Patronio, "this is a very dangerous situation, and so that you may better understand what you ought to do, I should like you to hear what happened in Tunis to two gentlemen who lived with Prince Don Enrique."

The count asked him to tell him about it.

"Sir Count," said Patronio, "two gentlemen who lived with Prince Don Enrique in Tunis were great friends and always lodged where he lodged. Now these two gentlemen each had a horse, and though the gentlemen were very fond of each other, their horses cordially detested each other. The gentlemen were not rich enough to maintain two lodgings, but because of the horses' dislike for each other, they could not stay in the same inn, and so their life was not at all agreeable. This situation lasted until they could stand it no longer, so they told their problem to Don Enrique and begged him as a favor to throw their horses to a lion owned by the king of Tunis. Don Enrique acknowledged their plea and spoke to the king. Even though the horses were very fond of their masters, they put them in a corral where the lion was.

"And when the horses found themselves in the corral, before the lion came out of the enclosure where he was kept, they fought as hard as they could. And while they were fighting, the door of the lion's cage opened, and when he came into the corral and the horses saw him, they began to tremble violently and little by little they approached each

64

other. And when they were together, they stood thus a while, and then faced the lion valiantly together; and they gave him so many bites and kicks that he had to be put back in his cage. The horses were unhurt, for the lion did them no harm. And afterwards these horses were so friendly that they ate out of the same manger, and lived in the same small stall, and their friendship was the result of their fear of the lion.

"And you, Sir Count, if you think your enemy is really afraid of this powerful lord, and needs you enough to forget the enmity between you, if without your help he cannot defend himself, I think that like the two horses who joined forces until they were no longer afraid and came to trust each other, you should gradually come to trust him and reach an agreement with him. And if you find honesty and loyalty in him so that no matter how much it might profit him he will not hurt you, then it will be wise and to your advantage to make common cause with him. In this way the third party can neither conquer nor destroy you. Men must indeed bear a great deal and endure much from relatives and neighbors lest they be ill treated by others. But if you think that your enemy, once you have helped him out of danger, will turn against you and cannot be trusted, then you would be ill advised to help him. You must avoid him then, as much as you can, for if you see that in the midst of danger he was not willing to forget his bad feeling toward you, and you realize that he was waiting for a chance to do you an ill turn, then you must not allow yourself to do anything that will help him to extricate himself from his present danger."

And Count Lucanor was much pleased with what Patronio said, and he thought he was giving him very good advice.

And because Don Juan thought this story a good one, he had it written down in this book and wrote these verses which run as follows:

Guard against the wily stranger,
And keep your goods from every danger.

. . .

Puybusque suggests somewhat convincingly that the origin of the story comes from the *Crónica de Alfonso X* in which is recorded the adventures of Alfonso's rebellious brother, Enrique, who escaped to Tunis and was placed in a *corral* with two lions; but similar events can be found in folktales and in other literatures such as the *Lamp of*

Princes of Abubéquer of Tortosa. Bromyard also used the motif, and it appears also in the *Gesta Romanorum* (chapter 133), with dogs substituted for horses. Thompson-Keller: J. 891, J. 1020, and K. 5218; Devoto: pp. 379-80; Ayerbe-Chaux: pp. 72-76.

10. What Happened to a Man Who on Account of Poverty and Lack of Other Food Was Eating Bitter Lentils

One day Count Lucanor was talking to Patronio, his adviser, in the following manner: "Patronio, I know that God has done me more good than I can ever repay Him. Indeed, I feel that in every way my estate is in good order and honorable; but sometimes I feel so weighed down with poverty that I think I would prefer death to life."

"Sir Count Lucanor," said Patronio, "in order to comfort you in these moods I should like you to hear what happened to two very rich men."

The count asked him to tell him about them.

"Sir Count Lucanor," said Patronio, "one of the men in question reached such a state of poverty that he had nothing left to eat. And although he tried very hard to find something, all he could get was a little bowl of bitter lentils. When he remembered how rich he had been and thought about the way his hunger and his need forced him to eat bitter lentils, which are very astringent and of bad flavor, he began to weep abundantly. Nevertheless, because of his great hunger he began to eat the lentils, all the while weeping and throwing the hulls behind him. And while he was in this anguish and this dismal mood, he noticed that someone was behind him. Now he turned his head and saw that this person was eating the hulls which he was throwing away.

"And when the first man saw him eating the hulls he asked him why he did so. And the man said that he had once been rich but that now he had come to such poverty and hunger that he was glad to find even the hulls that were being thrown away. Therefore, when the man who was eating the lentils saw this, his spirits rose, for he realized that there was someone poorer than he who had even less reason to be happy. And with this comfort he made an effort, and God helped him, and he found a way to rise above his poverty, and he did so and became prosperous.

"And you, Sir Count Lucanor, must know that this is the way of the world, for our Lord does not think it good for any man to have everything. Now in everything else God is good to you. You are respected and esteemed, and if sometimes you lack money or find yourself pressed, do not lose hope on that account. Be certain that others richer and more honorable than yourself have also been hard pressed, and these would think themselves fortunate if they could provide for their people by giving them even less than you give yours."

And the count liked what Patronio said, and he took heart and labored, and with God's help he rose from his despondency.

And Don Juan thought this a good story and he had it placed in this book and wrote the following verses:

> It matters not how poor you are,
> For other men are poorer far.

. . .

Quite probably the episode comes from the autobiography of Abdal-Rahman (tenth to eleventh century) and was told in a lost work of one Ibn Baskuwal and preserved in the anthology of Ibn Sa'id. However, such an autobiography could have contributed to folklore and could have been picked up by Don Juan Manuel through his associations with Moorish scholars and soldiers. Thompson-Keller: J. 883.1; Devoto: pp. 380-82.

11. What Happened to a Dean of Santiago and Don Yllán, the Grand Master of Toledo

On another day Count Lucanor was talking to Patronio, his adviser, and he told him his problem in this fashion: "Patronio, a man came to ask my help in a matter in which he requires assistance and has promised in return to do something to my advantage and honor. So I began to help him to the extent of my ability, but before the affair was over, when he felt that the business was all but concluded, something occurred to make me need his help, and so I asked him and he made excuses.

"Then another occasion arose when he could have helped me, and he made excuses as before. And he did this every time I asked him. And the problem for which he begged my assistance is still not settled and will not be unless I wish it. Now because I have faith in you and in your intelligence, I ask your advice as to what I ought to do about this."

"Sir Count," said Patronio, "in order for you to do as you ought to do, I should like you to hear about what happened to a dean of Santiago with Don Yllán, the great sage of Toledo."

And the count asked what had happened in that instance.

"Sir Count," said Patronio, "in Santiago there was a dean much skilled in the art of necromancy, and he heard it reported that Don Yllán of Toledo knew more of this science than anyone else in the land. Therefore he went to Toledo to learn the science, and when he got there, he went straight to Don Yllán's house, and found him reading in a secluded room. When he arrived he was greeted cordially, but Don Yllán said that he did not wish to talk about his reasons for coming until the dean had eaten. And Don Yllán thought well of him and gave him comfortable lodgings and everything that he needed, and let him know that he was glad to see him.

"When they had eaten, the dean took him aside, told him his reason for coming, and urged him to teach him his science, for he was very anxious to learn it. Don Yllán replied that since he was a dean and a man of high estate he might go far, but that men of high standing, when they obtain all they want, are likely to forget what others have done for them. For this reason Don Yllán was afraid that as soon as he had learned what he wanted to know he would not keep his promises. But the dean promised and assured him that all his resources would be at his disposal. Now they continued to talk from lunch time till dinner time, and when they had reached an agreement, Don Yllán told the dean that the science could only be learned in a remote place and that on that very night he would show him where they must stay until he had mastered what he wanted to learn. Therefore he took him by the hand and led him to a room, and withdrawing from all other company, he called a maidservant and told her to cook partridges for supper, but not to start roasting them until he gave the orders to do so. After saying this, he summoned the dean, and they went down an elaborately carved stone staircase, and descended for such a distance that it seemed as though they were down far enough to be below the river Tagus.

"When they reached the bottom of the stairs, they came to a comfortable lodging and a well-appointed room containing the books for the project in which they were about to engage. As soon as they were seated they began discussing which books to read first. Now while they were thus engaged, two men appeared at the door and handed the dean a letter from his uncle, the bishop, in which he informed him that he was very ill, and declared that if he wished to see him alive he must come at once. The dean was greatly troubled at this news, both for his uncle's suffering and because he was afraid that he might even have to give up the studies which he had begun. But he decided not to leave his most interesting study, and so he wrote a reply to his uncle, the bishop, and sent it to him.

"Three or four days later other men came bearing other letters to the dean informing him that the bishop had died and that the clergy at the cathedral were engaged in an election, and that *Deo volente* he, the dean, would be elected bishop. For this reason he need not trouble to go to the cathedral, as it would be better for him to be elected while he was in some other place than in the church.

"About a week later two very well-dressed and well-accoutred squires arrived, and when they approached the dean, they kissed his hand and showed him letters attesting that he had been elected bishop. And when Don Yllán heard this he told the successful candidate that he thanked God for the good news that had come to his house, and that since God had been so good to the dean, he asked to have the vacant deanship conferred on his son. The new bishop urged him to let him confer it on one of his own brothers, but he said that he would do right by Don Yllán in the cathedral and would reward him. Indeed he asked him to go to Santiago with him and bring his son along. Don Yllán agreed, and they went to Santiago.

"When they arrived they were received with much honor. And when they had been there a while some messengers came to the bishop from the pope naming him to the archbishopric of Toledo, and granting him permission to bestow the bishopric upon whomever he pleased. As soon as Don Yllán heard this, he mentioned pointedly what had happened the previous time, and asked that the bishopric be given to his son. But the archbishop urged him to allow it to go to one of his own uncles, a brother of his father. Don Yllán realized that great wrong was being done to him, but he agreed if only he would make amends in the future. The archbishop promised him faithfully to do so, and begged him to go with him to Tolosa and to bring his son along.

"When they reached Tolosa they were very well received by the counts and other nobles of the land. After they had lived there two years, emissaries from the pope arrived with letters showing that the pope had made the archbishop a cardinal and he graciously consented to his handing over the archbishopric of Tolosa to whomever he wished. Then Don Yllán went and told him how many times he had failed to do as he promised, and that now there could be no excuse for not conferring the dignity on his son. But the cardinal begged him to agree that the archbishopric should go to an uncle of his, the brother of his mother who was a very old man, but that since he was now a cardinal, Don Yllán should accompany him to the papal court, for there would be plenty of opportunities to do something on his behalf there. Don Yllán complained a great deal about this, but he agreed to do as the cardinal proposed and so he went with him.

"When they arrived they were very well received by the cardinals and everyone else and they stayed a long time. And every day Don Yllán kept urging the cardinal to do something for his son. While they were there the pope died, and the cardinals elected the former dean pope. Then Don Yllán went to him and said that now he could find no more excuses for not keeping his promise. The pope said not to insist so much, for there would always be an occasion for doing him a favor in the proper way. But Don Yllán complained, loudly, recalling the many things he had promised yet had never done, saying that he had feared something like this would happen when he first talked to him, and now that he had reached the pinnacle, and did not do as he had promised, there was no longer any reason to expect benefits from him at all.

"The pope objected to this complaint and began to abuse him, saying that if he persisted he would put him in a prison as a heretic and a necromancer, for he well knew that he had no other life nor trade in Toledo where he lived than to exercise the art of magic. And when Don Yllán saw how badly the pope rewarded him for what he had done for him, he bade him farewell. And the pope would not even give him provisions for the journey. At this, Don Yllán told the pope that since he had nothing to eat, he would have to return to the partridges which he had ordered roasted that night, and he called the servant woman and told her to roast them.

"Now when Don Yllán said this, the pope found himself back in Toledo and dean of Santiago, as he was when he came, and so great was his shame that he did not know what to say. Therefore, Don Yllán told him to take his leave, for he had shown well enough what he was like, and that he, Don Yllán, would consider the partridges wasted if the dean had any share of them.

"And you, Sir Count Lucanor, since you see how much you are doing for the man who asks you to help, and yet gives you little thanks for it, I do not think that you should do very much or take any risks only to come to the point of being rewarded as was Don Yllán by the dean."

And the count thought this good advice and he took it and profited from it.

And because Don Juan thought this a good story, he had it placed in this book and he wrote these following verses:

If one you help is thankless now,
He'll later keep no solemn vow.

. . .

The *Book of The Forty Viziers* has been cited as a source, but since that book dates from the fifteenth century, it cannot be the source— unless an earlier version existed and could have reached Spain. Most such stories as those found in the *Viziers* or in the so-called *Arabian Nights* or its Persian predecessor, the *Hazar Afsana*, had been assembled for ages from popular sources. Thus, many of the stories could have come into Don Juan's ken either as tales in Arabic books or from Arabic folktales, some of which might well have penetrated Spanish folklore by the time Don Juan began to write his stories. A possible source, also, is the thirteenth-century *Tabula Exemplorum*, cited by Ayerbe-Chaux. Thompson-Keller: H. 1565, D. 2031.5; Devoto: pp. 382-93; Ayerbe-Chaux: pp. 98-104.

12. What Happened to the Fox and the Rooster

Count Lucanor was talking to his counselor Patronio one day in this fashion: "Patronio, you know that, praise be to God, my lands are extensive, but not all adjoining each other. And although I have some localities that are very well fortified, others are less so, and there are even some lands that are quite distant from where my strength is greatest. Now when I quarrel with overlords and neighbors who are stronger than I, men who call themselves my friends, and others who pretend to be my advisers, try to frighten me by saying that under no circumstances should I establish myself in my distant lands, but that I should remain within the well-fortified holdings directly under my control. And because I know that you are loyal and know a great deal about such things, I want your advice as to what you think I ought to do under the circumstances."

"Sir Count Lucanor," said Patronio, "in important affairs, and doubtful causes advice is risky, for in most cases no one can express himself with certainty, since there is no reliable person before whom he can lay his case. Often we see that a man first thinks one thing and then another, and what a man believes to be wrong, sometimes turns out to be right, and what he thinks is right turns out to be wrong. Wherefore, anyone who gives advice, if he is loyal and well intentioned, is in great perplexity when he is called upon for advice, since if his advice turns out well, he gets no other thanks than to hear it said that he did his duty. On the other hand, if his advice turns out badly, he loses face and is shamed. And because I am much in doubt about this advice and foresee danger in it, I would like to avoid giving it; but since you demand my advice, and I must give it, I should like to have you hear what happened to a rooster and a fox."

The count asked what had happened.

"Sir Count," said Patronio, "a farmer had a house in the forest, and among the things that he raised were a great many hens and roosters. One day one of the roosters happened to be walking in a field, away from the house. He was walking quite confidently, when a fox saw him and sneaked up on him in hopes of catching him. The rooster saw him and flew up into a tree which stood a little apart from the rest. When the fox saw that the rooster was safe, he was much annoyed at not catching him, and he wondered how he might manage to. So he went up to the tree and began to ask questions, flattering the rooster and

72

urging him to come down and walk around in the fields as usual, but the rooster would not. Then when the fox saw that he could not deceive him by flattery, and since he realized that there was no way to deceive him, he began to threaten him, saying that since he did not trust him he would see to it that he came to a bad end. But the rooster knew he was safe and paid no attention to his threats or his assurances. Then the fox, seeing that he could not deceive him in any way, went up to the tree and began to gnaw it with his teeth and to hit it hard with his tail.

"Then the poor foolish rooster became unreasonably frightened, not realizing that his fear of the fox was groundless, and he grew needlessly terrified and tried to fly to some other trees where he might be safer. Now although he could not reach the forest, he did reach another tree. And when the fox saw his silly terror he went after him and chased him from tree to tree, until finally he drove him out of the trees and caught him and ate him.

"And you, Sir Count, if you need to go to your property and stay there, do not be unnecessarily concerned. And do not be frightened by vain threats, nor by what people say. Therefore beware of anything that can harm you. Fight always to defend and protect your farthest outposts and remember that as long as you have men and supplies no one can hurt you simply because a place is not well fortified. For if vain fear or anxiety cause you to desert your most distant possessions in this way, surely your enemies will begin to deprive you of place after place until they have taken everything. For the more fear and anxiety you and your followers display by deserting your territories, the more your enemies will try to take what belongs to you. For the more you and your followers see your enemies exerting themselves, the greater will be your dismay, and thus the affair will progress until you have nothing left in the world; but if you resist in the first instance, you may be safe as the rooster would have been if he had stayed in the first tree. Therefore, I think this is proper conduct for all who have fortresses, for if they but knew this story, they would not be unnecessarily afraid when attempts are made to frighten them with tricks or pitfalls or siege engines or similar things such as are conceived to frighten the besieged. And let me say one thing more to show you that I am telling the truth: a fortress can only be taken by scaling the walls with ladders, or by tunneling beneath them, but if the wall is high the ladders will not reach the top. And as for digging, you may well believe that those who must do the digging need a great deal of time. So it is that places are taken on account of fear or because of some defect in the defenders; nothing but irrational fears can bring them down.

"Certainly, Sir Count, people like you, and even others who are not as strong as you are, should study a situation well and approach it with great resolution before deciding what to do. You yourself cannot and must not fail in this, but once in the fray, you must be bold, and especially must you avoid unreasonable fear, for you may be certain that of those who are in danger many more escape unharmed among those who defend themselves, than among those who run away. Note, therefore, that if a small dog attacked by a huge hound stands firm and shows his teeth, he often escapes, however large the other dog may be; but if he runs away, he is caught and killed."

And what Patronio told him greatly pleased the count, and he acted accordingly and was happy.

And because Don Juan thought this a good story he had it placed in this book and wrote the following verses:

Do not give way to senseless fear,
But bravely keep what you hold dear.

. . .

The source is not known. Some authorities suggest folklore, others certain fables in the well-known collections, but no one can give the exact source. It has some similarities with a story in *Calila e Digna* entitled "De la golpexa e de la paloma e del alcaravan." The animal characters are different, however. Don Juan Manuel utilized *Calila e Digna* as a source for several stories. Until a better suggestion is brought forward, we believe that the story of the fox, the dove, and the stork in *Calila* is the source. Thompson-Keller: K. 815; Devoto: pp. 393-94; Ayerbe-Chaux: pp. 64-66.

13. What Happened to a Man
Who Was Hunting Partridges

On another occasion Count Lucanor was talking to Patronio, his adviser, and he said, "Patronio, some very clever men, and some who are less so, occasionally damage my property and harass my people; but then when we meet, they let on that they are sorry about it, that they acted only out of great necessity and great anxiety, and because they could not help themselves. And since I want to know how I ought to react when this happens, I should like to have your opinion."

"Sir Count Lucanor," said Patronio, "what you have asked me to give you advice about reminds me of what happened to a man who was out catching partridges."

The count asked him to tell him about it.

"Sir Count," said Patronio, "a man put out his nets for partridges, and when they had fallen into it, he came up to the net where the partridges lay. And as soon as he caught them, he killed them and took them out of the net. Now while he was killing partridges the wind blew so hard into his eyes that they began to water. And one of the partridges, still alive in the net, said to the rest: 'Look, friends, at this man: although he is killing us, see how sorry for us he feels. He is weeping about it!'

"But another partridge, which was smarter than the first and which, because of her cleverness, had avoided the net, answered her as follows: 'Friend, I thank God for saving me, and I pray Him to keep me and my friends from someone who wants to kill and hurt me, yet pretends to be sorry for me.'

"And you, Sir Count Lucanor, look out for the man who harms you and says he is sorry for it. But if someone hurts you, without meaning to harm or dishonor you, and the harm is not enough to distress you, and if he is a man from whom you have had kindness and honor, and he acts out of necessity and is sorry for it, then I advise you to overlook it, but to act in such a way that he will not do it often enough to harm you or shame you. But if he works against you in any other way, deal with him so that your goods and honor will always be safe."

And the count thought that Patronio's advice was good and he acted accordingly and profited from it.

And Don Juan, thinking the story good, had it placed in this book and wrote the following verses:

From one who hurts you 'gainst his will,
Guard yourself with utmost skill.

. . .

This story appears in the famous *Narrationes* or *Fabulae* of the English cleric, Odo of Cheriton, and in the *Libro de los gatos* which is a hispanification of Odo's fables. Don Juan Manuel could have drawn upon either. Thompson-Keller: J. 869.1; Devoto: pp. 394-95; Ayerbe-Chaux: pp. 63-64.

14. The Miracle of Saint Dominick
When He Preached against the Usurer

One day Count Lucanor was talking to his adviser Patronio in his residence, and he said to him: "Patronio, I have been advised to heap up as much wealth as I can, and having been told that it behooves me to do this more than anything else, come what may, I would like you to tell me what you think of this."

"Sir Count," said Patronio, "although great lords may think it behooves you to acquire wealth for many purposes, and especially to be able to do whatever you must do, do not believe that it is necessary to grow wealthy in such a way as to dissipate your talent, for in so doing you may fail to do your duty toward your people and protect your honor and estates, for if you do, the same thing may happen to you as happened to a Lombard in Bologna."

The count asked what had happened.

"Sir Count," said Patronio, "in Bologna lived a Lombard who had amassed a great fortune, and he did not care whether it came from a good source or not. He concentrated solely on heaping up money in every way possible. Now the Lombard suffered from a mortal ailment,

76

and one of his friends, when he saw him close to death, advised him to make confession to Saint Dominick, who was then in the city, and the Lombard agreed. And when they sent for Saint Dominick the latter realized that it was not God's will for that wicked man to avoid a punishment for the evil that he had done. Therefore, he did not want to go himself, but sent a friar instead. When the Lombard's sons knew that Saint Dominick had been sent for, they were very upset, thinking that the saint would make their father give away his possessions for the good of his soul, and that then nothing would be left for them.

"When the friar came they said that their father was sweating, but that when it was needful they would send for him. And in a short while the Lombard could no longer talk and he died in such a fashion that he had done nothing that he ought to have done for the sake of his soul. On the next day when they took him away for burial, they asked Saint Dominick to preach over him, and he did. Now when he came to say some words about that man, he spoke the word of the Gospel: *Ubi est tesaurus tuus ibi est cor tuum*, which means, 'where thy treasure is, there will thy heart be also.'

"When he uttered these words, he turned to the people and said: 'Friends, so that you may understand that the word of the Gospel is true, examine the heart of this man, and I tell you that you will not find it in his body, but in the chest where he kept his money.'

"Then they looked for the heart in the body and could not find it, but found it in the chest, as Saint Dominick had said. And it was full of worms and smelled worse than anything putrid or rotten.

"And you Sir Count Lucanor, although wealth is good, as mentioned above, be careful of two things: first, that the treasure that you amass is of good origin; and the other that you do not give your heart so completely to your treasure that you fail to do what you must do. Never fail in anything as regards your honor or duties, but amass a treasure of good works so that you may enjoy God's grace and a good reputation among men."

The count liked this advice of Patronio's very much, and he acted accordingly and profited by it.

And Don Juan, thinking this a good story, had it written down in this book and wrote the following verses:

Try an honest treasure to achieve,
Ill-gotten goods will but deceive.

Stories of usurers can be found in de Vitry, in the *Castigos e documentos para bien vivir* of Don Juan's cousin, King Sancho IV, and in many sermons and *exempla;* but the exact source is yet to be determined, in spite of what scholars have written. The Dominicans may have given the tale to Don Juan. Thompson-Keller: W. 153.1; Devoto: pp. 395-96; Ayerbe-Chaux: pp. 45-47.

15. What Happened to Lorenzo Suárez at the Siege of Seville

On another occasion Count Lucanor was talking to his counselor Patronio as follows: "Patronio, I happen to have a very powerful king for an enemy. The quarrel between us has lasted a long time, but we now find it to our advantage to become reconciled. Now although we are now in agreement and not at war, we are still suspicious of each other. And some of his people as well as some of mine try to frighten me by saying that he is looking for an excuse to attack me. So, since you are wise, I want you to advise me what to do in this case."

"Sir Count Lucanor," said Patronio, "this for many reasons is a very serious matter to give advice about. First, everyone who wants to engage in a quarrel has to prepare the ground very well. While claiming to seek your advantage, he disillusions you, gets you in the right frame of mind, and sympathizes with you about the harm that has been done to you, and always tells you things to make you suspicious. Because of this suspicion you take certain precautions and these are the beginning of a quarrel; yet no one can tell you not to do this, for anyone who tells you not to protect yourself gives you to understand that he does not value your life; and anyone who would tell you not to repair, guard, and strengthen your forts, makes it plain that he does not wish to protect your inheritance. Anyone who tells you not to have friends and vassals and reward them well to keep and hold them, makes it obvious that he cares neither for your honor nor your defense. Thus, by your failure to do these things you expose yourself to great danger, and you might even cause your own downfall. But since you want my advice in the matter, I should like you to hear what happened to a worthy gentleman."

The count asked him to tell him about it.

"Sir Count," said Patronio, "the sainted and blessed King Don Fernando was besieging Seville, and among the many fine men who were there with him were three gentlemen reputed to be the best men of arms in the world. One was named Don Lorenzo Suárez Gallinato, the second Don García Pérez de Vargas, and I cannot recall the name of the third. One day these three gentlemen had an argument as to which of them was most skilled at arms. And because they could not agree by any other means, they decided to arm themselves well and to go up to the gate of Seville and strike it with their lances.

"The next day in the morning they put on their armor and headed for the city. Now the Moors who were on the walls and in the towers, when they saw that they were only three, thought that they came to parley, so no one came out against them. And the three warriors passed over the moat and through the outer wall and reached the gate of the city and struck it with the butts of their lances. As soon as they had done this they gave their horses rein and turned back toward their army. And when the Moors saw that they had nothing to say, they thought they were being made fun of and they set out after them. But when they got the gate of the city open, the three warriors were already far away. Even so, more than 1,500 horsemen and more than 20,000 foot soldiers came out after them.

"When the three warriors saw that they were closing in on them, they turned their horses about and waited. When the Moors were a little way distant, the man whose name I have forgotten went up to them to attack them, but Don Lorenzo Suárez and Don García Pérez remained where they were. And when the Moors were still closer Don García Pérez de Vargas went to fight them. But Don Lorenzo Suárez stood his ground and did not go toward them, until the Moors came up and began to attack him. Now when they began to harass him, he went among them and wrought marvelous feats of arms. And when the royal army saw these warriors among the Moors, they went to their aid.

"Although they were hard pressed and wounded, it was God's will that none of them died. But the struggle between Christians and Moors was so great that King Don Fernando himself entered the fight, and his Christian soldiers were very gallant that day. When the king retired to his tent, he ordered the three warriors taken into custody, saying that they deserved death for risking themselves in so mad an adventure—first, for having the army attack without his command, and second, for risking the lives of three such excellent knights. But when the most excellent men of the army asked the king's pardon on their behalf, he let them go.

"When the king found out that they had done the deed because of an argument among themselves, he sent for the ablest men who were with him to judge which of the three was the best. And when they came together, there was a great argument among them, for some said the greatest effort was that of the first man who attacked the enemy; others that it was the second; and still others that it was the third. And each one argued so well that he seemed to be right. In truth, however, so fine was the deed itself that anyone could find reasons to praise it. But when the discussion was over, it was decided as follows: that if the Moors who came after them were so numerous that they could have been conquered by the strength or the virtue of those warriors, then the first to attack was the greatest warrior, since something was begun that could be ended; but since the Moors were so numerous that there was no way to conquer them, he that went toward them did not do so in order to conquer them, but to avoid the shame of flight; and since he could not escape, the anxiety within him made him strike them because he could not bear to seem afraid.

"And the second who went to attack them, who waited longer than the first, they thought superior because he could endure greater fear. But Don Lorenzo Suárez, who bore all the fear and waited until the Moors attacked him, they judged to be the greatest warrior.

"And you, Sir Count Lucanor, see yourself beset by fears and anxieties, for the quarrel is such that even if you begin it, you cannot end it. The more you suffer from these fears and terrors, the stronger you will be and the more sensibly you will act, since you will take care of your own and will do nothing hastily for fear of being harmed. I advise you not to yield to the anxiety within you. And since no great harm can come to you, wait until someone attacks you, and then perhaps you will see that the fears and anxieties that possess you are not real, but result from what people are saying to their own advantage, since they profit only by evil. And you must realize that those on your side like those on the other, desire neither war nor peace, for they do not wish to prepare for war, nor to have a total peace either. What they want is a period of confusion which they can use to do damage, holding you and yours as hostages so as to deprive you of all that you possess without fear of your chastising them for their actions.

"Therefore, although they act against you, they cannot make it much worse for you by laying the blame on someone else. In fact, a great deal of good may come out of it. First, God is on your side and helps in such cases; and second, everyone will think you did what was right. And if perchance you refrain from doing what you should not do, your adversary may not move against you and you will have peace and will serve God and the welfare of good people; and you will avoid giving satisfaction to the troublemakers, who would be little affected by any harm that might come to you incidentally."

And the count was pleased with the advice that Patronio gave him, and he acted accordingly and profited from it.

And because Don Juan thought this a good story he ordered it written down in this book and he wrote these verses:

Waging war no evil cures;
He conquers most who most endures.

．　　．　　．

Don Juan Manuel went to Spanish history for this story: there was a Don Lorenzo Suárez Gallinato and in the *Crónica del Santo rey don Fernando*, Don Juan's grandfather. Much is related about this knight; however, Don Juan has changed history to suit his purpose. The prince must have been an admirer of Don Lorenzo, for he appears also in *exemplo* 28. Thompson-Keller: J. 572.1; Devoto: pp. 397-98.

16. The Reply that Count Fernán González Gave to His Relative Nuño Laynes

Count Lucanor was talking one day to Patronio, his adviser, as follows: "Patronio, you know that I am no longer young, and that I have thus far endured many trials; therefore from now on I should like to rest, go hunting, and avoid labor and toil. And because you always advise me well, I should like you to tell me what in your opinion will be the best for me."

"Sir Count," said Patronio, "you speak well and reasonably, but I should like you to hear what Fernán González once said to Nuño Laynes."

The count asked him to tell him about it.

"Sir Count," said Patronio, "Count Fernán González was in Burgos and he had endured many trials to defend his land. Now once when he was somewhat relaxed and at peace, Nuño Laynes told him that from then on it would be well for him not to engage in so many dangerous activities, but to rest and allow his men to rest. The count replied that no one would like better to rest and be idle than he, if he could but afford to do so; however, that he knew there was a great war on between the Moors, the Leonese, and the Navarrese, and if people took it easy their enemies would be after them; and if they wanted to go hunting with good birds up above Arlanzón, or down below on good fat mules, and stop defending their land, they might well do so, but if so then what the old saying tells might happen: 'When death came, the man died and with him died his fame.' But if we are willing to forget recreation and work hard to defend ourselves and raise up our honor, they will say of us after our death: 'Dead the man's name but not dead his fame.' For after all, idle and lazy though we are, we must all die, and it would not look good to me, if through idleness or ease we should fail to act in such fashion that after our death, the reputation of our good deeds might live on.

"And you, Sir Count, since you know that you must die, following my advice, you will never fail through ease or idleness to do such deeds that even after your death the fame of your actions may live on."

And the count liked Patronio's advice and he took it and profited by it.

And because Don Juan liked this story he had it written down in this book and wrote the following verses:

> *If idle ways destroy our fame,*
> *Our life, though short, will bear the blame.*

.   .   .

The famous, and perhaps mythical knight, Fernán González was very much a subject of Spanish history. Don Juan Manuel could have taken the events he used from the hero's life as found in the *Crónica General*, sponsored by his uncle Alfonso X, or from the earlier *Poema de Fernán González* utilized in the writing of the *Crónica General;* but even so, as was his custom, Don Juan embellished the older accounts and inserted ideas of his own. Thompson-Keller: J. 674.2; Devoto: pp. 398-99; Ayerbe-Chaux: pp. 88-91.

17. What Happened to a Very Hungry Man Who Was Half-heartedly Invited to Dinner

On another occasion Count Lucanor was talking to his adviser Patronio in this manner: "Patronio, a man has come to me and said that he wants to do something that will greatly please me. But he said it in so half-hearted a manner that he would obviously prefer me not to accept his offer. On the one hand I would like very much to accept it, but on the other I am reluctant to accept his help, since he offers it so unenthusiastically. Now with the good mind that you have, please tell me what you think I ought to do in this situation."

"Sir Count Lucanor," said Patronio, "if you are to do what is to your advantage, I should like you to hear what happened to a man who was invited to dinner."

The count asked him what had happened.

"Sir Count Lucanor," said Patronio, "there was once a good man, formerly rich, who had reached a state of poverty, but he was ashamed to beg for food. For this reason he often went hungry and suffered a great deal. And one day as he was going about in some pain because he had had nothing to eat, he passed the house of an acquaintance of his who was dining. And when he saw him passing by, the acquaintance invited him rather half-heartedly to dine, and because of his great need he washed his hands and said: 'Truly, Mr. So-and-So, since you have urged me and insisted on my eating with you, it would surely be wrong to refuse or to have you ask in vain.' And he sat down to eat and overcame his hunger and the pangs that he had endured. Thus did God help him and give him a way of escape from his great suffering.

"And you, Sir Count Lucanor, since you think that what the man proposes is to your great advantage, tell him that you accept his proposal, and pay no attention to his half-hearted manner. Do not wait for him to insist, for if he should not mention it again, you would be more ashamed to make a request of him, than to have him make a proposal to you."

And the count thought this good advice and he followed it and profited from it.

And Don Juan thought this a good story and he had it written down in this book and wrote the following verses:

> *If you're seeking personal profit,*
> *When it's offered do not scoff it.*

· · ·

A timeless folk motif of world currency could be the origin of this tale. Later it would appear in *Lazarillo de Tormes* from the mouth of the poverty-stricken *hidalgo*. We may never know Don Juan Manuel's exact source. It might originate in Arabic literature or folklore. Thompson-Keller: J. 1340; Devoto: pp. 399-400.

18. What Happened to Pero Meléndez de Valdés When He Broke His Leg

Count Lucanor was talking to his adviser Patronio one day as follows: "You know that I have a quarrel with a neighbor who is a powerful and honorable man. Now we have agreed to go to a certain town, and that whichever one of us gets there first will occupy it and the other will be the loser.

"You know that my men are already assembled, and I trust in God's mercy that if I were to go, I would win honor and advantage thereby. But right now I am prevented from going, for I am not altogether well. And although the town will be a great loss to me, I would be much more upset by failing to win the honor that will accrue to him than I would be by the actual loss of the town. Therefore, because of the faith I have in you I beg you to tell me what to do."

"Sir Count Lucanor," said Patronio, "although you have a right to complain, I would like you to hear what happened to Pero Meléndez de Valdés, so that you can do what is best."

The count asked what had happened to him.

"Sir Count Lucanor," said Patronio, "Don Pero Meléndez de Valdés was a very distinguished gentleman in the kingdom of Leon, and he had a habit of saying, no matter what happened, 'God be praised. For what He does is all for the best.' And this Pero Meléndez was the counselor and favorite of the king of Leon. Now his adversaries, since they were very envious of him, plotted wickedly against him and employed such deceit with the king that he agreed to order his death.

"And while Pero Meléndez was in his home a summons from the king came. And those who were to kill him were waiting for him a half a league from his house. But Don Pero Meléndez, while making ready to ride to the king, fell downstairs and broke his leg. And when those who were to go with him saw what had happened at this time, they began to berate him saying, 'Well, Don Pero Meléndez, you are always saying that what God does is for the best. Look at this favor that God has done you!' And he replied that they could be certain that although they were very sorry for what had happened to him on this occasion, they would find out that since God had done it, it was for the best. And no matter what they said he would not change his opinion.

"And those who were waiting to kill him on the king's command, when they saw that he did not come, and when they learned what had happened to him, returned to the king and told him why they could not carry out their orders. For a long time Don Pero Meléndez was unable to ride, and while he was in this sorry condition, the king found out that what had been imputed to Pero Meléndez was really false, and he arrested those who had said it. And he went to see Don Pero Meléndez and told him the lies that had been told about him and how he had ordered him to be killed, and he asked his pardon for the harm that was to have been done him, and he treated him kindly and did honor to him to make amends. Indeed, he ordered the prosecution of those who had plotted against him.

"Thus God freed Don Pero Meléndez because he was guiltless and his everlasting saying was true, that everything that God does is for the best. And you, Sir Count Lucanor, do not complain about the setback that you have endured, but be convinced that everything that God does is for the best, for if you believe this, everything will turn out well for you. But you must realize that everything happens in two ways: first, a man encounters an obstacle about which he can take counsel; secondly, an obstacle arises against which he cannot take counsel. And in the case of obstacles about which one can take counsel a man should do his best to do so, and should not wait for the will of God or for matters to straighten themselves out by chance, for this would be tempting God. For since a man has reason and understanding, he ought to do everything possible to find a solution to what has happened to him, but when he cannot, he should believe that what happens is the will of God and all for the best. And since what has happened to you comes about by God's will, which cannot be changed, you must believe that since God does it, it is for the best, and God will make things happen according to your heartfelt desire."

And Count Lucanor thought that Patronio spoke the truth and gave good advice and he followed it and profited thereby.

And Don Juan thought this a good story and he had it written in the book and wrote the following verses:

What God hath wrought is all for thee,
Be patient, then, his will to see.

.   .   .

Historians do not identify the protagonist as any known historical character. This kind of coincidence in which someone is prevented by illness or physical hurt from going to a place at which he will be ambushed or killed is common in folklore. The story, but with different characters, would be utilized by Clemente Sánchez nearly two centuries later. Possibly a similar event might have occurred in Don Juan Manuel's own life. Thompson-Keller: N. 178; Devoto: pp. 400-402; Ayerbe-Chaux: pp. 96-98.

19. What Happened to the Crows and the Owls

One day Count Lucanor was talking as follows to Patronio, his adviser: "Patronio, I am having a disagreement with a very powerful man who is my enemy, and in my enemy's house is a relative, in the capacity of a retainer whom he has helped greatly. One day because of something that happened between them, my enemy mistreated this man and dishonored him, and the man who was so greatly indebted to him, seeing the harm he had received and trying to find a way to avenge himself, came to me; and this will be of great advantage to me, for this man can give me information and show me how best to hurt my enemy. But because of the confidence that I have in you and in your wisdom, I urge you to tell me what to do."

"Sir Count Lucanor," said Patronio, "first let me tell you that this man came to you only to deceive you. And so that you may know the manner of his deceit, I should like you to hear what happened to the owls and the crows."

The count asked him what had happened.

"Sir Count Lucanor," said Patronio, "the crows and the owls had a great quarrel among themselves, but the crows complained the most. The owls, because it is their custom to fly about at night and remain by day in caves where they are hard to find, came at night to the trees where the crows were, and hurt and killed many of them. And since the crows had suffered so much, one of them who was very wise, and who grieved greatly over the harm done to them by the owls, their enemies, spoke to the crows, his relatives, and showed them a way to vengeance. And this is how it was. The crows should pluck a crow of most of his feathers except for a few with which he could barely fly. And when he was in this pitiful condition he was sent to the owls to tell them in detail all the bad things the crows had done to him. He said he did not wish to turn against the crows, but that since they had done him so much harm he would show the owls many ways of taking vengeance on them, and of doing them a great deal of harm. And when the owls heard this, they were very pleased, and they thought that this crow's presence stood them in good stead. Therefore, they were kind to the crow and trusted him in all their actions and private affairs. But among the owls was a very old one who had suffered much, and when he saw what the crow was doing he understood the trick. And he went to the other owls and told them that it was plain that the crow was there only to hurt them and to spy upon them, and that they ought to drive him away. But the others did not believe it. And when he saw that they would not listen, he went away to a place where the crows would not be able to find him. But the rest of the owls thought well of the crow. And when his wings had grown out he told the owls that now since he could fly, he would go and find out where the crows were and would come and tell them so that they could rally to kill them, and the owls liked this.

"And as soon as the crow was with the other crows, a lot of them got together, and knowing all the ways of the owls, they came upon them by day when they do not fly and were safe and confident, and killed and destroyed so many of them that the crows were victorious in their war. And all this misfortune happened to the owls because they trusted one crow, who was their natural enemy.

"And you, Sir Count Lucanor, since you know that this man who has come to you is indebted to your enemy, naturally he and all his family are your enemies. Therefore, I advise you by no means to admit him to your company, for you may be sure that he came to you only to deceive you and harm you. But if he wishes to serve you, without becoming close to you so that he can neither obstruct your actions nor learn anything about your affairs, and if he should indeed harm your enemy and work against him, to whom he is united by gratitude, so that you see that he will never be reconciled to him, *then* you may trust him, but always trust him in such a way that no harm can come to you."

And the count thought this good advice, and he took it and profited from it.

And because Don Juan thought this a good story he had it written in this book and wrote the following verses:

> *Beware to trust a former foe,*
> *For sure as fate 'twill bring thee woe.*

. . .

The source of this story is undoubtedly a version of a tale found in the Spanish version of *Calila e Digna*. Since the Arabic original, *Kalilah wa-Dimna*, must have been extant, Don Juan could have drawn upon the Arabic. The oldest written version is that found in the *Panchatantra*, book 3, entitled "the Crows and the Owls." Novelesque in length in the original Sanskrit, as well as in the Arabic and Spanish versions, in the hands of Don Juan Manuel it is reduced to a story of only a few pages. Thompson-Keller: A. 2294.5.7, B. 263.3, K. 2042; Devoto: pp. 402-4.

20. What Happened to a King for Whom a Man Promised to Perform Alchemy

One day Count Lucanor was talking to Patronio, his adviser, as follows: "Patronio, a man has come and told me that he can help me to win great advantage and great honor, and for this purpose he asked to look into my affairs for a place to begin; and when he had concluded, he told me that for one piece of money spent there would be ten. And for the sake of the good intelligence that God has given you, I beg you to tell me what in your view I should do in this matter."

"Sir Count Lucanor," said Patronio, "there was once a man who was very dishonest and very anxious to grow rich and to give up the hard life that he was living. And he knew of a not-very-sophisticated king who was trying to perform alchemy. So the swindler took 100 doubloons and filed them, and with the filings that he collected, and with other things that he added to them, he produced 100 pellets, each of which weighed a doubloon, in addition to the mixture of other things that he added to the filings. And he went to the town where the king was, and dressing himself appropriately, he took the pellets and sold them to a grocer. And the grocer asked what the pellets were for, and the swindler told him they had many uses, and especially that without that substance one could not perform alchemy, and he sold him the 100 pellets for two or three doubloons. And the grocer asked him what the pellets were called and the swindler said they were called *tabardie*. And the swindler lived in the town quietly for a while, and he went around telling people quietly that he knew how to perform alchemy. And the news reached the king. And the king sent for him and asked if he knew how to perform alchemy. And the swindler, although he made a show of wanting to keep it quiet and pretended that he did not know anything about the subject, finally let it be known that he did; but he advised the king not to trust anyone with the fact, nor to risk much of his money on it, although if he wanted him to, he would personally show him what he knew about it. And the king thanked him heartily, for he thought that since it was to be explained to him, there could be no trickery involved. Then the swindler sent for the things he needed, and they were all things that were available, and among other things he sent for a coin made of *tabardíe*. And all the things he sent for cost no more than a few pennies.

"And after they had brought them, he melted them in the king's presence, and it came to about one doubloon of fine gold. And as soon as the king saw something that cost but two or three pennies come out as a doubloon, he was delighted and thought himself the most fortunate of men; and he told the man who performed it that he thought him an excellent man and he asked him to make some more. And the swindler replied as if he knew nothing more: 'Sire, I have shown you all that I know. From now on you can do it as well as I, but you must realize that if one of the ingredients is lacking one cannot make gold.'

"And when he had said this he took his leave of the king and went home. And the king tried to make gold without the swindler, and he doubled the recipe, and it came out weighing two gold doubloons. Then he doubled it again and got four doubloons. And when the king saw that he could make as much gold as he wished, he sent for enough materials to make a thousand doubloons. And they found all the materials except the *tabardíe*. And when the king saw that *tabardíe* was lacking, and that he could not make gold, he sent for the man who had showed him how to do it, and told him that he could not do it anymore. And he asked him if he had all the ingredients that he gave him in writing. The king said yes, except that the *tabardíe* was missing. Then the swindler told him that if anything was missing he could not make gold, as he had told him on the first day. Then the king asked if he knew where to get more *tabardíe*. And the swindler said yes. Then the king said that since he knew where it was, he should go and get it and procure enough for him to make all the gold he wanted. And the swindler told him that anyone at all could do this as well or better than himself, but if the king demanded it as a favor, he would go and get it, and would find enough in his own country. Then he told the king how much it would cost and it came to a large sum.

"And when the swindler had the money in his possession he went his way and never came back. Thus the king was deceived through bad advice. And when finally he thought that the swindler was taking longer than he should, he sent to his house to get news of him. In his house nothing was found but a locked chest, and when they opened it they read the following message: 'Now hear this: there is nothing in the world called *tabardíe*, for I have deceived you, and when I told you that I would make you rich, you should have told me that if I first made myself rich you would believe me.'

"In a few days' time men were laughing and joking about the matter and decided to write down a list of the names of all the people they knew together with their qualities: the tricky ones are such and such, the rich are x and y, and the wise ones Jack and John, and so on, revealing the whole story, good and bad. And when they came to write about men who had been ill advised, they put down the name of the king. And when the king heard of it, he sent for them and assured them that he would do them no harm on that account, if they told him why they depicted him as a man who had been ill advised. And they said that it was because he had given so much money to a stranger for whom he had no guarantee. And the king admitted that he had made a mistake, but that if the man who had taken the money returned, they would no longer think him so ill advised. And they said that for their part they had lost nothing, for if the other returned they would no longer apply their saying to the king but to the other man.

"And you, Count Lucanor, if you do not wish to be thought ill advised, do not risk any of your resources on something risky, for you would be sorry to lose it through hope of winning great profits while still in doubt."

And the count liked the advice, and he took it and profited by it.

And Don Juan, seeing that this story was good, had it written down in this book and wrote these verses:

> *Risking wealth is badly done,*
> *Advised by one possessed of none.*

This story, probably of oriental origin, appeared in the Spanish *Caballero Cifar* finished probably in 1300, and was therefore available to Don Juan Manuel. But Arabic sources were probably available, too. Thompson-Keller: K. 111.4; Devoto: pp. 404-6; Ayerbe-Chaux: pp. 20-24.

21. What Happened to a Young King and a Philosopher to Whom His Father Commended Him

Once again Count Lucanor was talking to Patronio, his adviser, in this manner: "Patronio, I once had a relative of whom I was very fond, but he died and left a small son whom I have reared. And because of what I owed his father and my great affection for him, and also because of my expectation of what he will do for me when he is able, I have brought him up well, and God knows I love him as if he were my own son. The boy is intelligent, and I trust to God that he will turn out to be a good man; but because appearances are often deceptive and boys do not achieve what they should, I shall be happy if youth and inexperience do not lead him astray. Now, through the good sense that you have, I beg you to tell me how to guide him so that he may do what is best for him and for his estate."

"Sir Count Lucanor," said Patronio, "in order for you to handle the boy's affairs as I think best, I should greatly like you to hear what happened to a great philosopher and a boy-king, his ward."

The count asked what had happened.

"Sir Count Lucanor," said Patronio, "a king had a son whom he entrusted to a philosopher to rear. Now when the king died, his son was still a small boy, and the philosopher cared for him until he was more than fifteen years old. But when he became an adolescent, he began to despise the advice of his tutor and heeded the advice of other boys' mentors, and listened to those who owed him little duty, hoping they would keep him out of harm's way. And as he handled his affairs in this fashion, things soon reached a point that both in his care of his person and his property, matters had fallen to a sorry state, and everyone said it was too bad that the lad was losing his health and property. Now things went so badly that the philosopher who was responsible for the boy's upbringing was greatly concerned and worried and did not know what to do. After all, he had frequently tried admonishing him, urging him, and even punishing him; but to no avail, for his youth led him astray. And when the philosopher could find no way to reach him, he thought of a plan that I shall now tell you. The philosopher began little by little to let it be known in the king's household that he was the world's greatest diviner and soothsayer. And so many people heard about it that the young king did also. And the king asked the philosopher if it were true that he knew how to read auguries as well as he was reputed to do. And the philosopher, although he pretended to deny it, finally said it was true, but that no one should know about it.

"And as boys are anxious to know and to try everything, the king, being a boy, was very eager to see how the philosopher foretold the future. And the more the philosopher postponed it, the more the boy-king was anxious to know, and he kept insisting until the philosopher finally agreed to go out with him some morning very early to read the signs, but secretly so that no one would know. And they got up very early in the morning, and the philosopher led him through a valley where there were some deserted villages. And when they had passed through a number of them they heard a crow cawing in a tree. And the king pointed him out to the philosopher who gave a sign that he had heard him. And another crow began to caw in another tree, and the two crows kept it up, first one cawing and then the other. And when the philosopher had listened for a while he began to weep bitterly and tore his clothing and showed signs of overwhelming grief.

"Now when the boy-king saw it, he was astounded and asked the philosopher why. And the philosopher said that he had rather not tell. But when the king insisted, the philosopher said that he would rather be dead than alive, for not only men but the birds also understood how through his king's bad conduct his land was lost and his body desecrated. And the boy-king asked how this could be. And he told him that those two crows had planned to marry the son of one of them to the daughter of the other, and that the crow who had first begun to talk, said that since the wedding was planned, they might as well marry. And the other replied that it was true that the wedding was planned, but that now the female was richer than the other, for thanks be to God, since the beginning of the reign of the present king all the towns of the valley are deserted, and that in the deserted houses there are many snakes, lizards, and toads, and other such creatures as live in deserted places, wherefore there is more to eat than usual, and therefore the wedding was not between equals. And when the other crow heard this, he began to laugh and told him that he was talking nonsense if he wished to postpone the wedding for this reason, for if God permitted the king to live, soon the second crow would be richer than her neighbor, for soon the valley in which she lived would be deserted too; and in it there were ten times as many villages as in the other valley, and so there was no reason to postpone the wedding on this account. Therefore they authorized it. And when the king heard this he was sad, and he realized that it was his fault that his land was deserted. And when the philosopher saw the grief and concern of the boy-king and his willingness to attend to his affairs, he gave him such good advice that in a short time his affairs were again in order, both in his person and in his kingdom.

"And you, Sir Count, since you are rearing this boy and you want him to straighten out his affairs, find some way either by examples or by well-chosen words and flattery to make him understand his situation. But by no means upset him with punishment or ill treatment, thinking thus to straighten him out, for it is the way of most boys to detest the one who punishes them, especially if he is a man of importance, for they regard it as a kind of scorn, not realizing how wrong they are, because no man is a greater friend than he who corrects a boy to keep him from harm. But boys do not take it thus, but in the worst possible way. And thus a disaffection might arise between the two of you, which would harm you both from now on."

And this advice that Patronio gave him pleased the count, who followed it to his profit.

And because Don Juan was pleased with this story he had it placed in this book and wrote the following verses:

> *Don't spank a boy for his misdeeds,*
> *But show him rather how to please.*

. . .

The motif of an animal or animals which speak and think like humans, or, in some cases, which speak only what they have been taught to say with no knowledge of the meaning, is ancient. One reads of such creatures in Pliny, and Aesop's fables abound in speaking animals. The *Libro de los engaños* contains a story of an intelligent parrot set to spy upon its master's wife and tricked by her; in *Calila* there is a story of parrots taught to malign their master's wife by a servant whom she rejected. But the most likely source of Don Juan Manuel's tale 21 may be the *Book of the Forty Viziers*. The likelihood of his having heard it from oral tradition is not to be discounted, however. Thompson-Keller: B. 216, J. 816.1, J. 1075; Devoto: pp. 406-8.

22. What Happened to the Lion and the Bull

On another occasion Count Lucanor was talking to his adviser Patronio, and he said to him: "Patronio, I have a distinguished and powerful friend, and although up to now I have seen in him nothing but good works, I am now told that he is not so fond of me as he once was and is even looking for a way to oppose me. I am therefore in great perplexity: first, because I am afraid that if he should turn against me he might hurt me badly; and secondly, because I am afraid that if he thinks I suspect him and I start protecting myself, he will do the same, and then suspicion and alienation will grow between us until we begin to quarrel. And for the sake of the great trust that I have in you, I beg you to advise me as to what I ought to do."

"Sir Count Lucanor," said Patronio, "in order for you to protect yourself, I should very much like you to hear what happened to the lion and the bull."

And the count asked him to tell him what had happened.

"Sir Count Lucanor," said Patronio, "the lion and the bull were very good friends, and because they are strong and vigorous animals, they ruled and lorded it over all the other animals, for with the help of the bull the lion oppressed all the animals that eat meat, and with the lion's help the bull oppressed all those who eat grass. And because they all knew that the lion and the bull held them down by mutual coopera-tion, and saw that for this reason they had to bear great oppression and great harm, they talked together about finding a way to escape from their oppressors. Now they realized that if they could make the lion and bull fall out they would avoid being tyrannized by them. And because the fox and the sheep were more in the confidence of the lion and the bull than the other animals, they asked them to try to bring about a disagreement between them. And the fox and the sheep said they would work at it as hard as they could. Then the fox, who was the adviser of the lion, told the bear, who was the bravest and strongest of all the meat-eating animals after the lion, to tell the lion that he was afraid the bull was looking for a way to harm him, that they had previously reported this, when perhaps it was not true, but that he now should pay some attention to it. And the sheep, who was adviser to the bull, said the same thing to the horse, who was the strongest of the grass-eating animals. And the bear and the horse each repeated these things to the lion and the bull. And although the latter did not believe it, still they suspected something, since those who were saying these things were the most honorable of their lineage and company and yet they were talking in this fashion in order to bring some mistrust between them. Nevertheless, they became somewhat suspicious of each other. And each one talked with the fox and the sheep, their confidential agents. And they said that although perhaps the bear and the horse had told them these things with some deceitful purpose, it would be wise to pay attention henceforth to the words and deeds of the bear and the horse, and according to what they saw they could act. And with this a greater suspicion arose between the lion and the bull, and as soon as the animals heard that the lion and the bull were becoming suspicious of each other they let it be known more openly that each of them was afraid of the other, and this was only for the ill will that they hid in their hearts. And the fox and the sheep, like false counselors seeking their own advantage and forgetting the loyalty due to their lords, instead of telling them the truth, deceived them and accomplished so much that the love that used to exist between the lion and the bull turned into great disaffection.

"And when the animals saw this, they began to egg on their leaders until they got a quarrel going, each of them letting his principal think that they were helping him, and they were careful not to hurt each other, and caused all the harm to fall on the lion and the bull. And finally the quarrel came to this, that although the lion did the most harm to the bull and greatly lowered his power and prestige, ever afterward the lion was left so much lessened in power that he could not rule the other beasts nor control them, whether of his own lineage or any other. And thus, because the lion and the bull did not understand that through their mutual love and help they were honored by and masters of all the other animals, they did not maintain the useful affection that they had felt toward each other, and were not able to avoid the bad advice they were given by those who wished to escape from their control and then control them. The lion and the bull came out of their quarrel so badly that just as they had previously ruled the other animals, they were afterward ruled by them.

"And you, Count Lucanor, beware lest those who give you reasons to suspect your friend, are doing to you what the animals did to the lion and the bull. For this reason I counsel you that if your friend is loyal, and you have always found in him good and faithful ways, and you trust him as a man should trust a son or a brother, not to believe what is reported against him. I advise you rather to tell him what is being said about him, and then he will tell you what is being said about you. Thus will you so disgrace those who try to stir up trouble by their intrigue that no one will ever dare to try it again. But if your friend is not of the sort I have described, or is one of those friends who loves you for a time only, or by chance or through necessity, guard against such a man and never do or say anything to let him believe that you suspect him. Even overlook certain of his faults, for no great harm can come to you so unexpectedly that you cannot observe the signs before anything happens. If you are forewarned by trickery or slyness, as described above, tell such a friend that you should come to each other's aid, doing good deeds and showing a kindly disposition and not becoming suspicious without reason or on the say-so of evil men, overlooking his mistakes; and show him that as he carries out his obligations to you, you will carry out yours in similar fashion. In this way affection between you will last, and you will be prevented from falling into the mistake that hurt the lion and the bull."

And the count liked this advice of Patronio and heeded it and profited from it.

And Don Juan, believing this a good story, had it written down in this book and wrote these verses as follows:

Beware to lose by wicked lies
A man whose friendship you should prize.

This story is an abbreviation and revision of chapter 3 of *Calila e Digna*, entitled "Del leon e del buey e de la pesquisa de Dina e Calilla." It goes back, of course, to the *Panchatantra*. Thompson-Keller: K. 2131.2; Devoto: p. 408; Ayerbe-Chaux: pp. 39-43.

23. How the Ants Provide for Themselves

Another time Count Lucanor was talking to Patronio, his adviser, as follows: "Patronio, praise be to God, I am fairly well off and some people advise me, since I am able to do so, to have no concern but to eat, drink and be merry, for I have enough for myself and enough to leave my children well provided for. And out of the good intelligence that you have, I wish you to advise me as to what I ought to do."

"Sir Count Lucanor," said Patronio, "although relaxing and taking one's ease is pleasant, if you would do what is most profitable, I should like you to hear how the ant looks after herself."

The count asked about this, and Patronio told him.

"Sir Count Lucanor, you see how small an ant is, and therefore one might not expect her to have much intelligence, but you will discover that every year at the season of the wheat harvest, the ants come out of their anthills and go to the threshing floors to carry away as much wheat as they can for food, and they store it in their dwellings. And when the first rains come they bring it out, and people say they do this in order to dry it, but they do not know what they are talking about, for that is not true. For when the ants bring the wheat out of their anthills, you can tell that the first rains are coming and winter is about to begin, for if every time it rained they had to bring out the wheat to dry it, they would have hard work; and besides there would be no sun to dry it, for during the winter the sun shines rarely. But the real reason for their bringing it out the first time it rains is this: they set aside as much grain as their storehouse will hold at one time, and their sole concern is to fetch as much as they can. And when they have it in safekeeping, they think they have made provision for that year. And when the rain comes, and the grain gets wet, it begins to germinate, and they realize that if the grain germinates in the anthills, instead of their controlling it, it may kill them and thus cause a terrible disaster, so when they bring it out, they eat the heart of each wet grain from which the seed comes, and leave the rest of it. After that, however much it rains, the wheat cannot germinate and they live on it all year.

"And you will also discover that although they have all the grain they need, every time there is good weather they do not fail to heap up all the grains they can find. And they do this for fear that what they have will not be enough; and since they have it they do not wish to waste it nor lose the time God gives them, since they can profit by it.

"And you, Sir Count, since the ant, which is such a small creature, has so much understanding and does so much to provide for herself, you should realize that it is not reasonable for a man, especially for one who has to maintain a large estate and govern a great many others, always to eat what is on hand; for you may be certain that however great is the supply from which one takes each day's supplies, and into which one puts nothing, that this cannot last long. Furthermore, to do so seems like great stupidity and lack of intelligence. But my advice is that if you wish to eat and take your ease, do so while always maintaining your estate, guarding your honor, and looking to and being careful of how you will have what you will require. For if you have a great deal and wish to do what is right, there are plenty of places where you can spend your wealth to your honor, and to the service of God, which is still more important."

And the count liked very much this advice that Patronio gave him, and he followed it and profited by it.

And because Don Juan was pleased with this story he had it placed in this book and wrote verses as follows:

Eat not all you've laid aside;
Live with honor, die with pride.

.   .   .

It would seem that this story came from Pliny's *Natural History*, which Don Juan might have read in Latin. But so long had the story been in literary and oral currency that it would be hazardous to suggest the exact source. Thompson-Keller: J. 711.5, Q. 86.1; Devoto: pp. 408-11; Ayerbe-Chaux: p. 271.

24. What Happened to the King Who Wanted to Test His Three Sons

One day Count Lucanor was talking to Patronio, his adviser, and he said to him: "Patronio, in my house we bring up many boys of good family and some that are less wellborn, and I see in them many different characteristics and some rather strange ones. And out of the great understanding that you have, I want you to tell me how to predict which boy will turn out to be the best man."

"Sir Count," said Patronio, "what you ask is a very difficult question to answer with certainty, for one can never know for sure what is to come; but although this is true, some things can be known by certain inward and outward signs to be seen in boys. The outward signs may be seen in the figure and face, the carriage, the complexion and shape of the body and its members, for these things give evidence of the nature of the chief organs, which are the heart and the marrow and the liver. But these are signs one cannot be certain of, for seldom do all the signs agree, since if some signs show one thing, others show the opposite; but on the whole, according to these signs will the man turn out.

"And the most certain signs are those of the face, especially the eyes, and the bearing, for these signs seldom fail. By bearing is not meant whether a man is handsome or homely, for many men are attractive and handsome and do not have the bearing of gentlemen, while others are homely yet have the bearing to become proper men. But the shape of the body and the members gives an indication of the temperament and shows whether one is to be valiant or quick. And such things as the shape of the body and the members do not show for certain what are to be the deeds, for after all these are the signs, and I mean signs merely, and do not say certainties, for a sign always indicates of itself what is to be, but it is not foreordained that it will be so. And these are the inward signs which are always very doubtful with regard to answering your question. But boys may be judged by inward signs, which are more reliable, and so I should like you to hear how a Moorish king once tested his three sons to determine which one would be the finest man."

And the count asked him to tell him about it.

"Sir Count Lucanor," said Patronio, "a Moorish king had three sons. And because a father can decide which of his sons is to rule, and since he was already old, the leaders of his country begged him kindly to indicate which of his sons he desired to have rule after him. And the king said that he would give his answer within a month. And eight or ten days later one afternoon he told the oldest son that the next morning bright and early he wanted to ride out and wanted him to go along. And the next day the oldest son came, but not so early as the king his father had said. When he arrived the king said that he wanted to get dressed, and for him to bring him his clothes. And the son told the chamberlain to bring the clothes, and the chamberlain asked him what clothing he wanted. The prince turned to the king and asked him what clothing he wanted. And the king said the *jubba* and he turned to the chamberlain and said that the king wanted his *jubba*. And the chamberlain asked what kind of cloak he wanted, and the prince turned to the king and asked him. And he did this for each article of clothing, and he came and went for each question until the king had all his garments. Then the chamberlain came and dressed him and helped him put on his shoes.

"And when he was fully dressed, the king ordered the prince to fetch his horse, and he told the man who kept the king's horses to bring out the horse, and the keeper of the horses asked which horse to lead out, and the prince returned with this question to the king. And he did the same with the saddle, the bridle, the sword, the spurs, and everything that was needful for riding. For each object he went and asked the king. And when he was equipped, the king told the prince he did not intend to ride, but for him to go through town and observe everything that he saw in order to report it to him. And the prince rode off and with him all the important men of the kingdom, and they were accompanied by trumpets, cymbals, and other instruments. And the prince, having ridden around the town for a while, returned to the king who asked him his opinion of what he had seen. And the prince told him that he thought the instruments made a lot of noise.

"And a few days later the king sent word to his middle son to come to him the next morning, and the prince did so. And the king put him through all the tests to which his elder brother had been submitted, and the prince spoke and acted like his elder brother.

"A few days later he sent for his youngest son to go out with him early in the morning. And the prince was up before the king was awake and waited for him to wake up. And when he awoke, the prince went in and bowed with proper courtesy, and the king asked him to bring his clothes. Now the prince asked what clothing he wanted, and once and for all asked about all that he needed in order to be fully dressed, and he went and brought it all. And he did not permit any chamberlain to dress him or help him or help with his shoes, for he expressed the idea that he would consider himself fortunate if the king his father should take pleasure in his efforts; and since he was his father, it was right and intelligent to do for him as much service and kindness as he could.

"And when the king was dressed, he ordered the prince to bring him his horse. And he asked him which horse he wanted, with what saddle and bridle, what sword and all the things necessary for riding, and whom he wanted to have ride with him, and he did all that was required. And after he had done everything, he did not ask more than once, but brought the horse and prepared him as the king had asked. And when everything was done, the king said he did not wish to ride himself, but that the prince should ride and then come and tell him what he had seen. And the prince rode off and everybody went with him as with his two brothers, but neither he nor his brothers nor anyone else knew why the king was doing this. And while the prince was riding, he ordered them to show him everything inside the town, the streets, where the king kept his treasure, and all the mosques, and all the nobility of the town, and all the people who dwelled there. Then he went outside the town and he ordered out all the men of arms, on horse and on foot, and he commanded them to drill and show him their war games and weapons, and he observed the walls and towers and fortresses of the town. And when he had seen all this, he returned to the king his father. And when he got back it was already very late. And the king asked him what he had seen, and the prince replied that if he did not mind, he would not tell him what he thought of it all. And the king commanded him under pain of losing his blessing to tell him what he thought. And the prince told him that although he was a good king, it seemed to him that he was not so good as he should be, for if he were, since he had many good people and such great power and so many possessions, he need but exert himself a bit more for the whole world to be his.

"And the king liked the report that the prince gave him, and when the time came for him to give his reply to his countrymen, he said that he intended to give them that son as their king. And he did this on account of the signs that he saw in the others and the signs that he saw in this one. And although he would have preferred one of the others as king, he did not think it advisable to name one of them because of what he saw in each one.

"And you, Sir Count, if you want to know which boy will be best, pay attention to such things and thus you will gain some insight and perhaps have a fair idea what the boys will be like."

And the count liked what Patronio told him.

And because Don Juan thought it a good story he had it written down in this book and wrote these verses as follows:

> *By deeds not words you 'll come to see*
> *Which lad the finest man will be.*

.　.　.

Many books contained this story, and the folklores of many nations include it also. It appears in the *Scala Coeli* and in the *Book of the Seven Sages* (the Western branch), as well as in the *Thousand Nights and a Night*, although none of these incorporates the exact sequence of events related by Don Juan. Thompson-Keller: L. 10; Devoto: pp. 411-12; Ayerbe-Chaux: pp. 150-54.

25. What Happened to the Count of Provence and How He Was Freed from Prison by the Advice of Saladin

Count Lucanor was talking one time with his adviser in this fashion: "Patronio, one of my vassals told me the other day that he would like to arrange a marriage for one of his relatives, and it is my duty to counsel him as best I can. He asked me as a favor to advise him as to what I understood to be his greatest asset, and he told me about all the marriages he has arranged. And because he is a man whom I should like to see succeed, and because you know a great deal about such things, I urge you to tell me your opinion, so that I may give him advice that he will profit by."

"Sir Count Lucanor," said Patronio, "in order to advise a man who is about to arrange the marriage of a relative, I should like you to hear what happened to the count of Provence with Saladin, the sultan of Babylonia."

And Count Lucanor asked him how that was.

"Sir Count Lucanor," said Patronio, "there was once a count in Provence, a righteous man, who desired to act in such a way as to win God's grace for his soul and earn the glory of paradise by doing such deeds as might redound to his honor and that of his estate. And to accomplish this, he took many people with him, intelligent men, and went overseas to the Holy Land, resolved in his heart that no matter what happened to him he would always be a man of goodwill, standing upright in the service of God. And because God's judgments are marvelous yet hidden, our Lord thinks it well to test His friends frequently, and if they are able to resist temptation, our Lord always manages to turn the problem to the honor and advantage of the man who is tempted. And for this reason our Lord thought it well to tempt the count of Provence, and consented to his capture by the sultan during his pilgrimage. And although he was a captive, because Saladin knew the great goodness of the count, and his high lineage, he showed him much kindness and honor, and all the tasks that he had to perform he did by his advice. And the count advised him so wisely and the sultan trusted him so much, that although he was a prisoner, he had a high position and happiness and his bidding was done in the whole land of Saladin just as if it were his own. And when the count departed from his own country, he left behind a very small daughter.

"Now he had remained a prisoner so long that she was already of age to be married, and the countess, his wife, and his relatives sent word to the count that many kings' sons and other important men were asking for her hand in marriage. One day when Saladin came to talk to the count, and after they had decided the matter for which Saladin came, the count addressed him as follows: 'Sir, you do me so much kindness and honor and you trust me so much that I consider myself fortunate to serve you. And since you, sir, are pleased to have me advise you in all the matters that arise, relying on your kindness and trusting in your wisdom, I entreat you to advise me in a personal matter.'

"And the sultan was grateful to the count and told him that he would advise him willingly and would even help him gladly in anything that he might ask. Then the count told him about the wedding plans that were afoot for his daughter and asked him to kindly advise him as to whom she should marry.

"And Saladin replied as follows: 'Count, I know that your intelligence is such that in the few words that a man may speak, you will understand the matter fully. Wherefore I shall advise you in this case according to my comprehension of it. I do not know the men who ask for your daughter's hand, or their lineage or their power, or what they are like personally, or what local ties they have with you, or what superiority some have over others. For this reason, I cannot advise you specifically, but my advice is this, that you marry your daughter to a man.' And the count was grateful and understood very well what was meant. And the count forwarded to the countess, his wife, and to his relatives the advice that the sultan had given him, and said that they should find out concerning all the gentlemen in his region, what their manners and customs were, what they were like personally, and to pay no attention to their wealth or power, but to send to him in writing what the suitors, whether kings' sons or sons of great nobles in his country, were like. And the countess and the count's relatives marveled greatly at this, but they did what the count commanded them to do and they set down in writing all the manners and customs, good and otherwise, of all who asked for the hand of the count's daughter and described all the other conditions to be found in them. Similarly they wrote down what the gentlemen of the region were like and sent the report to the count.

"As soon as the count saw the report, he showed it to the sultan. And when Saladin saw it, although all the men were good, he found in each of the sons of the king and in the great lords alike some fault, either as to his being ill bred in eating or drinking, or in being bad-tempered or standoffish, or uncivil toward people, or enjoying bad company, or slow to keep their word, or some such fault among the many that men can have. And he discovered that the son of a certain middle-class man of no great power seemed from the report to be the most excellent and most accomplished man, and with the least faults of any he had ever heard of. And when the sultan saw this he advised the count to have his daughter marry that man, for he understood that although the others had greater honors and greater nobility, that this was the best marriage, and the count would marry his daughter more wisely to that man than to any of the others in whom there was a fault, and all the more so if they had many other faults; and he found that

that man was more to be esteemed for his deeds and for his nobility of his lineage than for his wealth.

"And the count sent word to the countess and to his relatives to have his daughter wed the man whom Saladin commended. And although they wondered greatly at this, they sent for the son of the middle-class man and told him the count's command. And he replied that he knew that the count was more noble and richer and more honored than he, but that, if he himself had such great power, he thought any woman would be well married to him, and furthermore if they said what they did with no intention of carrying it out, he felt that they were doing him a great injury and wished to destroy him. But they told him they intended to carry out the plan in any event, and told him the reason: that the sultan had advised the count to offer him his daughter before any of the sons of the kings or any of the other great lords, especially since they chose him for his manhood. And when he heard this he realized that they spoke truly regarding the marriage and thought that since Saladin chose him for his manhood, thus honoring him, that he would not be a man if he did not do what it behooved him to do. Then he told the countess and the count's relatives that if they wanted him really to believe what they had told him, they should at once give him authority over the whole territory of the count and all its income. But he told them nothing of what he intended to do.

"What he said pleased them, and so they turned everything over to him right away. And seeing himself provided with money, he took a great many things with him and in great secrecy armed a fleet of galleys at once and loaded his goods under guard. And when this was done he ordered his wedding prepared for a certain day, and when the wedding was over and done, and it was a rich and honorable one, the night when he was to go to his wife's house, before they went to bed, he called for his mother-in-law, the countess, and her relatives and told them in great secrecy that they well knew that the count had chosen him from among others better than himself and that he had done so because the sultan advised him to have his daughter marry a real man; and since the sultan and the count, his lord, did him so much honor as to choose him for a man, that he thought he would not be one if he did not do what he had to do, and that he was leaving and that he left his betrothed and the count's territory, and that he trusted in God to guide him so that the people might know that he was doing a man's deeds. And having said this, he rode off confidently. He set out for the kingdom of Armenia and stayed there long enough to learn the language and all the customs of the land. And he found out that Saladin was a great hunter. And he took many good birds and many good dogs and made his way to Saladin. And he divided his galleys, placing one in each port, with orders not to leave until he gave the word.

"And when he came to the sultan he was very well received, but he did not kiss his hand nor do him the reverence that a man is supposed to do his lord. And Saladin ordered him to be given everything that he needed and he thanked him properly, but he refused to take anything from him, and said that he had not come to take anything of his, but on account of all the good he had heard spoken of him, and that if he were willing, he would like to live for some time in his house to learn something of the good there was in him and his people; and because he knew that he was very fond of hunting, he had brought many birds and a pack of good dogs, and if he chose to do so, he should take as many as he wanted, and with what he had left he would arrange to go hunting with him and would do him such service as he could in that way and in every other.

"And this pleased Saladin very much and he took what he thought right, but in no way could he get the other to take anything from him, nor tell him anything about his affairs, nor was there between them anything which alarmed Saladin, so that he needed to have him guarded. And thus he remained in the household a long time. And since God brings about those things that He wishes, it was His wish that they came upon some falcons and cranes. And they rode off to kill one of the cranes in a seaport where one of the galleys lay that the count's son-in-law had anchored there. And the sultan who was riding a good horse, and a man with him, got so far separated from their people that neither of them saw where they were headed.

"Now when Saladin got to where the falcons were, with the crane, he dismounted rapidly to come upon them. And the count's son-in-law who got there with him, as soon as he saw him on foot, called to the men in the galley. But the sultan who was paying no attention except to feed his falcons, when he saw the men of the galley around him, was very frightened. And the count's son-in-law put his hand to his sword and let him understand that he meant to strike him with it. When Saladin saw this, he began to protest violently, calling it great treason. And the count's son-in-law told him it was not God's will, that he well knew that he had never taken him for his lord, nor had he been willing to accept anything from him nor to take from him any assignment for which there might be any reason to hold him, but that he knew that Saladin had assumed all that. And when he had said this, he took him, and placed him in the galley, and when he had him aboard, he told him that he was the son-in-law of the count, and that he was the one whom he had chosen among others better than himself for a man; and that since he had chosen him for a man, he realized that he would not be one if he had not done this, and he begged him to release his father-in-law to him, so that he might know that the advice that he had given him was good and true and that he had profited by it.

"When Saladin heard this, he gave thanks to God because he was as glad that he had been right in his advice as if he had acquired some advantage or honor, however great. And he told the count's son-in-law that he would surrender him gladly, and the count's son-in-law trusted the sultan and released him from the galley and went with him. And he ordered the men in the galley to sail out of the port so far that they could not be seen by anyone who appeared. And the sultan and the count's son-in-law fed their falcons, and when their party arrived they found Saladin very happy and he never told anyone what had happened to him.

"And when they reached the town he dismounted at the house where his prisoner the count was and took him to his son-in-law. And he, when he saw the count, began talking happily, 'Count, I thank God for his kindness in letting me hit the mark as I did it in the case of the advice I gave you regarding the marriage of your daughter. Behold your son-in-law who has rescued you from prison.'

"Then he told him all that his son-in-law had done and of the loyalty and great effort he had shown in capturing him and then in trusting him. And the sultan and the count and all those who heard the story greatly praised the intelligence, the energy, and the loyalty of the count's son-in-law, and in like fashion they praised the goodness of Saladin and the count and thanked God for bringing the affair to such a good conclusion. Then the sultan gave many rich gifts to the count and to his son-in-law. And for the suffering that the count had endured as a prisoner he gave him twice the income that he could have gained in his land during the time that he was in prison and he sent him away wealthy, honored, and in good health to his country. And all this came to him through the good advice that the sultan gave him to the effect that his daughter should marry a man.

"And you, Sir Count Lucanor, since you have to advise your vassal regarding the marriage of his relative, advise him that the principal thing to look for in the marriage, no matter who the man is, is that he should be a man of and by himself; for if this is not so, neither by his honor, his wealth, nor his nobility can she ever be well married. For a man who is good increases honor, increases his nobility, and multiplies his wealth. For if a man is noble and rich, if he be not good, everything will soon be lost. And in this connection one could cite the great deeds of many estimable men whose fathers left them rich and honored, and who, since they were not so good as they should have been, ill-used their lineage and their patrimony, while other men of high and humble estate, by the great goodness that was in them, greatly increased their honor and their possessions, so that they were more praised and more appreciated for what they did and what they were than for their family. Therefore, I say that all good and all harm arises from what a man is of and by himself, whatever his social standing. Wherefore, the first things to be looked at in a marriage are the manners, the customs, the understanding, and the works that a man possesses either in himself or in the woman who is to be married, and this having been first looked to, if in addition they are of noble lineage, are wealthy and of satisfactory standing, and if their associations are close, all the better is the marriage."

And the count liked this advice which Patronio gave him, and he thought that it was true as he presented it.

And Don Juan, seeing that this story was good, had it written down in this book and wrote these verses:

A worthy man can build a life,
A lesser one finds failure rife.

．　．　．

The story, minus Saladin and the count of Provence, whom Don Juan Manuel inserts for the effect their names would engender, is to be found in Valerius Maximus from whom Clemente Sánchez de Vercial in the fifteenth century translated it almost literally. Stories of the poor young man of high moral quality who is superior to unworthy sons of rich men are also related in *Barlaam and Josaphat*. Thompson-Keller: 640, 9.3, R. 154.4; Devoto: pp. 412-13; Ayerbe-Chaux: pp. 124-37.

26. What Happened to the Tree of Lies

One day Count Lucanor was talking to Patronio, his adviser, and he said: "Patronio, I am in the midst of great difficulty and a fierce quarrel with some men who do not much care for me. And these men are so quarrelsome and dishonest that all they do is lie to me and to everyone else with whom they have any dealings. And the lies they tell are so well placed for their profit that they do me much harm, and in this way they increase their power and make people angry at me. And you may well believe that, if I were willing to act as they do, perhaps I would be as good a liar as they are, but because I believe lying is a bad business, I have never done it, and now out of the good intelligence that you have I want you to advise me as to how I should act toward these men."

"Sir Count Lucanor," said Patronio, "if you are to do what is best and most to your advantage, I should very much like you to hear what happened to Truth and Falsehood."

The count asked him to tell him about it.

"Sir Count Lucanor," said Patronio, "Falsehood and Truth were companions, and when they had been together for some time, Falsehood, who is more eager, said to Truth that it would be a good idea to plant a tree from which they could pick fruit and where they could enjoy the shade during hot weather. And Truth, since she is a frank and willing creature, agreed. And when the tree had been planted and had begun to grow, Falsehood said to Truth that they should each choose her part of the tree, and Truth agreed. And Falsehood gave very pointed and appropriate arguments to the effect that the roots are the part that gives life and sustenance to the tree and are therefore the best and most appropriate part. Falsehood advised Truth to choose the roots, which are underground, while she would take the little branches that were to grow above the ground, although they were in danger of being cut or defoliated by men, or gnawed by animals, or clipped by birds with their claws and with their beaks, or dried by great heat, or nipped by great cold. She said that the roots did not take all these risks.

"And when Truth heard the arguments, because she knew little about it and because she is a naive and trusting creature, she trusted Falsehood, her companion, and believed her and thought Falsehood was advising her to choose the better part, so she chose the roots and was very well pleased. And when this was done Falsehood was very happy about the deceit that she had practiced on her companion by telling her such beautiful and appropriate lies. So Truth went underground to live where the roots were, and Falsehood stayed above ground where men live and where all things move. And since she is a great flatterer, in a short time everyone was fond of her.

"And the tree began to grow and to throw out great branches and broad leaves, making a beautiful shade, and there appeared upon the tree fine flowers of beautiful colors and pleasing appearance. And when the people saw the beautiful tree, they eagerly gathered around and enjoyed its shade and its beautifully colored flowers; and most people were usually there, and even those who were not said to each other that if you wish to take your ease and be happy, to stay in the shade of the tree of Falsehood. And when the people were gathered under the tree, since Falsehood is very attractive and clever, she did many nice things for the people and taught them what she knew.

"And the people were delighted to learn her art. In this way she gathered to herself most of the world's people. To some she showed simple lies; to others, more complex, double lies; and to the still more learned, triple lies. And I must explain that a simple lie is when a man says to another: 'Mr. So-and-So, I will do such and such a thing for you,' and does not intend to do it. And a double lie is when he takes an oath and does homage and gives hostages and gets others to perform promises, and while giving these assurances, he has already thought of a way to turn the whole thing into a lie and a cheat. But the triple lie, which is mortally deceptive, is that which lies and cheats by telling the truth. And Falsehood knew how to do this so well, and was so gifted in teaching it to those who basked in the shade of the tree, that she taught them to achieve by knowledge most of the things they wanted. And there was no one possessing this skill who did not use it to his purpose, one for the beauty of the tree, and another for the great skill that Falsehood taught him. And people were anxious to enjoy the shade and to learn what Falsehood taught. And Falsehood was much honored and appreciated and followed by the people, and anyone who approached her but little, and knew least about her skill, was despised by all and even prized himself least.

"And while Falsehood was in such a fine situation the wretched and despised Truth was hidden underground, and no one knew anything about her, nor cared about her, nor tried to seek her out. And she, seeing that she had nothing to live on except the roots which Falsehood had advised her to accept, since she had nothing else to eat, she began to gnaw and cut and live on the roots of the tree of Falsehood. And although the tree had very good branches and broad leaves, and gave good shade, and had many flowers of fine colors, before it could bear fruit all the roots had been cut, for Truth had to eat them, as she had nothing else to live on. And when the roots of the tree of Falsehood were all cut, with Falsehood sitting in the shade of her tree with all the people who were learning her skill, a wind came up and struck the tree; and because the roots were cut it was easy to uproot it, and it fell on Falsehood and injured her badly, and all who were studying her art were killed or badly wounded or damaged. And from the trunk of the tree Truth, who had been hidden, came out, and when she returned to earth, Falsehood and those who sided with her were very unfortunate and found themselves in bad straits to the extent that they had learned and used the art that Falsehood taught them.

"And you, Sir Count Lucanor, know you that Falsehood has many great branches, and her flowers are her sayings, thoughts, and flattery, which are very pleasant and attractive to people, but it is all appearance and never bears good fruit. Wherefore, if your antagonists use the skills and tricks of Falsehood, guard yourself as best you can against them and do not try to equal them in their art. Be not envious of the debonair manner which they have, because they use the art of Falsehood, for it will not last them long and they will come to no good, even though they think they are in a most agreeable posture, for it will fail them just as the tree of Falsehood failed those who imagined themselves well off in its shade. For although truth is scorned, embrace her well and esteem her highly, for through her you will find yourself well situated and will come to a good end, and will win God's grace so that He will give much goods in this world and honor for your person, and salvation for your soul in the next."

And the count liked Patronio's advice, and he took it and it turned out well for him.

And Don Juan, thinking this a good story, had it written down in this book and wrote these verses as follows:

Follow truth, avoid all lies,
For liars' problems grow in size.

. . .

No exact source can be found. A story in which Truth and False-
hood are protagonists appears in *El libro de los gatos*, the rendition of
Odo of Cheriton's *Narrationes*. Thompson-Keller: K. 171.1, K. 1635,
H. 659.13.2; Devoto: pp. 413-14.

27. What Happened to an Emperor and to Don Alvarfáñez Minaya and Their Wives

Count Lucanor was talking to Patronio, his adviser, one day, and he
spoke as follows: "Patronio, two of my brothers are married and each
one lives in a fashion diametrically opposed to the other. For one is so
fond of his wife that we can scarcely get him to leave her for a day, and
he does nothing except what she wants or with her permission. And the
other we cannot persuade to see his wife or go into the house where she
is. And because this makes me sad I beg you to tell me how we can put
things to right."

"Sir Count Lucanor," said Patronio, "from what you tell me both of
your brothers are wrong in their actions, for the one ought not to show
such great affection nor the other such great disaffection as they show
their wives; but although they are wrong, perhaps it is the wives' fault.
Wherefore, I should like you to hear what happened to the emperor
Fadrique and Don Alvarfáñez and their wives."

The count asked what had happened.

"Sir Count Lucanor," said Patronio, "because I cannot tell two
stories at one and the same time, I shall first tell you what happened to
the emperor Fadrique and then I will tell you what happened to Don
Alvarfáñez.

"1. Sir Count, Emperor Fadrique married a girl of very high rank, as
he should have done; but nevertheless it did not turn out well for him,
since he did not find out her ways before the marriage. And after they
were married, although she was a very fine woman and modest in
appearance, she became the crudest, strongest, and most cross-grained
of all women, so that, when the emperor wished to eat she said she

113

wanted to fast, and when the emperor wanted sleep, she wanted to get up, or if the emperor was fond of something, then she disliked it. What more can I say? Everything the emperor liked she made a point of disliking, and whatever he did, she always did the opposite. After the emperor had stood this a while and had found no way to change her by pleas or threats, nor kindness or harsh treatment, he realized that his frustration and unhappiness was a burden upon his household and his people and that he could not straighten it out. And when he realized this he even went to the pope and told him his problem, relating the life he was living, and the harm that he and his country endured because of the empress's bad ways. And he was very anxious to find out whether the pope would let him divorce her. But he saw that according to Christian law they could not be parted, nor could they bear to live together because of her evil ways, and the pope understood that such was the case.

"And since no other solution could be found, the pope told the emperor that he commended the problem to the intelligence and the subtlety of the emperor, for he could not assign penance before the sin had been committed. And the emperor left the pope and went home, and tried every way he knew by flattery, threats, advice, disappointments and every way that he and those around him could imagine to make her change her ways. But nothing worked, no matter what they said, to get her to change. Every day her conduct was more contrary. And when the emperor saw that there was no way to right matters, he told her one day that he was going deer hunting and that he would take with him a bit of the herb used on arrows with which they kill deer and would leave the rest for another hunt, and for her to avoid by all means putting that herb on an itch or on a scab or any place where she might bleed, for the herb was so powerful that there was nothing in the world that it would not kill. And he took another very good and helpful ointment and very useful for wounds and annointed himself with it in several places that needed it.

"And the empress and all those with her saw that he was cured. And he told her, if need be, to put it on any cut that she might have. He said this in the presence of a group of men and women. And when he had said it, he took the herb for killing deer and went hunting as he intended. And when the emperor was gone, the empress began to get angry and rave saying: 'Did you hear what that deceitful emperor said to me? Because he knows that my rash is not like his, he told me to use the ointment he used, for he knows that it will not do me any good, but the good ointment which he knows will cure me he told me not to use at all. To spite him I shall use it, and when he returns he will find me cured. For I know there is no way to irritate him more. So I shall do it.' And the gentlemen and ladies who were with her urged her not to, and begged her weeping bitterly to refrain, for if she did so she would die. But for all that she would not stop. She took the herb and annointed her sores with it; and soon the madness of death was upon her and she would have repented, but it was too late. And she died, for her stubborn ways led to her own destruction.

"2. But the very opposite of this happened to Don Alvarfáñez, and so that you may know what happened, I shall tell you about it. Don Alvarfáñez was a fine man and an honorable man who settled down at Yxcar. Now Count Don Pero Ansúrez, who had three daughters, had settled in Cuéllar and dwelt there. And one day Don Alvarfáñez went into his house without misgivings and Count Don Pero Ansúrez liked him very much. And when they had eaten, he asked him why he came thus unannounced. And Don Alvarfáñez said that he came to ask for the hand of one of his daughters in marriage, but he wanted to see all three and talk to each one and would then make his choice. And the count, seeing that the Lord was kind to him in this, said that he would be pleased to do as Don Alvarfáñez asked.

"Don Alvarfáñez took the eldest girl aside and told her that if she were willing he would like to marry her, but that before they talked about it he wished to tell her something about himself. He wanted her to know, in the first place, that he was not young and that because of the many wounds he had acquired in battle if he drank any wine he would lose his head completely, and that while out of his mind he was so irrational that he did not know what he was saying and he sometimes struck people, and when he came to himself he was very sorry for what he had done; also that even in bed he did things that were unappealing.

"And he told her so many things of the sort that any woman who was not fairly mature might think herself not very well married. And when he had told her all this, the count's daughter said that marriage was not for her to decide, but was up to her father and mother. Then she left Don Alvarfáñez and went to her father. And when her mother and father asked her decision, because she was not so bright as she should have been, she told them what Don Alvarfáñez had said, and said that she would rather be dead than married to him. And the count did not want to repeat this to Don Alvarfáñez but said that his daughter did not wish to get married.

"Then Don Alvarfáñez talked to the middle daughter and told her what he had told her elder sister. Then he talked to the youngest daughter and told her everything that he had told her two sisters. And she replied that she thanked God that Don Alvarfáñez wanted to marry her, and as for what he had told her about what wine did to him, that if by any chance he happened to be shunned by anyone, for the reason mentioned or any other reason, she would hide the fact better than anyone else. And as for his being old, she would not be deterred from the marriage by that reason, for she was pleased with the profit and honor of the marriage, and with being married to Alvarfáñez; and as for his going mad and striking people, this was no major obstacle, for she would never give him a reason to hit her or if he did, she would be able to bear it. And to everything that Don Alvarfáñez said she had such excellent replies that Don Alvarfáñez was very pleased and thanked God that he had found a woman of such judgment. And he told Count Don Pero Ansúrez that he wished to marry her. And the count was delighted, and the wedding took place at once. And he was happy with his wife. And the lady's name was Vascuñana.

"After Don Alvarfáñez took his wife home, she was such a fine woman and so sensible that Don Alvarfáñez considered himself happily married and thought it proper to do everything that she wished. And he did so for two reasons: first, because God was so good to her and she loved Don Alvarfáñez so much and so appreciated his intelligence that everything he did or said was truly for the best; and the second, because she approved his every remark and never did she contradict him in anything that he liked. And do not think that she did this to flatter, or to win his favor, or to deceive. She did it because she truly liked everything that Don Alvarfáñez did and said, for in nothing could he make a mistake, nor could anyone improve upon him. First, because that was the greatest possible good and second, because he was of such understanding and of such good works that he always did the best thing. And for these reasons Don Alvarfáñez loved her and esteemed her to the degree that he thought it proper to do everything that she wished, since she always loved him and advised him to his honor and advantage. And she never thought by disposition or will that there was anything that Don Alvarfáñez did except what was best for him, and most to his honor and advantage.

"One time while Don Alvarfáñez was at home a nephew came to visit him who lived in the house of the king. And Don Alvarfáñez was very pleased with him. And when he had been with Don Alvarfáñez a few days, he told him that he was a fine man and an accomplished one and that he could find but one fault with him. And Don Alvarfáñez asked what that might be. And the nephew said that the fault was that he did a great deal for his wife and supported her in all her handling of the estate. And Don Alvarfáñez answered that within a few days he would give him a reply. And before Don Alvarfáñez saw Vascuñana, he rode off and went to another place and stayed there a few days, and he took his nephew with him. Then he sent for Doña Vascuñana, and arranged for them to meet on the road, but without time to discuss anything together. And Don Alvarfáñez went ahead with his nephew. And Doña Vascuñana came after them.

"And when they had gone some distance, Don Alvarfáñez and his nephew met a great herd of cows. And Don Alvarfáñez said: 'Do you see, nephew, what beautiful mares we have in our country?' And when the nephew heard this, he marveled greatly at it and thought he was joking, and he said, as one might, that they were cows. Then Don Alvarfáñez seemed greatly astonished and said he was afraid that the nephew had lost his mind, for it was plain that they were mares. And when the nephew saw that Don Alvarfáñez insisted and was saying it seriously, he was very much frightened and thought that Don Alvarfáñez had lost his mind. And Don Alvarfáñez stuck to his opinion until Doña Vascuñana appeared on the road. And when Don Alvarfáñez saw her he said to his nephew: 'Well, nephew, here is Doña Vascuñana to settle our argument.' The nephew agreed.

"And when Doña Vascuñana came up, he said to his aunt: 'Señora, Don Alvarfáñez and I are having an argument, for he says that these cows are mares and I say they are cows. And we have stuck to our opinions, so that he thinks me mad and I think that he is not in his right mind. And so, Señora, please settle this argument for us.

"When Doña Vascuñana heard this, although she knew them to be cows, since her nephew told her that Don Alvarfáñez claimed they were mares, she really believed in her heart that he was mistaken and did not recognize them; but since Don Alvarfáñez could never be mistaken in so recognizing them and since he said they were mares, then by all means they must be mares and not cows. And so she addressed her nephew and all those present: 'For goodness sake, nephew, what you say pains

117

me greatly, and God knows I should like you to return to the king's house where you so long lived with full intelligence and to greatest advantage, because one can see that you lack understanding and vision, claiming that these mares are cows.'

"And she began to show by their colors, their appearance, and many other things that they were mares and not cows and that what Don Alvarfáñez said was the truth, since in no way could the reason or the word of Don Alvarfáñez be wrong. And she affirmed this so stoutly that the nephew and all the rest began to wonder if they were wrong, and if Don Alvarfáñez spoke the truth and that what they took to be cows were mares.

"Then after this, Don Alvarfáñez and his nephew went on ahead and met a great herd of mares. And Don Alvarfáñez said to his nephew: 'Ha, nephew, here are the cows and not the ones that you previously saw, for I told you they were mares.' When the nephew heard this he said to his uncle: 'For God's sake, Don Alvarfáñez, if you are right, it was the Devil who brought me to this country, for certainly if these are cows I have lost my mind, for in every possible way these are mares, not cows.'

"Then Don Alvarfáñez began to insist very sternly that they were cows, and the argument lasted until Doña Vascuñana arrived. When she came up, they told her what Don Alvarfáñez had said and what the nephew had said, and although it seemed to her that the nephew was right, she could in no way imagine that Don Alvarfáñez could be mistaken, nor that anything could be the truth except what he said. And she began to find reasons to prove that what Don Alvarfáñez said was right.

"And she gave so many reasons and such good ones that her nephew and everyone else thought that their judgment and their vision erred and that what Don Alvarfáñez said was true. And so it was. And Don Alvarfáñez and his nephew went on ahead until finally they came to a river that had a number of windmills. And while their animals were drinking in the river Don Alvarfáñez began saying that the river was flowing in the opposite direction from its point of origin, through the mills from downstream. And Don Alvarfáñez's nephew thought himself lost when he heard this, for he thought that he was wrong in the matter of the cows and the mares and that he was wrong in the same way now by thinking that the water was running in the opposite direction from that which Don Alvarfáñez said. But they persisted in their opinions until Doña Vascuñana came up. And when they told her the argument in which Don Alvarfáñez and his nephew were engaged, even though it seemed to her that the nephew was right, she did not trust her own mind, but considered as true what Don Alvarfáñez said; and she knew how to back up her reasoning in so many ways that the nephew and everyone else believed that it was so. And from that day forth there is a saying that if a husband says a river is running upstream, a good wife should believe it and say so too.

"And when Don Alvarfáñez's nephew saw that by every argument that Doña Vascuñana gave she proved that Don Alvarfáñez was right and that he was wrong in not seeing things as they were, he found himself in a very bad way, believing that he had lost his mind. And when they had gone on along the road a way and Don Alvarfáñez saw that his nephew was sad and in great perplexity, he said to him, 'Nephew, now I have given you the reply that you asked for the other day when you told me that people thought it blameworthy of me to do so much for Doña Vascuñana, my wife, for you must realize that everything that has happened to you and me today was all done to show you what she is like, and that what I do for her, I do quite properly; for you should know that I knew that the first cows we saw, which I said were mares, were indeed cows as you said. And when Doña Vascuñana came up and heard you say that I said they were mares, I am certain that she knew you were speaking the truth; but she trusts my judgment so that she believes that for nothing in the world could I make a mistake, and so she thought that you and she were wrong in not recognizing things as they were. Wherefore, she gave so many and such good arguments that she made you and all the rest who were there believe that what I said was true, and she did the same with the mares and with the river. And I tell you in truth that from the day that she married me at no time have I seen her do or say anything that could make me think that she desired anything or took pleasure in anything except what I desire. Nor have I seen her take umbrage at anything that I have done. And always, according to her way of thinking, everything that I do is for the best, and what she has to do, or what I recommend that she do, she knows well how to do; and she always does it to my honor and advantage, wanting people to know that I am her lord and that my will and my honor must be served. She wants for herself no advantage nor reputation except what is known to be my advantage and that I take pleasure in it. And I hold that if even a Mooress beyond the sea acted thus, I ought to love her greatly and appreciate her and do a great deal according to her advice. Furthermore, being married to Doña Vascuñana and considering her lineage, I consider myself well married. Now, nephew, I have given you a reply as to the fault of which you spoke the other day.'

"And when Don Alvarfáñez's nephew heard this reasoning he was greatly pleased and understood that since Doña Vascuñana was such a woman and had such an intelligence and such goodwill, his uncle acted properly in loving and trusting her and doing for her all that he did and even more if he wished to.

"Thus the emperor's wife and Don Alvarfáñez's wife were the exact opposite of each other.

"And you, Sir Count Lucanor, if your brothers are so dissimilar that one does everything that his wife desires and the other the opposite, perhaps it is because their wives are like the empress and Doña Vascuñana. And if this is the case, you ought not to wonder at nor blame your brothers. But if their wives are neither so good nor so bad as the two that I have talked about, doubtless your brothers are wrong; for although your brother who does a great deal for his wife does well to do so, he ought to do so sensibly, but no more; for if a man, because of his great love for his wife, wants so much to be with her that for this reason he fails to go to the places to which he ought to go or to do the deeds that he should do to his advantage and honor, he acts very wrongly, for if to please her or to satisfy her wishes, he fails to do anything that pertains to his estate, or his honor, he acts unwisely. But observing in these matters all honor, all goodwill, and all the confidence that a husband can show his wife, anything is possible; and everything should be done, and it is his duty to do it. On the other hand he should be very careful about what he does lest it work against his interest or cause him harm, and lest it cause him grief or irritation, especially as regards anything in which there is sin. For from this comes great harm: on the one hand there is the sin of evil doing; and on the other one, the making of amends and causing of pleasure in order to be rid of irritation. Thus one may do things that will harm both his property and his reputation. Similarly, he who by his ill fortune has a wife like the empress, since at first he did not know how to control nor to advise her, he can do nothing but accept his fate as long as God wishes him to endure it. But know that in both cases it is very important on the first day of a man's marriage for him to let his wife know that he is master and make her understand what sort of life they are to have together.

"And you, Sir Count, as I see it, by reflecting on these things, will you be able to advise your brothers how to get along with their wives."

And the count liked very much what Patronio had told him and thought that he spoke the truth and made very good sense.

And because Don Juan thought these two stories were good he ordered them written down in this book and wrote these verses:

If you'd have your wife obey,
Lay down the law without delay.

．　．　．

Really these are two separate stories told under one title for the sake of comparison and contrast between the good wife and the bad wife. The motif of the bad wife, like Kate in the *Taming of the Shrew*, is of worldwide currency. Surely the queen of Frederick Barbarosa was never a part of these events, but Don Juan Manuel knew the power of name-dropping and therefore attributed the events to that king of the Germanies who was a famous knight and crusader and about whom many Spaniards knew. Thompson-Keller: T. 251, T. 251.2; Devoto: pp. 414 and 426-34; Ayerbe-Chaux: pp. 76-81.

The second part, that of the perfect wife, is also current in the oral traditions of many peoples. The use of the famous Alvarfáñez, cohort of the Cid Campeador, is again a distortion of history for effect. If there ever lived a Doña Vascuñana, no historian can place her. The story of *Patient Griselda*, of course, belongs to this tradition. Quite probably Don Juan took the motifs of the shrewish wife and the perfect wife and spun two remarkable stories which he combined under one heading. Thompson-Keller: T. 223; Devoto: pp. 414 and 426-34; Ayerbe-Chaux: pp. 81-86.

28. What Happened in Granada to Don Lorenzo Suárez Gallinato When He Beheaded the Renegade Chaplain

Count Lucanor was talking one day to Patronio, his adviser, as follows: "Patronio, a man has come to take refuge with me, and although I know that he is a reputable man, yet some people tell me that he has done rather unwise things. And on account of the great wisdom that you possess, I beg you to advise me as to what to do in this matter."

"Sir Count Lucanor," said Patronio, "in order for you to do what I think most suitable, I should like you to hear what happened to Don Lorenzo Suárez Gallinato."

The count asked what had happened.

"Sir Count Lucanor," said Patronio, "Don Lorenzo Suárez Gallinato lived with the king of Granada and had lived there a long time. And when it pleased God for him to come to the aid of King Don Fernando, the king asked him one day, since he had done a great disservice to God by helping the Moors against the Christians, whether he thought God would have mercy on him and not condemn his soul. And Don Lorenzo Suárez answered that he had not done anything to prevent God from giving him His grace except for the fact that he had once killed a mass-saying priest. And King Don Fernando thought this very strange and asked him how that could be.

"And he replied that while he was living with the king of Granada that monarch had trusted him and had made him his bodyguard. And one day while he was riding with the king through the city, he heard the sound of shouting, and because he was the king's guard he set spurs to his horse and reached the point where the noise was, and he came upon an unfrocked priest. Now you must know that this bad priest was a Christian who was turning Moor. And one day to please the Moors he told them that if they liked he would give them the God the Christians believed in and trusted and held to be God. And the Moors asked him to do it. Then the wicked, traitorous priest had some vestments made, and had an altar built, and said mass and consecrated a Host. And when it was consecrated he gave it to the Moors. And they went dragging it through the mud and making a great mockery of it.

"Now when Don Lorenzo Suárez saw this, although living with the

Moors, he remembered that he was a Christian, and believing truly that that was the body of God, and since Jesus Christ died to save sinners, it would be quite proper if he died to avenge Him and to extricate Him from the dishonor that those false people did to Him. And thinking thus, with the joy and sorrow that he felt, he went against the treacherous renegade priest who was performing such a great treason and cut off his head. And he got off his horse and got down on his knees and adored God's body which the Moors were dragging through the mud. And while he was on his knees the Host that was beside him shot up from the mud and landed in the lap of Don Lorenzo Suárez Gallinato. And when the Moors saw this, they were greatly disturbed and put their hands to their swords, and with swords and clubs and stones they all went for Don Lorenzo Suárez to kill him. And he put his hand to the sword with which he had cut off the evil priest's head and began to defend himself.

"Now when the Moorish king heard the uproar and saw that they were trying to kill Don Lorenzo Suárez, he ordered that no one should harm him, and he asked what was happening. And the Moors, who were in a state of excitement and anger, told the king what had happened. And the king was angry and grieved and he asked Don Lorenzo Suárez why he had done what he did without his command. And Don Lorenzo Suárez told him that he well knew that he was not of his faith, that he was a Christian, and that in spite of this he knew him and entrusted his person to him, thinking him loyal, and knowing that for fear of death he would not fail to guard him. And if he thought him loyal enough to do that for a Moor, then he ought to realize what, as a loyal man, he ought to do as a Christian to guard the body of God who is King of Kings and Lord of Lords, and that if the king wished to kill him for this he would never find a better occasion. And when the king heard what Lorenzo Suárez had done, it pleased him very much and he loved him and esteemed him much more from that day forward.

"And you, Sir Count Lucanor, if you believe that the man who seeks refuge is a good man, and you can trust him, although they tell you that he has done some unreasonable things, you ought not for that reason put him out of your company, for perhaps what men consider was unreasonable in him was not so, just as King Don Fernando thought it ill advised for Don Lorenzo Suárez Gallinato to kill a priest until he knew the reason for it. And so we can say that Don Lorenzo

Suárez Gallinato did the most excellent of all deeds. But if you know that what this man did was ill done, you would do well not to keep him with you."

And what Patronio said pleased the count greatly and he took his advice and profited by it.

And Don Juan thought this story was good and he had it written down in this book and he wrote these verses as follows:

> *Many a meaning seems quite dense*
> *Which, better known, will make good sense.*

.   .   .

A century earlier Etienne de Bourbon had used this story, but had made its protagonist a knight who lived during the reign of Philip Augustus. Others also before Don Juan Manuel had told the same story—de Vitry, Saint Bernard of Sienna, for example—and Don Juan might have used any of these ecclesiastics as his source, or could have used an oral version which he hispanified. Thompson-Keller: Q. 221.1.3, Q. 222.1.1; Devoto: pp. 414-16; Ayerbe-Chaux: pp. 86-88.

29. What Happened to a Fox Who Lay down in the Street to Play Dead

Another time Count Lucanor was talking to Patronio, his adviser, and he said to him: "Patronio, a relative of mine lives in a country where he has so little armed strength that he cannot take exception to all the tricks that are played on him, and the powerful men in the land would be very glad to see him do something to give them a pretext for turning against him. And my relative thinks it a serious matter to have to suffer these insults, and he would prefer to risk everything rather than suffer so many daily indignities. And because I want him to find the best solution, I beg you to tell me how to advise him, so that he may get along as best he can in his country."

"Sir Count Lucanor," said Patronio, "if you are to advise him most advantageously in this case, I should like you to hear what happened to a fox who played dead."

And the count asked what had happened.

"Sir Count," said Patronio, "a fox went into a yard one night where there were some hens. Now he was prowling about among the hens, and when he thought he had better escape, it was daylight and people were already walking the streets. And when he saw there was no place to hide, he went out stealthily into the street and stretched himself out playing dead. And when the people saw him, they thought he was dead and paid no attention to him.

"Finally a man who went by said that the hair from a fox's forehead was useful to put on the foreheads of little boys to keep them from being bewitched. And with his shears he cut off the hair of the fox's forehead. Then another man came and said the same thing about the hair of his back, and another of the hair of his sides. And so many spoke and acted in similar vein that at last they had shorn him bare. Yet for all this the fox did not move because he knew that it would not harm him to lose his hair.

"Then another man came and said that the toenail of the big toe of the fox was a good cure for an inflammation of the toe, and he removed it. And the fox did not move. Finally, after a while, another man came and said that the heart of a fox was good for heart pains, and he put his hand to his knife to take out his heart. And when the fox saw that they wanted to remove his heart, he knew that if they did so, he could not recover and that his life would be lost, and so he thought it better to take a risk than to suffer from something that might destroy him. So he took a chance and escaped very well.

"And you, Sir Count, advise your relative that if God has placed him in a land where he cannot avoid the way he is treated as he would like to or as he should, so long as what is done to him is such that he can bear it without great harm or loss, let him make it known that he does not mind the indignities but accepts them. For so long as he lets it be understood that he does not consider himself ill treated by what is done to him, he is not shamed thereby; but if he lets it be known that he considers himself ill treated, and if from then on he does not do all that he must do so as to keep from being ill treated, his standing is not what it should be. Wherefore toward unimportant things he need not react strongly. It is better to let them pass. But if a case arises whereby he can be greatly harmed or ill used, then he must take a risk and refuse to bear it, for destruction or death is better while defending one's rights and honor and estate, than living to endure slights in a dishonorable fashion.

And the count thought this good advice.

And Don Juan had it written down in this book and wrote these verses as follows:

Accept such ills as you can bear,
Repel the rest with utmost care.

. . .

Probably the source is a version of the *Book of the Seven Sages of Rome*, which goes back to Arabic, Persian, and perhaps even to the literature of India. But there is a Greek version, and this seems closer to that of Don Juan Manuel than the others. No one will ever know which of the many written and oral versions the prince utilized. As usual, he made changes and added or altered details. His contemporary, Juan Ruiz, archpriest of Hita, told the same story with more fidelity to some of the known sources. Thompson-Keller: J. 351.2; Devoto: pp. 416-18; Ayerbe-Chaux: pp. 66-69.

30. What Happened to King Abenabet of Seville and Ramayquía His Wife

One day Count Lucanor was talking to Patronio, his adviser, as follows: "Patronio, it happens that a certain man has often asked me, and even begged me, to help him and give him some of my goods. And although when I do so he declares that he is grateful, the next time he asks a favor if I do not at once do as he asks, he grows angry and makes it plain that he is not grateful and has forgotten everything that I have done for him. Now from the wisdom that you possess I urge you to counsel me as to how to deal with this man."

"Sir Count Lucanor," said Patronio, "it seems to me that what has happened to you with this man is like the case of King Abenabet of Seville and his wife Ramayquía."

The count asked what had happened.

"Sir Count," said Patronio, "King Abenabet was married to Ramayquía and loved her more than anything else. And she was a very good wife, and the Moors tell many good stories about her; but she had one bad habit, which was that she sometimes took notions of her own. And one day in Córdova, in the month of February, the snow fell, and when Ramayquía saw it she began to weep. And the king asked her why. And she said it was because he never let her live in a land where she could see snow. And to please her the king had almond groves planted all over the mountains around Córdova, for Córdova is a hot country and it does not snow there every year, and in February the almond groves in flower would look like snow and make her forget her desire for snow.

"Another time, when Ramayquía was in a room overlooking the river, she saw a barefoot woman gathering mud near the river to make adobe bricks. And when Ramayquía saw this she began to weep, and the king asked her why she was weeping. And she said it was because she could never please herself by doing what that woman was doing. So to make her happy the king ordered the great reservoir of Córdova filled with rosewater; and instead of water and mud he had it filled with sugar, cinnamon, and spice, and musk, and amber, and civet, and all the good spices and odors. And instead of straw he had sugar cane placed there. And when the reservoir was full of these things, and of the kind of mud that I have told you, the king told Ramayquía to take off her shoes and stockings and to shape the mud and make as many adobe bricks as she liked.

"And another day, because of another notion of hers, she began to weep and she said she was crying because the king never did anything to please her. And the king, seeing that, after all he had done to please her and to fulfill her desires, did not know what more he could do; so he spoke a word that is spoken in Arabic as follows: '*Vâ la nahar el-tin,*' which means 'Not even the day I provided the mud?' as if to say that if she had forgotten all else, she should not forget the mud that he made to give her pleasure.

"And you, Sir Count, if you perceive that no matter what you do for that man, if you do not do everything else that he asks, he then forgets and is ungrateful for all you have done, I advise you not to do so much for him that it will be injurious to your own affairs. And I advise you also if anyone does anything to satisfy you and then afterwards does not do everything that you ask, you must never forget the good that came to you from what he did do."

And the count thought it good advice and he took it and profited thereby.

And Don Juan, thinking this a good story, had it written in this book and he wrote the following verses:

Who e'er forgets a kindness soon,
Does not deserve another boon.

.   .   .

Moorish Spain interested Don Juan Manuel. The plot of this story probably comes from the *Analectas* of a certain Al-Makkari, who relates the same anecdote and who, it is believed, borrowed it from a story about the Abbasids of Seville, written in the twelfth century by Ibn Kasim. Most authorities agree that the monarch in the story was Abderraman III, king of Córdova (912-961); but others think that the protagonist was Muhammad ibn al-Mutamid ibn Abbad, king of Seville (1040-1095), and that Ramayquía, actually Rumayqiya (that is 'slave of Rumaiq') was the lady in the story. Thompson-Keller: T. 261.3, F. 771.2.4.1; Devoto: pp. 418-19; Ayerbe-Chaux: pp. 119-24.

31. How a Cardinal Judged between the Canons of Paris and the Friars Minor

Another day Count Lucanor was talking to his adviser Patronio as follows: "Patronio, a friend of mine and I wish to do something to our mutual advantage and honor, and I should like to go ahead but I dare not do so until he arrives. Now with the good understanding that God gave you, I beg you to advise me in this."

"Sir Count," said Patronio, "if you are to act as seems most to your advantage, I would like you to hear what happened to the canons of the cathedral church and the lesser friars of Paris."

The count asked him what had happened.

"Sir Count," said Patronio, "the canons of the church were saying that since they were the head of the church, they should be the first to sound the hours. And the friars said that they had to study and get up for matins and prayers so as not to miss their studies, and besides they were exempt and had no reason to wait for anyone. And the argument about the point was great and it cost both parties a great sum of lawyers' fees, and the suit lasted a long time in the papal court. At long last a pope who came along commended the affair to a cardinal with orders to settle it in one way or another. And the cardinal ordered the documents in the case brought to him, and they were so numerous they were frightening to look at. And as soon as the cardinal had all the papers before him he set a time when on another day they were to hear his sentence. And as soon as they were all before him, he ordered the papers burned, and spoke as follows: 'Friends, this lawsuit has lasted a long time and you have all spent a good deal and have received great harm from it, and I do not wish to prolong this lawsuit; therefore, I pronounce the following decree: Let him who first wakes up ring the bell!'

"And you, Sir Count, if the lawsuit is profitable to you both and you can carry it on alone, I advise you to do so, and do not postpone it, for because of delay lawsuits are often lost which might be concluded. And later, when a man wants to undertake them, they may or may not be feasible."

And the count thought himself well advised and he acted accordingly and profited by it.

And Don Juan, thinking this a good story, had it written down in this book and wrote the following verses:

> *Seek fortune now, if you know how,*
> *For if you wait, 'twill be too late.*

.   .   .

María Rosa Lida de Malkiel was certain that the Dominicans told this story to Don Juan or gave him a written account of it, since it reflects the animosity the Dominicans had for other preaching friars. We shall never know with certainty the exact source used by the prince. Thompson-Keller: J. 1179.18; Devoto: pp. 419-20; Ayerbe-Chaux: pp. 419-20.

32. What Happened to the King and the Tricksters Who Made Cloth

Again Count Lucanor spoke to his adviser Patronio and said to him: "Patronio, a man has come to me about an important transaction and he gives me to understand that it will be of great advantage to me, but he tells me not to tell a soul in the world, no matter how much I trust him. And so strongly does he insist on my keeping the secret until he releases me, that he says that if I tell a single soul, my entire estate and even my life may be in jeopardy. And since I know that no man can say anything, whether honestly or deceitfully, that you don't understand, I urge you to tell me how this matter seems to you."

"Sir Count Lucanor," said Patronio, "so that you may know what in my opinion would be best to do in this case, I should like you to hear what happened to a king with three tricksters who came to him."

The count asked him how it was.

"Sir Count," said Patronio, "three tricksters came to a certain king and told him that they were skillful weavers of fabrics, and that above all they could weave a cloth which no man could see, unless he were truly the son of the man he, as well as other people, considered to be his father. The king was delighted, believing that by means of the cloth he would be able to distinguish in his realm who were the rightful sons of their supposed sires and who were not, and that in this way he might vastly increase his wealth, since the Moors inherit nothing from their fathers if they are not verily their sons.

"Therefore the king had a room turned over to them for the making of the cloth. And they told him, so that he might see that they had no desire to deceive, that he should have them locked up in the room until the cloth was finished. Now this greatly pleased the king, and as soon as the men had collected much gold and silver and silk and a great quantity of what was required, they entered the room and were locked up inside.

"They set up their looms and gave everybody to understand that they were weaving cloth. Then, after a few days, one of them went to tell the king that the cloth was begun and that it was the most remarkable thing in the world, and he explained to him what designs and what stitches they were using and that if he liked, he could come to see it, but that no man could enter the room with him.

"Wishing to test the cloth on someone else, the king sent one of his chamberlains to inspect it, but he was unaware that the men were deceiving him. Now as soon as the chamberlain saw the artisans and heard what they said, he was afraid to admit that he could not see the cloth. And when he returned to the king, he said that he had seen it.

"Later the king sent another man, and he said the same thing. And since all whom the king sent told him that they had seen the cloth, the king went himself. And when he entered the room, he saw the artisans weaving and saying 'this is such and such a design, this is such and such work, this is such and such a figure, and such and such a color.' They all insisted upon each detail, but in reality they were weaving nothing at all.

"Now when the king observed that they were weaving nothing and that as they described the makeup of the fabric he could not see it, when others had done so, he considered himself as good as dead, for he thought that he was not the son of the king whom he thought was his father, and for this reason he could not see the cloth; and he was afraid that if he admitted it he would lose his kingdom. For this reason he began to praise the cloth and he memorized what the artisans said about it as it was being woven. And once he was back in his house with his people, he began to say wonderful things about how fine and how marvelous the cloth was, and he described its designs and patterns, but he was actually very suspicious.

"After two or three days he sent his constable to see the cloth and he described to him the marvels and peculiarities which he had seen in it. And when the constable went in and saw the men weaving and expounding upon the figures and patterns of the fabric, while he himself saw nothing, he believed that he was not the son of his father, and that on this account he could not see it, and he believed that if people found it out, his reputation would be destroyed.

"Therefore, he began to extol the cloth as much as the king had done and even more. And he returned to the king and told him that he had seen the cloth and that it was the finest and most gorgeous thing on earth. Then the king considered himself to be even more unfortunate, assuming that the constable had actually seen the cloth and that he himself had not, and he had no doubt that he was not the son of the father he thought he was. Therefore he began to praise the cloth even more and to insist even more upon its excellence and quality and he praised the artisans who were skilled in producing it.

"The next day the king dispatched another of his confidants, and the same thing happened to him as had happened to the king and the others.

"What more is there to tell? In this manner and through this same fear the king and all the people of his realm were deceived, for no one dared to say he could not see the cloth. And so time passed until a great holiday arrived. And everyone told the king that he ought to wear the cloth in the festivities. Now the artisans brought the cloth to him wrapped in fine sheets and explained that they were unwrapping it and asked the king what he wanted them to make for him. And the king told them what garments he desired, and they made him think that they were cutting and measuring the garments to size, and then that they were sewing. And when the holiday arrived, the weavers came to the king with their fabrics cut and sewn and made him think they were dressing him and clothing him in the garments. And in such fashion did they continue until the king believed that he was dressed, for he dared not say that he could not see the garments.

"Now when the king was clothed as you have heard, he mounted his horse to ride through the city, but well it was for him that it was summer. And when the populace saw him riding as he was and knew that those who did not see the cloth were not the true sons of their fathers, everyone thought that his neighbors saw it, and that if they did not, and said so, they would be ruined and disgraced.

"For this reason the secret was kept, since no one dared to reveal it, until a Negro who held the king's horse and who had nothing to lose, approached the king and said, 'Sire, it matters little to me whether or not you consider me the true son of the man I regard as my father or someone else; therefore, I say that either I am blind or you are naked.'

"Then the king began to beat him, saying that because he was a bastard he could not see the cloth. But once the Negro had said this, another person who heard it said the same thing, and soon everyone was saying it, until the monarch and everyone else ceased to be afraid of knowing the truth and they understood the deceit which the tricksters had performed.

"And when they went to look for them they could not find them, since they had made off with everything that they had received from the king by means of the stratagem of which you have heard.

"And you, Count Lucanor, since this man tells you that nobody whom you trust can know anything of what he tells you, you may be certain that he plans to deceive you, for you must realize that he has no desire for your well-being, since he does not have so close a relationship with you as do those who live with you and receive from you many favors and gifts which make them desire your well-being and your protection."

And the count regarded this as fine advice and he did as Patronio said, and the results were good.

And since Don Juan saw that this was a good story he had it set down in this book and composed the verses which run:

If bid to keep a secret from your friends,
'Tis sure the bidder wickedness intends.

.   .   .

This version of the famous story best known in the Western world as "The Emperor's New Clothes" is of Eastern origin, most probably from the *Forty Viziers*. But again, as in the case of so many of the stories of Eastern origin used by the prince, the exact source has not been found. Thompson-Keller: K. 445, J. 2312; Devoto: pp. 420-21; Ayerbe-Chaux: pp. 140-49.

33. What Happened to Don Juan Manuel's
Saker Falcon and an Eagle and a Heron

Again Count Lucanor and his counselor Patronio were talking, and in this manner: "Patronio, it quite often happens that I get into disputes with various men, and when the disputes are over, there are those who advise me to start quarrels with other people, while some advise me to rest and be at peace, while still others tell me to start a war and fight with the Moors. And since I know that no one can better advise me than you, I beg you to advise me as to what to do in this situation."

"Sir Count Lucanor," said Patronio, "so that you may hit upon the best way of dealing with this situation, it might be well for you to know what happened to some very good heron falcons and especially to a saker falcon belonging to Prince Don Juan Manuel."

And the count asked what had happened.

"Sir Count Lucanor," said Patronio, "Prince Don Juan Manuel was out hunting one day near Escalona and he loosed a saker falcon against a heron. And as the falcon rose toward the heron, an eagle came at the falcon. And being afraid of the eagle, the falcon left the heron and began to fly away. And the eagle, when he saw that he could not catch the falcon, flew away also. Now as soon as the falcon lost sight of the eagle, it went back after the heron and began to pursue her in earnest to kill her. But while the falcon was chasing the heron, back came the eagle, and off flew the falcon as before; then away went the eagle, and the falcon turned again to the heron. And this happened some three or four times, for every time the eagle departed the falcon pursued the heron again, and each time this happened back came the eagle to kill the falcon. So, when the falcon saw that the eagle would not let him kill the heron, he left it and rose against the eagle and flew at him several times, wounding him so badly that he made him leave the area.

"Then when he had driven the eagle away, the falcon again flew at the heron, flying high in the sky after it, yet once more the eagle came after him to kill him. So when the falcon saw that there was no other way, he flew upward once again toward the eagle and attacked it and struck it such a blow that he broke its wing. And as soon as he saw the eagle falling with a broken wing, he went to the heron and killed it. And he did so because he believed that he should not abandon his catch as soon as he was free of the eagle which kept getting in the way.

"And you, Count Lucanor, since you know that your hunting and your heron and all your fortune in body and in soul is serving God, and you know that in your position there is nothing for you to do that is so profitable as to wage war on the Moors and thus enhance the true Catholic faith, I advise that as soon as you are safe from other parties, you should go to war against the Moors. For thus will you accomplish much good: in the first place you will serve God, and will keep your honor and live in your place and duty and will not eat your bread without earning it, which is unseemly for any great lord. For you lords, when you have no duty to perform, do not have as high an opinion of people as you should, nor do you do for them all that you ought. You busy yourselves with unnecessary matters. And since it is good and advantageous for you nobles to have a cause, of all the duties you could perform, plainly none is so good, honorable, or advantageous as war with the Moors. And if you will kindly heed the third parable which I related to you in this book, about the leap which King Richard of England made, and how much he gained by it, then consider in your heart that you have to die and that during your life you have grieved God greatly, and that God is the lawgiver and of such great justice that you cannot avoid paying the price of the sins you have committed. But if you are of goodwill, and find an act by which you may have pardon for all your sins, since in a war with the Moors you must die in a state of true penitence, you will be a martyr and blessed. And even though you do not die in battle, your good works and good intent will save you."

And the count considered this good advice and he carried it out and he begged God to guide him in this service.

And because Don Juan understood that this story was good he had it written in this book and wrote these verses:

> *If God to thee is ever kind,*
> *Then thou must keep Him on thy mind.*

. . .

A similar tale exists in the *De Natura Rerum* of Alexander Neckham (died 1217), but it is not safe to attribute a reminiscence from Neckham to Don Juan Manuel's diligence in reading. The story is well known as a traditional tale, and the prince might have found it in a number of places, both in writing and in oral lore. That he personalized it, using his own father as the owner of the falcon, is but another example of his originality. One last possibility exists, but scholars who have written about the matter seem never to admit it: why could not the falcon of Don Juan Manuel's father have had such an experience with an eagle? Polygenesis is a definite possibility, for anyone's falcon could have had a fight with an eagle. Thompson-Keller: L. 315.9; Devoto: pp. 422-23.

34. What Happened to a Blind Man
Who Was Leading Another

On another occasion Count Lucanor was talking with Patronio, his counselor, in this way: "Patronio, a kinsman and friend of mine whom I trust and who, I am sure, truly loves me, advises me to go to a place about which I am rather fearful. And he insists that I should not be afraid, since he would rather die than see any harm come to me. And now I beg of you to advise me in this matter."

"Sir Count," said Patronio, "as to this advice, I'd like very much for you to hear what happened to two blind men."

And the count asked him what had happened.

"Sir Count," said Patronio, "a man who was a town-dweller lost the sight of his eyes and went blind. And while he was thus blind and poor, another blind man who lived in the same town came to him and said that the two of them ought to go to town close by, where they could beg in God's name, and thus they might obtain the wherewithal to support and care for themselves.

"Now the first blind man told the second that he knew the road to that town and that it was full of holes, gullies, and risky places and that he was afraid of it. But the second blind man told him not to be afraid, since he would go with him and keep him safe. And so much did he assure him and so many advantages did he point out about the journey that the first blind man believed him, and they set out.

"And as soon as they arrived at the bad and dangerous spots, the blind man who was leading the other fell, and the one who had been afraid to undertake the journey could not keep from falling also.

"And you, Sir Count, if you have reason to be afraid and the path is dangerous, do not go into danger because your relative and friend tells you that he would rather die than see you harmed, for little would it profit you if he were to die and you were to suffer and die also."

The count took this to be good advice and he followed it and found himself well off because of it.

And since Don Juan realized that this was a fine tale, he caused it to be written in this book and wrote these verses:

Never tread the slippery way
No matter what a friend may say.

.   .   .

The parable of the blind leading the blind may have been the source out of which the prince created this brief tale. Other medieval writers— de Vitry, for example—had related similar accounts. The exact source the prince used cannot be determined. Thompson-Keller: J. 2133.9; Devoto: pp. 423-25; Ayerbe-Chaux: pp. 45-47.

35. What Happened to a Young Man Who Married a Strong and Ill-tempered Woman

On another occasion Count Lucanor was talking to his adviser Patronio, and he said to him: "Patronio, one of my wards told me that a marriage was being arranged for him with a very rich woman who is also of a higher social standing than he is. He says that it is a good marriage except for one thing. He says they have told him that the woman in question is about as strong and ill-tempered as any woman on earth. And now I want you to advise me whether to tell him to marry the woman, since he knows the sort of person she is, or whether to tell him not to."

"Sir Count," said Patronio, "if he is like the son of a certain Moor, tell him to go ahead; otherwise he had better not."

And the count asked him to tell him about it.

Patronio said: "In a certain town there was a worthy man who had a son, a most excellent fellow, but he was not rich enough to carry out as many plans as he felt that he should. And for this reason he was in a quandary, for he had a strong desire to succeed but lacked the where-withal to get ahead. Now in that same town there was another Moor, richer and more distinguished than his own father, and this man had an only daughter. And she was the exact opposite of the young man, for just as the young man's ways were good, hers were bad and she was shrewish. For this reason no one wanted to marry her.

"One day the young man went to his father and said that he knew that he was not rich enough to provide him with what he needed for a good life, and so he would have to lead a needy and impoverished existence unless he left the country. Or, perhaps with his approval, it might be a good idea if he got married. In this way he might get enough to live on. His father said the idea was all right if he could find the right girl. Then the son told his father he wanted him to make arrangements with the man with the ill-tempered daughter for him to marry her.

"When the father heard this he was astonished and asked his son how he could even think of such a thing, since no one he knew, however poor, wanted her. But the son begged him to arrange the marriage and insisted, so that the father, even though he thought it mad, agreed to do it. So he went to the good man, who was a friend of his and told him his son's idea, saying that since his son had the courage to marry the girl, he hoped he would be kind enough to agree.

"And when the man heard this he answered: 'For God's sake, my friend, if I did a thing like that I would not be much of a friend, for your son is a good lad. It wouldn't be right to let him get hurt or killed, for if he marries my daughter I am certain that he will either be dead or wish he were. But so that you won't think I am saying this just to get out of doing you a favor, if you truly want me to, I will be delighted to let your son marry her—or anyone else who will take her out of my house.'

"The father thanked him for his offer, but said that since his son had requested it, he urged him to do as he had asked.

"The wedding took place, and they took the bride to the groom's house, for it is a Moorish custom to prepare a meal for a young couple and set the table and then leave them alone until the next day. And they did so, but the parents of both the bride and groom were very fearful, thinking that the next morning they would find the groom either dead or badly hurt.

"When they were alone in the house the couple sat down at the table, and before the wife could say anything her husband looked around the house and, seeing the dog, he yelled at it roughly: 'Dog, bring us water to wash our hands.'

"And the dog did not do it. Then he began to grow angry and he told the dog even more roughly to bring water for their hands. And the dog did not. When he saw this, he got up from the table angrily, took his sword and went for the dog. When the dog saw him coming he began to run, with the groom after him, and they ran over carpets, and over the table and through the fire, until the young man caught him, struck off his head and legs, and cut him to pieces, bloodying the house and the curtains and the table.

"And then still angry and covered with blood, he sat down again and looked around till he saw the cat. He told the cat to give them water to wash their hands, and because he did not, he said: 'What, false Sir Traitor, didn't you see what I did to the dog when he wouldn't do what I told him? I swear that if you keep on I'll do to you what I did to the dog!'

"But the cat did nothing, for it is hardly the custom for cats any more than for dogs to provide water for washing. And because the cat would not, he took him by the legs and struck him against the wall and smashed him into a hundred pieces, screaming at him even louder than he had at the dog. And so, wild and angry and making horrible faces, he came back to the table and looked around again. And his wife, watching him, thought he was crazy or out of his mind and said nothing. And when he had looked all around he noticed his horse standing there, and it was the only horse he had; but he told him roughly to bring water for their hands. And the horse did not do it, and when he saw that he did not do it, he said: 'What, Sir Horse, do you think that because you are the only horse I have that I will spare you if you do not do as I say? Don't believe it, for it will be to your sorrow if you fail to do what I tell you. I swear to God I'll kill you as I did the others. For there is no living creature who fails to do what I say that I will not treat in the same fashion!'

"And the horse just stood there. And when he saw that he did not do as he was told, he went and cut off his head, putting on an

139

appearance of frenzied anger. And he cut the horse to pieces. And when his wife saw that he had killed the horse, having no other, and heard him say that he would do the same to anyone who didn't obey him, she decided it was no joke, and she was so frightened she did not know whether she was dead or alive. And the husband, still frenzied and angry and bloody, came back to the table, swearing that if a thousand horses or men or women in his house refused to obey he would kill them all. And he sat down, holding his bloody sword in his lap. And when he had looked everywhere and saw no other living creature, he turned to his wife and said to her very angrily, sword in hand: 'Get up and get me water for my hands.'

"And the woman, who surely expected nothing but to be cut to pieces, quickly got up and brought the water. And he said: 'Ah, thank God that you did as I asked, for on account of my anger at the others I would have done the same to you.'

"Then he ordered her to serve him food, and she did. And every time he said something she thought her head was already forfeit. And so things went between them that night. And the wife never spoke, but did her husband's bidding. They went to bed, and after they had slept a while he said: 'Last night's anger is keeping me awake. Don't let anyone wake me, but keep me well supplied with food.'

"And the next morning their parents and relatives came to the door, and since they heard no voices they thought the husband must be dead or wounded. And when they looked inside and saw the bride, but not the groom, they were all the more convinced. And when the wife saw them at the door, she came quietly and fearfully and said: 'Mad traitors, what are you doing? How dare you come to the door and talk. Be quiet! Otherwise all of us, including myself, are as good as dead!'

"And when they heard this they marveled greatly, and after they had learned briefly what had happened, they thought well of the young man for having known how to rule his household. And from that day on his wife was well behaved and they had a good life together.

"A few days later the groom's father-in-law decided to do what his son-in-law had done, and so he killed a rooster. But his wife said: 'Well now, Mr. So-and-So, you are a little late. It wouldn't matter to me now if you killed even a hundred *horses*. You should have begun sooner, for now we know each other.'

"And so, Sir Count, if your protegé wants to marry a woman of this sort, and if he is like this young man, tell him to marry, for he will certainly know how to manage his household; but if he is the kind who will not know what to do, he had better not. And I advise you in all your dealings with others, always to let them know what you expect of them."

And the count thought this good advice and he took it and profited from it.

And because Don Juan thought this a good story he had it written down in this book and wrote these verses to go with it:

> *Rules you want folks to obey*
> *You'd better state without delay.*

. . .

The most famous version of this story is Shakespeare's *The Taming of the Shrew*. Don Juan Manuel seems to have used a Moorish story, which in its turn may go back through Arabic literature or folklore to a version in Persian or even in Sanskrit. Other medieval writers—de Vitry and Etienne de Bourbon, to name but two—related accounts about shrewish wives, but they are not from the same source, it would appear, as Don Juan Manuel's story. The elements of Moorish daily life with which the prince decorated his own version do not, of course, prove that he had the story from Moorish folklore or Moorish writing. We must simply conclude that we do not know the exact source, but that we think it was oral. Thompson-Keller: T. 251, T. 251.2; Devoto: pp. 426-34; Ayerbe-Chaux: pp. 155-61.

36. What Happened to a Merchant When He Found His Son and His Wife Sleeping Together

One day Count Lucanor was talking to Patronio, and he was very angry about something people told him, since he considered it much to his dishonor; and he told him that he wanted to do something important about it, something so important that it would always be considered phenomenal.

And when Patronio saw him so enraged and so disturbed, he said to him: "Sir Count, I very much want you to know what happened to a merchant who went out one day to buy wisdom."

And the count asked him how that was.

"Sir Count," said Patronio, "there lived in a certain town a great master whose only occupation was the selling of wisdom. And that merchant of whom I spoke before, because he had heard of this, went to see that sage who sold wisdom and asked him to sell him some. And the sage asked him what price he wanted to pay, since he must pay according to the quality of the wisdom he wanted. And the merchant told him that he wanted a farthing's worth. The sage took the farthing and said: 'Friend, when someone invites you to dinner, if you don't know what dishes you will have to eat, eat well of the first one he sets before you.'

"And the merchant told him that he hadn't given him much wisdom. Then the sage told him that he hadn't given him enough money for a large portion of wisdom. Then the merchant told him to give him a doubloon's worth, and he gave it to him. And then the sage told him that when he became very angry and planned to do something violent, that he should not vex himself nor become upset until he knew the whole truth.

"Now the merchant considered that if he kept learning such sayings he could waste all his doubloons, and so he had no desire to buy any more wisdom, but even so he treasured what he had bought in his heart. And it came about that the merchant went seafaring to a very distant land, and when he departed he left his wife pregnant. And the merchant tarried, as he plied his trade, for so long a time that his son, the fruit of the pregnancy of his wife, reached the age of twenty years. And the mother, since she had no other child and because she believed that her husband was not alive, comforted herself with that son of hers, loving him like a son and, because of the great love she had borne for her husband, she called him ' husband.' And he always dined with her and even slept with her, just as when he was only a year or two old. And thus she spent her life like a very virtuous woman and yet in great sadness, since she never had word of her husband.

"Now it came to pass that the merchant finished all his trading and turned homeward wealthy. And on the day that he arrived at the gates of that village where he had once lived, he said nothing to anyone but went incognito to his home and hid himself in a secret place in order to see what had been happening there. And when it was evening the son of his good wife came home, and his mother said to him: 'Tell me, husband, where you have been today.'

"And the merchant, when he heard his wife call that young man husband, was deeply grieved, for he most certainly believed that he was a man with whom she sinned, or at best, that she had married. But he clung more to the belief that she was living in sin than that she was married because the man was young. And he desired to slay him on the spot, but recalling the wisdom that had cost him a whole doubloon, he held his temper. And as night came on they sat down to supper. And when the merchant saw them that way, he was even more minded to kill them, but on account of the wisdom he had paid for, he remained calm; however, when night came and he saw them get into bed, it seemed more than he could bear, and he made his way forward to murder them. But as he made for them in great fury, he was again mindful of the wisdom he had purchased, and he calmed himself.

"Now just before they extinguished the lamp, the mother began to weep bitterly and to say to her son: 'Alas, husband and son, they have told me that a ship has just arrived in port from that land where your father went, and for God's sake go early tomorrow morning and perchance God will allow you to learn some tidings about him.'

"And when the merchant heard that and recalled how he had left his wife pregnant, he realized that this was his own son. And you will not be surprised at the great joy he knew. Likewise, he was most grateful to God because He had prevented him from slaying his son as he had desired to, a deed by which he would have been ruined; and he considered himself fortunate, indeed, that he had spent the doubloon for the wisdom he had remembered and that he had not acted violently in anger.

"And you, Sir Count, no matter how much you think it may be an insult to endure what you mention, it would be best to be certain about the matter; but until you are certain, I advise you not to rush into anything, whether in wrath or in haste, for this is not something you will lose on account of time and suffering. While you are waiting to learn the truth, you will lose nothing at all, but you would quickly repent a hasty action."

And the count held this to be good counsel and he acted in accordance with it and the results were happy.

And Don Juan, considering it a good parable, had it written down in
this book and he made verses which read as follows:

If you seem a fool at first,
People always think the worst.

. . .

The idea of this story—that is, of knowledge bought and used
later—is old, and other medieval writers had utilized it before the time
of Don Juan Manuel. Something similar appears in the *Gesta Romanorum*, Number 103, and in the *Exempla of the Rabbis*. But not one of
the many suggestions made by scholars can be proved conclusively.
That part of the story which tells of the son and the mother asleep
innocently together and discovered by the long-absent husband thought
long-dead is also a part of the *exempla* lore of many European coun-
tries. Most probably Don Juan read it in some Latin collection of
exempla, or perhaps even heard some Dominican relate it in a sermon.
Thompson-Keller: J. 163.4, J. 21.2; Devoto: pp. 434-36.

37. What Happened to Count Fernán González with His Men after He Had Won the Battle of Hacinas

On a certain occasion the count came out of battle tired, miserable,
and poor; but before he could take his ease and rest, a messenger
arrived in haste from an invasion which was just beginning. Now most
of his men urged him to rest awhile and then decide what to do. And
the count asked Patronio how to handle the emergency.

Patronio replied: "If you are to solve this problem, I should very
much like you to know of the reply which Count Fernán González
once gave to his vassals."

And the count asked Patronio how that was.

"Sir Count," said Patronio, "when Count Fernán González defeated
King Almanzor at Hacinas many of his men perished, and he and all

who were spared were badly wounded. Now before they could recover, he realized that the king of Navarre was making inroads upon his territory, and he commanded his troops to make ready to do battle with the Navarrese.

"All of his followers said that their horses were exhausted, as they were themselves, and although on this account he could not fail to act, still for this reason he ought to do so, for he and all of them were badly wounded, and he should therefore wait until they had all recuperated.

"When the count saw that they all wanted to follow the same course, more interested in life than in honor, he spoke to them as follows: 'Friends, let's not pull back because of our wounds, for the wounds they will inflict upon us will make us forget those we have already received.'

"And as soon as they saw that the count gave no thought to his own person in the defense of his country and his honor, they went with him. And he won the battle and was very successful.

"And you, Sir Count Lucanor, if you want to do what you should, when you understand what is best for the defense of your property, and people, and honor, you will never complain of suffering or toil or danger. So act in such a way that the present dangers and sufferings will make you forget the past."

And the count considered this good advice and followed it and came out of it all successfully.

And when Don Juan realized that this was a good story, he had it written in his book and composed these verses which say:

> *Learn this truth and learn it well:*
> *That sloth with honor cannot dwell.*

.   .   .

Fernán González, the epic hero of the *Poema de Fernán González*, did indeed win the Battle of Hacinas, but the chronicles do not include the incident related by Don Juan. It would seem that he either created an interesting account from whole cloth or borrowed from some other story. Or perhaps some other writer had long since associated the tale with the hero of the battle and thereby had launched it into the current folklore of Don Juan's time. Thompson-Keller: J. 673, J. 350.1; Devoto: p. 437; Ayerbe-Chaux: pp. 88-91.

38. What Happened to a Man
Who Was Loaded down with Precious Stones
and Drowned in the River

One day the count told Patronio that he wanted to go to a certain place because there he would be given a sum of money, and he hoped to do well for himself there; but he was very reluctant to go because if he stayed there, he might undergo much danger, and he begged Patronio to advise him as to what he should do.

"Sir Count," said Patronio, "so that you may do what in my opinion will be best for you, it would be useful for you to know what happened to a man who was carrying valuables on his back while he was crossing a very deep river."

And the count asked him about it.

"Sir Count," said Patronio, "a man was carrying a heavy load of jewels on his back, and there were so many of them that they were hard to carry. Now it happened that he had to cross a wide river. And since the weight was great, he was sinking more than he would have without the load. And when he was in the deepest part of the river, he began to sink even more. And a man on the bank started yelling to him that if he did not drop his burden, he would drown. But the foolish man did not realize that if he drowned in the river, he would be lost as well as the load he was carrying, but that if he dropped it, he would lose only the load, but not his life. But on account of his great greed for the value of the jewels he did not drop them and so he perished in the river, losing his life as well as his load.

"And you, Count Lucanor, even though the money and the other considerations which would accrue to you would be advantageous, I advise you, if you see danger to life and limb in the business, not to stay there out of desire for money or any other inducement. And furthermore I advise you never to risk your life except for something which would either redound to your honor or would be a great disgrace to you if you failed to do it, for I say that he who thinks little of himself and who through greed or vanity risks his life, is one who plans to do little with his life; for a man who truly values himself should strive to make others value him also. A man is not esteemed through the value he puts upon himself, but because he does such deeds as to make others esteem him.

"Now if a man acted in this way, you may be certain that he would set a great store by his own life and would not risk it out of greed or for any act from which he would gain little honor; but as to when he should risk it, be assured that no man on earth risks his life so readily and so deliberately as one who esteems himself highly and values himself greatly."

And the count held this to be good advice and he acted in accordance with it and succeeded in his enterprise.

And because Don Juan realized that this was a very good exemplary tale he caused these verses to be written down in his book:

He who risks his life through greed,
His way to death will surely speed.

. . .

The idea of losing one's life because of refusing to throw away valuables, often in the case of one swimming or about to drown, is old, and evidently it stemmed from actual events. It is well known that centuries later some of the soldiers of Hernán Cortés, as they retreated from Tenochtitlán, were drowned by the weight of the gold and jewels they carried. Don Juan Manuel could have witnessed similar drownings in the wars in which he took part. Or he may have found an account of such a happening. Thompson-Keller: J. 651.2, J. 2159.1; Devoto: pp. 437-38; Ayerbe-Chaux: pp. 48-50.

39. What Happened to a Man and a Swallow and a Sparrow

Once again Count Lucanor was speaking to Patronio as follows: "Patronio, there is no way that I can avoid trouble with either the one or the other of my neighbors. But it so happens that my closest neighbor is not so powerful as the more distant one. And now I ask you to advise me as to what I should do."

"Sir Count," said Patronio, "in order to understand what is most advantageous, it would be well for you to know what happened to a man and a sparrow and a swallow."

And the count inquired about that.

"Sir Count," said Patronio, "a man was very tired and he was highly annoyed by the shrillness of some bird calls, and he asked one of his friends for advice, since he could not sleep for the noise made by the sparrows and swallows. And his friend told him that he would not be able to get rid of all the birds, but that he knew a magic spell by which he could free himself of one variety—either the sparrows or the swallows.

"And the weary man replied that although the swallows make more noise, even so they go and come, while the sparrows stay around the house constantly; therefore he preferred the swallows, even though they are louder, because they aren't always there.

"And you, Sir Count, even though the man who lives farther away is the more powerful, I advise you to contend with the one who is nearby, although he is not so strong."

And the count considered this good advice and he followed it and all went well for him.

And because Don Juan was pleased with this fable he had it written in his book and composed these verses:

If quarrels seem ordained, choose first
The distant one, though it seems worst.

. . .

In the *Speculum Laicorum*, Number 557, a somewhat similar tale is told of Saint Francis. Such stories entered the lore of ancient fables (this story does not appear in the classical fables of Aesop and Phaedrus) and came from man's observations of the habits of animals. Surely some such tale existed in Spain in Don Juan Manuel's time, either in some book or in oral tradition. Thompson-Keller: J. 215.1.4; Devoto: p. 438.

40. Why the Seneschal of
Carcassonne Lost His Soul

Count Lucanor was again speaking to Patronio as follows: "Since I am aware that no one can escape death, I would like to live in such a way that after death I may leave something special for my soul's sake, something that will last forever, so that all men may know that I have done it."

"Sir Count," said Patronio, "although good works, no matter of what kind, or for what reason, are always excellent, even so you ought to know what a man ought to do for his soul's sake and to what end. Wherefore I would be pleased to have you hear what happened to a seneschal of Carcassonne."

And the count asked him about that.

"Sir Count," said Patronio, "a seneschal of Carcassonne was taken ill, and when he realized that he could not recover, he sent for the prior of the Preaching Friars and arranged with them for the salvation of his soul. And he commanded that as soon as he was dead they should carry out all his commands, and they did so.

"Now he had promised a great sum for the state of his soul. And because his vow was so ably and quickly carried out, the friars were gratified and had high hopes of his salvation.

"But it happened that a few days later a devil-possessed woman came to town, and she said marvelous things; and because the devil spoke through her, she knew everything that was done and everything that was said. And when the friars to whom the seneschal had entrusted his soul learned what the woman was saying, they thought it a good idea to go and see her and ask her whether she knew anything about the seneschal's soul. And they did so, and when they came to the possessed woman's house, even before they could ask her any questions, she told them she knew exactly why they were there, and that they should know that the soul they wanted to ask about had gone to hell shortly after it had left the body.

"Now when the friars heard this, they said that she was lying, for it was a fact that the man had made proper confession and had received the sacraments of the Holy Church; and since the Christian faith was a true one, it was impossible for what she said to be true. And she told them that of course the Christian faith was entirely true, and if the man had died and had done all that a real Christian ought to do, that his soul would have been saved; but that he had not acted as a good Christian because even though he had promised much for the sake of his soul, he had done not what he should have, nor had he had the proper intention, since he had ordered it carried out after his death; his intent being, in case he did not die, but lived on, that none of it should be carried out. And so he ordered things done after his death, since he could not keep his goods or take them with him. And thus his bequest was made so that the fame of his action would last forever and he would be esteemed by all men.

"Therefore, even though he did a good work, he did not do it well, because God does not reward good works alone, but only those works which are done properly. For good works lie in good intentions, and since the seneschal's intention was not good, since it was not as it should have been, he did not receive a reward for it.

"And you, Sir Count, since you ask me to counsel you, I tell you to accomplish the good you desire to do in your lifetime. And so as to have a proper reward for it, it behooves you first of all to make amends for the wrongs you have done, since it does little good to steal a lamb and then as charity donate the feet in God's name. Nor will it avail you much to keep things you have stolen and then bestow alms out of what you have taken illegally from others. Moreover, for alms to be good, five things are required: in the first place, they must be derived from fairly earned sums; secondly, they must be given while one is in full penitence; thirdly, they must be sufficient to make the giver suffer from privation, or even want, through the giving; fourth, they should be given in this life; and in the fifth place, they must be given honestly for God and not for vainglory, nor worldly pride.

"And, Sir Count, by observing these five conditions all good works and all alms will be perfect and will have a great reward; but even though neither you nor anyone else is able to perform as perfectly as he should, do not fail to do good works, believing that since you cannot accomplish them in the five aforementioned ways, you will have no advantage from them, for it is certain that no matter how one does good works, they are always worthwhile; for good works help one to avoid sin and accomplish penitence and the body's welfare, and to attain riches and honors, and have high repute among men, and enjoy every temporal reward. And therefore every good thing that a man may do is always good, no matter what his intent may have been; but it is much better for the salvation and betterment of his soul if he has observed the five requirements cited above."

And the count believed that what Patronio told him was true and he resolved to follow his advice; and he begged God to help him to do exactly as Patronio said.

And Don Juan, seeing that this exemplary tale was excellent, had it written in this book and composed these verses:

> *If God's reward you hope to win,*
> *Throughout your life abstain from sin.*

.   .   .

Several proverbs and even several *exempla* have been suggested by scholars but none of these can with safety be considered the direct source of Don Juan's story. The account smacks of the *exempla* so often told in sermons and in the alphabets of tales, but this particular tale has not been found in such sources as early as Don Juan's time. Since avarice is one of the seven deadly sins, it is easy to see how a wide variety of such tales came into being. Perhaps the Dominicans gave the prince the version he related or suggested it. Thompson-Keller: U. 236.1, V. 511.2; Devoto: pp. 438-39; Ayerbe-Chaux: pp. 45-54.

41. What Happened to a King of Córdova Named Al-Haquem

One day Count Lucanor was conversing with Patronio, his counselor, in this way: "Patronio, you know what a hunter I am and that I have discovered many ways of hunting formerly unknown. Indeed, I have even contributed helpful parts, never before used, to the leashes and the hoods of falcons; and now people try to make fun of me, and when they praise the Cid Ruy Díaz or Count Fernán González for the number of battles they have won, or when they praise the holy and blessed King Ferdinand for all his fine conquests, they praise me too, saying that I did a fine thing indeed by adding some parts to falcons' hoods and leashes. Now because I realize that such a compliment as this is meant to reflect more scorn on me than praise, I beg you to advise me what I can do to keep people from mocking my improvements."

"Sir Count," replied Patronio, "in Córdova lived a king named Al-Haquem. Now in spite of ruling his realm well, he did not strive to do any particularly honorable or famous thing out of all those that good kings usually do or should do. For not only are kings expected to protect their kingdoms, but if they wish to be good, they should do deeds to improve their realms and so act that during their lifetimes they shall be praised by men. Then after their death excellent accounts of their good works will endure.

"Now this king bestirred himself only to eat and drink, and take his ease, and live in luxury. And it happened that one day as he was practicing on a musical instrument, one very popular among the Moors and called a flute, this king listened to it and realized that it was not producing so fine a tone as it should, and so he added another hole directly above the others, and thenceforth the flute played much better than it had before. And although this was well done for a thing of the sort, because it was not the kind of great deed a king should do, people began to praise it in jest and say when they praised something: *Va he de ziat Alhaquim* which means 'just like King Al-Haquem's invention.'

"Now this saying was bruited about so much throughout the land that the king finally heard about it, and he inquired why folks said such a thing. And the more they tried to hide the words from him, the more he insisted that they tell them to him.

"As soon as he heard the saying he was greatly grieved; but since he was a good king, he had no desire to harm those who explained it to him, but resolved instead to make another invention for which men would have to praise him. And on this occasion, because the mosque of Córdova was not finished, the king added to it all that was needed to complete it. And it is the largest and most perfect mosque of the Moors in Spain, and thank God, it is now a church called Saint Mary of Córdova; for when the blessed King Don Ferdinand took Córdova from the Moors, he consecrated it to Holy Mary. And when that Al-Haquem had the mosque finished and excellent additions made to it, he said, since up until that time they had praised him in mockery for his improvement to the flute, that he believed it would be proper thereafter to praise him for his addition to the mosque of Córdova. And he was highly praised, and the mocking praise ceased and became true praise. And to this day the Moors say, when they desire to praise something fine, 'this is the addition of Al-Haquem.'

"And you, Sir Count, if you are sad and believe that they are praising you only to make fun of you for the improvement you made in the hoods and leashes and other inventions for the chase, make a point of performing some great, good, and noble deeds which are worthy of great men. Then of necessity people will praise your good works, just as now they praise you sarcastically for the improvements you have made in things pertaining to hunting."

And the count considered this to be good counsel and he followed it and profited because of it.

And because Don Juan understood that this was a good story he had it written in his book and composed the following verses:

> *Small steps of progress you may take,*
> *Then build on them for goodness' sake.*

. . .

Some scholars believed that the king in the story was Al-Hakem II of Córdova, but no one has found a chronicle of the Arabs which contains the events related by Don Juan Manuel. It has the ring of a local legend or a folk anecdote. Thompson-Keller: J. 370.1, J. 372; Devoto: pp. 439-40; Ayerbe-Chaux: pp. 119-24.

42. What Happened to a Woman of Sham Piety

Again Count Lucanor was talking to Patronio, his adviser, in the following way: "Patronio, I have been talking to a number of people, and we were asking each other what sort of habits an evil man or woman could possess in order to do the most harm to everyone else. Now, some said he could do it by being a troublemaker, others said it was by being a plotter. Others said it was by being a malcontent, while others asserted that the way to do most harm was by speaking calumny

—Todos son sinonimos   153

and bearing false witness. Now, on account of your great knowledge, I want you to tell me which of these evils will do people the most harm."

"Sir Count," said Patronio, "in a certain town there was a very fine young married man, and he and his wife lived so happily together that no discord ever came between them. Now the Devil, because he is always displeased by what is good, was greatly grieved by this, and for a long time he tried to stir up trouble between them, but could not. Now one day as he was returning sadly from the town where the man and his wife lived, he met a wicked woman who pretended to be pious. After they had become acquainted she asked him why he was so sad, and he told her that he had just come from the town where the husband and wife lived, and that for a long time he had tried to make them do evil against each other, but to no avail. Moreover, his superior knew this, and since he had spent so much time on the matter without success, he realized that he would be held in low esteem by him. For this reason he was sad.

"The woman told him that she was surprised that he knew so much yet could accomplish nothing, for if he would follow her advice she would bring it about. The Devil replied that he would do anything she suggested, provided he could sow discord between the man and the woman. And so, the Devil and the woman of false piety joined forces.

"The wicked woman then went to the couple's house and was so persistent that she made the young woman's acquaintance, and convinced her that she had been her mother's servant and that because of her friendship for her she felt obliged to serve the daughter in any way possible. The good wife believed her and took her into the house, and she and her husband trusted her with their affairs.

"After she had lived with them for a long time, and was completely in their trust, she came one day to the trusting young woman and said sadly: 'I am terribly grieved for I have heard that your husband is much more interested in another woman than in you. I beg you to be nice to him and please him so much that he will not like the other woman as much as he does you, for more harm can come to you through this than from anything else.'

"When the good wife heard this, even though she did not believe it, she was sad, and worried a great deal. Now as soon as the wicked old woman realized that the wife was unhappy, she went to a place where the husband was sure to be. And when she met him, she said that she was much disturbed to hear that he loved another woman more than his wife, when his wife was as good as she was. She said his wife knew all about it and was terribly upset. She also said that his wife had asked her, who served her so well, to find her a man to love her as much as her husband loved her or even more. And she begged him not to tell his wife that he knew about this or she would be as good as dead.

"When the husband heard this he grew sad, even though he did not believe it. And when the wicked woman had told him all this, she went directly to his wife, and feigning grief, said to her: 'Daughter, I do not know what the trouble is, or why your husband is displeased with you, but you can see for yourself that it is true. Notice how sadly he comes home and how angry he is, which is not at all like him.'

"Leaving her in this unhappy state she went to the husband and told him another story, and so when he came home he found his wife sad, and since they had none of the happiness they were used to having from each other, he was worried. And when he had gone out, the wicked woman told the good wife that if it was agreeable to her she would go and find a great doctor who would cause her husband to lose the evil feelings that he had for her. The wife, desiring a good life with her husband, told her she liked the idea and was grateful.

"A few days later the old woman came back to say that she had found a very wise man who had told her that if she could get a few of the hairs that grew on her husband's throat, he would prepare a charm to make her husband stop being angry, and then they would have the same kind of life they used to have, perhaps even better. And the old woman told her to get her husband to lie down and sleep with his head in her lap, and she gave her a razor with which to cut the hair. And the good woman, because she loved her husband so much and sorrowed because of the coolness between them, and because she wished above all to return to the good life they had had, agreed to do it. So she took the razor the wicked woman had given her.

"Then the wicked woman went back to the husband and told him she was so concerned over his imminent death that she could not hide the fact from him that his wife was planning to murder him and run off with her lover. And so that he might know that she was telling the truth, she said his wife had agreed with her lover to kill him as follows: as soon as he came in she would let him sleep with his head in her lap, and when he fell asleep she would cut his throat with a razor that she had for the purpose.

"When the husband heard the old woman's false words, he was so

155

frightened and alarmed that he determined to find out the truth. He went home, and when his wife saw him she was kinder to him than on the previous day. She told him that he was working too hard and that he did not take enough rest. She told him to stretch out beside her and put his head in her lap so that she could pick off his fleas. Now when the husband heard this he thought that what the wicked woman had told him was true. But to be certain of what she would do, he lay down with his head in her lap and pretended to be asleep. When his wife thought he was asleep she took out the razor to cut his hair just as the wicked woman had told her to do. When the husband saw the razor in his wife's hand, close to his throat, believing that what the wicked woman said was true, he snatched the razor from her hands and beheaded her with it. And he made so much uproar as he cut off her head that her father and brothers came. And when they saw the woman beheaded, and when they remembered that until that day neither her husband nor any other man had heard anything bad about her, they went up to the husband and killed him in their anger. At this uproar, the husband's relatives came running and killed those who had slain their kinsman. And so the affair progressed until the majority of the dwellers in the town were dead.

"And all this evil came from the false words of the woman of sham piety. But because God never wants an evildoer to live unpunished, even though his sin be hidden, he caused it to be known that all the trouble had come about through that evil woman. So they sentenced her and put her to death in a cruel manner.

"And you, Lord Count Lucanor, if you want to know who is the worst man on earth, and the one who does the most harm to people, you must know that he is the one who pretends to be a good and devout Christian while his life is false, going about spreading his lies so as to create discord among people. Therefore I advise you always to watch out for those who act like pious cats, for the majority of them are steeped in wickedness and treachery. And when you actually meet people of this sort follow the advice of the Gospel, which says: '*A fructibus eorum cognoscetis eos,*' which means 'By their fruits shall ye know them.' For rest assured that there is no one on earth who can very long conceal the deeds that he plans to do. He can hide them for a while, but not for long."

And the count believed that what Patronio said was true, and he resolved to follow his advice and begged God to protect him and all his friends from such an evil man and such an evil woman.

And since Don Juan understood that the tale was good, he had it set down in his book and composed the following verses:

Not looks but deeds will surely test a friend;
Know this and foil what wicked men intend.

Actions Speak Words

.   .   .

Etienne de Bourbon, Number 225, may have written the oldest medieval version of this tale. It also appeared in Rabanus Maurus and in the *Scala Coeli*. The oldest known version may be that of Joseph ibn Sebara, a Jew of Barcelona, who wrote in Arabic. It appears in the *Speculum Laicorum*, Number 463, and in Jacques de Vitry. Therefore, Don Juan could have taken it from any number of sources or even from oral lore. Thompson-Keller: T. 452, J. 2301, K. 1085; Devoto: pp. 440-42; Ayerbe-Chaux: pp. 13-20.

43. What Happened to Good and Evil and the Wise Man and the Madman

Count Lucanor was talking with Patronio, his counselor, in this way: "Patronio, I happen to have two neighbors; one is a man I'm very fond of and there are many ties between us to cause my affection. And I can't say for what devilish reason or cause he often hurts me and cheats me to my great annoyance. But the second is not a man with whom I have close ties, nor for whom I feel deep affection, nor is there any reason why I should be especially fond of him, and this man likewise sometimes does things to me that I do not like. Now through the great knowledge you have, I beg you to advise me as to how I should deal with these two men."

"Sir Count," said Patronio, "what you mention is not one matter, but two, and the two are the very opposite of each other. And so that you may act in this case as befits you, I would like you to know two things that once took place: one of them happened to Good and Evil; and the other to a wise man and a madman."

And the count asked how that was.

1

"Sir Count," said Patronio, "Good and Evil agreed to live together. Now Evil, who is more clever than Good and always full of guile, is never happy except while plotting some trick or evil deed. He told Good that it would profit them to have a flock of sheep to help them make a living, and Good liked the idea, and they agreed to get some sheep. And as soon as the sheep were bred, Evil told Good that each of them should choose his share from the produce of the sheep. And Good, since he is virtuous and prudent, did not want to choose but asked Evil to choose first.

"Now Evil, because he is wicked and deceitful, was delighted, and he told Good to take the lambkins as they were born, and that he would take the milk and the wool. And Good gave him to understand that he was satisfied with this division.

"Then Evil said that it was a good idea for them to keep pigs, and Good was pleased. And as soon as the pigs littered, Evil said that since Good had taken the offspring of the sheep and Evil the milk and the wool, that now Good should take the milk and the wool and that he, Evil, would take the offspring. And Good accepted that arrangement.

"Later Evil said that they should set out a garden, and they planted turnips. Now as soon as they sprouted, Evil told Good that he did not know what there was that could not be seen, but so that Good could see what he was taking, he should take the tops of the turnips, which could be seen and were above the ground, and that he, Evil, would take what was underground. And Good agreed.

"And later they planted cabbage. And as soon as it came up, Evil said that since Good had the other time taken the parts of the turnips which were above ground, that he should now take the part of the cabbage that was underground, and Good did so.

"Later Evil told Good that it would be advantageous for them to have a woman servant, and Good was pleased with the idea. And as soon as they had her, Evil told Good to take her from the waist to the head, and that he, Evil, would take the parts from the waist to the feet, and Good took these parts. And Good's half of the woman did what was needful around the house, and Evil's part was wed to him and had to sleep with her master. And the woman became pregnant and bore a son, and after he was born, his mother wanted to suckle him.

"Now when Good saw this, he said that she could not do so, since the milk came from his part and that he would in no way consent to the suckling. And when Evil came in joy to see his newborn son, he found him crying, and he asked his mother why. And the mother told him that it was because he wasn't getting milk. And Evil told her to feed him, but the woman replied that Good had forbidden it, saying that the milk came from his part.

"Now when Evil heard this, he went to Good, and laughing and joking, told him to let them have milk for his son; but Good told him that the milk was from his part and that he would not permit it. When Evil heard this he began to become insistent. And when Good observed the straits Evil was in, he said: 'Friend, don't think that I was so simple that I didn't recognize the kind of parts you always picked and the kind you gave me while I never asked of you anything from your share and I got along wretchedly with what you gave me, while you never stinted yourself nor showed any generosity toward me. And since God has now placed you in a predicament where you need something of mine, don't be surprised if I refuse to give it to you. Remember what you did to me, and take what is coming to you.'

"And when Evil realized that Good was telling the truth and that his son would die, he was most grief-stricken, and he commenced to beg and beseech Good's mercy in God's name for the child's sake and asked Good to overlook his wrongdoing, and henceforth he would do all that Good asked of him.

"And when Good understood this, he realized that God had favored him greatly in putting him in a position where Evil could not live without his kindness, and he regarded this as a great victory. So he told Evil that if he, Good, agreed to allow his wife to suckle her son, then Evil would have to put the child on his back and go through the city proclaiming, so that all could hear him: 'Friends, know that Good conquers Evil.'

"If he would do this, Good would consent to give him the milk. This satisfied Evil who considered that he had successfully bargained for the life of his son. And Good felt that he had done very well.

2

"But it happened in another fashion with a good man and a madman. The good man operated a bathhouse, and the madman came to

159

the bathhouse while people were bathing and hit them so hard with buckets, stones, and sticks, and whatever else he could lay his hands on, that no one dared go to the good man's establishment, and he lost his income.

"Now when the good man realized that the madman was causing him to lose his income from the bath, he got up early one day and entered the bath before the madman arrived. And he undressed, and picked up a bucket of very hot water and a large wooden shovel. And when the madman who kept coming to the bath to hurt people arrived, he went straight to the bath as usual. And when the good man, who was waiting naked for him, saw him come in, he went straight for him and very fiercely and angrily hit him over the head with the bucket of hot water, and he took the shovel and struck him so many blows on the head and body that the madman thought he was dead and that the good man was insane.

"And he fled screaming and met a man who asked him why he was yelling so and complaining so much. And the madman replied: 'Friend, look out, believe me there is another madman in the bath!'

"And so, you, Sir Count Lucanor, get along in this way with your neighbors: with the one with whom you have such ties that you think you will always be friends, always be kind, and even if he annoys you somewhat, forgive him and always help him when he needs it; but always do so while making him understand that you are doing so because of the ties and affection that you have for him and not because you are afraid or annoyed. But in the case of the man with whom you do not have such ties, never take anything from him, but make him realize that whatever he does for you is for his own good."

And the count thought this very good advice and he followed it and all went well for him.

And because Don Juan regarded this as a good exemplary tale he had it written in his book and wrote these verses:

> *Goodness always takes the prize,*
> *To bear a bad man is unwise.*

.   .   .

The deceitful division of crops or herds is well known in folklore, both in the Old and in the New worlds. A tale about good and evil as characters appears in *El libro de los gatos*, the hispanification of Odo of Cheriton's *Narrationes*, either of which collections of *exempla* Don Juan might have read; but that story is not actually the same as the one told by the prince. The second tale, that of the madman at the bathhouse, may have been suggested to the prince by certain proverbs, but no undisputed source has been found. Thompson-Keller: 171.1; Devoto: pp. 442-45.

44. What Happened to Don Pero Núñez the Loyal, to Don Ruy González de Zavallos, and to Don Gutier Roiz de Blaguiello with Don Rodrigo the Generous

Count Lucanor was talking with Patronio, his counselor, and he said to him: "Patronio, I have happened to be involved in many wars and my estate has been in great danger. Now when I was in greatest need, some of those whom I had brought up and treated well deserted me and even set out to do me a great deal of harm. And they did such things to me that I assure you that I have come to expect less of people than I did before. And because of the fine mind that God gave you, I beg you to counsel me as to what you think I ought to do."

"Sir Count," said Patronio, "if those who sinned against you were like Pero Núñez de Fuente Almexir and Don Ruy González de Zavallos and Don Gutier Roiz de Blaguiello, they would not have done what they have done if they had known what would happen to them."

And the count asked him what that was.

"Sir Count," said Patronio, "Count Don Rodrigo the Generous was married to a fine lady, the daughter of Don Gil García de Azagras; but the count, her husband, bore false witness against her. And as she denied it, she asked God if she were condemned to perform a miracle for her sake, so that if her husband was accusing her falsely it should be revealed in him.

"Now after her prayer by some miracle, the count, her husband, was stricken with leprosy and she left him. And as soon as they were separated, the king of Navarre sent a messenger to the lady, and married her and she became queen of Navarre.

"Now the count, realizing that he was a leper and incurable, went to the Holy Land on pilgrimage to die. And although he was highly esteemed and had many loyal vassals, only the three knights mentioned above went with him, and they dwelt there so long that all the supplies they had brought with them from home were used up and they were so poor that they had nothing to give the count, their master, to eat. And in their need two of them hired themselves out in the plaza while one stayed with the count; and with what they earned from their toil they provided for the count and themselves.

"Every night they bathed the count and cleansed the cankers of his leprosy. And it came to pass one night that while they were washing his arms and legs they had to spit and they did so. And when the count saw this, thinking that they did this from disgust, he began to weep and bemoan his awful plight and the suffering he bore. And in order to persuade the count that they were not nauseated at his disease, they took in their hands some of the water that was full of the pus and scabs from the count's sores and they drank a fair amount of it.

"And enduring such a life with the count, their master, they stayed with him until he died. And because they believed that it would be wrong to go back to Castile without their lord, alive or dead, they refused to do so. And although they were told to boil his body and scour his bones, they would not allow anyone to touch their dead master any more than if he were alive. They refused to let him be boiled, but buried him and waited a sufficient time for his body to decompose. Then they placed his bones in a coffer and carried them on their backs. And thus they made their way, begging their food, with their liege lord on their backs, and they bore testimony of all that had happened to them. And traveling in poverty but happy, they came to the region of Toulouse, and as they came into the city they met a multitude of people who were taking a noble lady to the stake because of an accusation of her husband's brother. And it was proclaimed that if some knight did not save her, her sentence would be carried out, but no knight had come forward.

"Now when Don Pero Núñez the Loyal, of noble fame, heard that for lack of a knight a sentence was being carried out against the lady, he told his companions that if he could be certain of her innocence, he would save her. And he went immediately to her and asked for the truth. And she told him that she positively had not committed the sin of which she was accused, but that she had wanted to. And Don Pero

Núñez, although he understood that since she had wished to do what she should not have done, only harm could come to anyone who tried to save her, because he had made a beginning and knew that she had not committed the entire sin of which she was accused, he said that he would save her.

"Now when the accusers tried to refuse to let him, saying that he was not a knight, as soon as he proved that he was, they could not refuse. And the lady's relatives provided him with a horse and weapons; but before he went into the jousting field he told her relatives that with God's grace he would win honor and save the lady, but it could not be without some accident's happening to him because of what the lady had done. When the fight began God aided Don Pero Núñez and he won the encounter and saved the lady, but he lost an eye, and thereby what he had said before the fight came to pass.

"And the lady and her relatives gave him such a good sum that he was able to carry the bones of the count, his lord, in a manner less wretched than before. Now when the tidings reached the king of Castile about the approach of those honorable knights and that they were bringing with them the bones of the count, their master, he was greatly pleased and thanked God that men from his kingdom had done such a deed. And he had them summoned on foot and poorly dressed as they were. And on the day when they were about to enter the kingdom of Castile, the king went out on foot to meet them a good five leagues before they reached his realm, and he was so generous to them that to this very day their descendants are heirs of the king's largesse. And the king and all those with him, in order to honor the count, accompanied his remains to Osma, where they buried them.

"And when the funeral was over, the knights went to their home. Now on the day that Don Ruy González reached his home, as he was sitting at the table with his wife, as soon as the good lady saw the food on the table, she said, 'I thank Thee, O God, that Thou hast permitted me to see this day, for well dost Thou know that after Don Ruy González departed this land, this is the first morsel of meat that I have eaten and the first wine I have drunk!'

"Don Ruy González was saddened by this and he asked her why she had done it. And she told him, and he replied that he well knew that he had told her he would not come back without the count and that she should live as a good wife should, for bread and water would never be wanting in her home; and that since he had put it that way, that it was right for her not to disobey his order and that for this reason she had not eaten anything except bread and water.

"Likewise, when Don Pero Núñez got home and was with his wife, the good lady began to laugh. And since Don Pero Núñez believed she was laughing at him in mockery of his lost eye, he covered his head and threw himself on his bed. Now when the good lady observed how sad he was, she was greatly grieved, and so anxious did she appear to learn the reason for his sadness that he told her that he was suffering because he felt that she was laughing at him because his eye had been put out.

"When the good lady heard this, she ran a needle into her own eye and put it out, and told Don Pero Núñez that she had done it so that if she ever laughed again, he would never think that she was laughing to shame him.

"And so God blessed those noble cavaliers for the good works they had done. And I believe, Count Lucanor, that if those who are not serving you well were like those knights, and if they realized all the good things that could come to them through their actions, they would not sin against you as they have. But even though people who should not harm you have done so, you, Sir Count, should never stop doing good works, because the very ones who sin against you, do more harm to themselves than to you. And note well that if people sin against you, many others serve you well, and the good deeds which the latter do for you are more important than the lessening of your power by those who hurt you. Therefore, do not expect to be well served by all whom you have supported. For it may turn out that one man will serve you in such a way that you will consider yourself well served in spite of all you have done for the others."

And the count held this to be good and true counsel.

And Don Juan, considering this a good story, had it written in this book and composed these verses:

If you by men have been ensnared,
Do not therefore go unprepared.

.   .   .

The events of this story probably all come from tradition and the customs of medieval society. The story might well be historical. Men

164

did go on crusades and their servitors might well have acted as did those in the story Don Juan relates. But no definite source that he might have used has been discovered. Devoto: pp. 445-49.

45. What Happened to a Man Who Became the Devil's Friend and Vassal

Once again Count Lucanor talked with Patronio, his counselor. It was in this fashion: "Patronio, a man has told me that he has great knowledge not only of augury but also of other arts by which I can know the future, and he says that through these things I can increase my estate, but I am afraid that in doing these things I would be sinning somewhat. Now because of my confidence in you, I beg you to advise me what I should do in this case."

"Lord Count," said Patronio, "so that you may do what is of the greatest profit to you in this regard, I would like you to know what befell a man with a demon."

Count Lucanor asked how it happened.

"Sir Count," said Patronio, "a man had been very wealthy and he fell into such great poverty that he had not the wherewithal to live. Now since there is nothing in the world more wretched than a man once well-off who has become poor, this man who had been so wealthy and had come to such great want, grieved mightily. One day he wandered sad and alone through a forest, deep in bitter thought, and he met the Devil. And since the Devil knows everything that has happened, he knew how great the man's grief was and he asked him why he was so sad. And the man asked him why he should tell him, since he could give him no counsel for all the grief he had. But the Devil told him that if he would obey him, he would provide a cure for his unhappiness, and that as a sign that he could do this, he told him that he would reveal to him the reason for his sadness. Then he related the man's entire case to him and the reason for his sadness, just like one who was perfectly familiar with it. He told him that if he would obey his commands, he would save him from poverty and would make him the wealthiest member of his entire lineage, for he was the Devil and had the power to do so.

"When the man learned that this was the Devil, he was terrified; even so, due to his extreme grief, he replied that if the Devil would show him a way to wealth, he would do whatever he wished.

"Now you can well believe that the Devil chooses a time for deceiving men when he sees that they are in some difficulty, or in need, or poverty-stricken, or afraid, or desirous of doing his work. It is then that he obtains from them all that he covets, and so it was that he lighted upon a way to deceive that man at a time when he was in such trouble.

"Thus it was that they drew up their contract, and the man became his thrall. And when all the conditions had been set up, the Devil told the man to steal thenceforth, that he would never find a door or a house locked against him, no matter how tightly they had been secured, and that he, the Devil, would open them for him immediately. And if ever by chance the man should find himself in difficulty or should be arrested, he should call to him and say, 'Help me, Don Martín,' and he would come to him straightway and would deliver him from any danger he encountered.

"Having made this bargain, they took leave of one another. The man went to a merchant's house on a dark night—for those who plan to commit evil always shrink from the light—and as soon as he reached the door, the Devil opened it for him and also the money chests, and he carried away a great haul. Then another day he committed another great robbery, and after that still another, until he became so rich that he couldn't remember the poverty he had endured.

"And so the wretch, unmindful of how fortunate he was to be free from want, began to steal all the more, and he did this so frequently that he was captured. And when they took him, he called for Don Martín to rescue him, and Don Martín came quickly to his aid and released him from prison.

"And when the man realized that Don Martín had been so reliable, he began to steal as he had formerly and committed a great many thefts, so that he was even richer than he had been poor. And following such a career, he was again arrested, and again he called Don Martín; but Don Martín didn't arrive so quickly as he wished, and the judges of the town where he had committed the robbery started legal proceedings over the crime.

"In the midst of this trial, Don Martín arrived and the man said to

166

him: 'Oh, Don Martín, what a scare you gave me! Why were you so slow?'

"And Don Martín replied that he had been engaged with other pressing affairs and had delayed on this account, but he removed him from prison right away. And the man returned to the way of the robber, and after many robberies he was again arrested, and after trial he was sentenced. Don Martín saved him, and he stole again because he saw that Don Martín would always help him.

"Then, on another occasion, he was captured and he called Don Martín and he didn't appear, and he even delayed until the sentence of death was handed down; but although Don Martín arrived after the sentence had been given, he obtained a pardon from the palace, took the man from prison and freed him.

"He again returned to theft, was captured, called Don Martín, who didn't arrive until they had sentenced him and sent him to the gallows. And at the foot of the gallows, Don Martín came to him.

"The man said: 'Ah, Don Martín, I hope you realize this is hardly a jest, for upon my word I was frightened to death!'

"Don Martín told him that he had brought him an alms purse of five hundred *maravedís* and that he could give them to the judge, and he did so.

"Now the judge had already ordered them to hang him, but they didn't find a rope for it. And when they were looking for the rope to hang him, the man called the judge and gave him the alms purse with the money. As soon as the judge saw that he had given him five hundred *maravedís*, he said to the people who were there: 'Friends, who ever saw a rope missing for a hanging? Certainly his days have not run out and God doesn't want him to die, and therefore caused the rope to be missing. Let's hold him until tomorrow and we shall investigate further, for if he is guilty justice will be done tomorrow.'

"The judge did this so as to free the man in return for the five hundred *maravedís* which he had given him. With this agreed upon, the judge stepped aside and opened the alms purse, expecting to find five hundred *maravedís*, and he found no money, but he did find a rope in the purse. When he saw this, he ordered the man hanged. As they put him on the gallows, Don Martín came up and the man asked him to help him. Don Martín said he always helped his friends until they came to the gallows.

"So the man lost his body and soul, believing the Devil and trusting him. And be very certain that there is no man who trusts him who does not come to a bad end. But if you doubt it, consider all the augurers and soothsayers, and those who cast lots and those who weave spells and enchantments and other things of that sort, and you will observe that they always come to bad ends. If you don't believe me, remember Alvar Núñez and Garcilaso, men who put all their faith in augury and the like, and you will see to what an end they came.

"And you, Lord Count, if you really want to arrange your life for the good of your body and your soul, trust in God and place all your hope in Him; help yourself as much as possible, and God will help you; but do not believe in nor trust soothsayers nor any other such foolishness, but realize that of all the sins in the world that grieve and wrong God, the greatest is to observe auguries and the like."

The count considered this to be good counsel and he followed it and good came to him through it.

And because Don Juan realized that this exemplary tale was good he caused it to be inscribed in his book, and he wrote these verses which say:

> Who does not on the Lord rely,
> Will badly live and badly die.

. . .

The pact with the devil is old indeed, and it had been included in many medieval books. The oldest may be the legend of Theophilus, first written in Greek, but soon translated into Latin and thence into the vernaculars. A version appears in the *Summum Praedicantium* and in the *Speculum Laicorum*, and there are similar accounts in the *Romulus* and in the *Lais* of Marie de France. And Don Juan's contemporary Juan Ruiz told the same story in verse, but with elements different enough to suggest a different source from the prince's. Closer still to Don Juan Manuel were Gonzalo de Berceo's *Milagros de Nuestra Señora* and the *Cantigas de Santa María* of King Alfonso X, both of the thirteenth century. Thompson-Keller: M. 212.2; Devoto: pp. 449-51; Ayerbe-Chaux: pp. 7-13.

46. What Happened to a Philosopher Who by Accident Went down a Street Where Prostitutes Lived

Again Count Lucanor was talking to Patronio and he told him his problem: "Patronio, you know that one of the things men should most strive to do is win a good reputation and see that no one questions it. And because I know that in this as in everything else no one can advise me better than you, I ask you to tell me how best I can increase, publish, and protect my reputation."

"Sir Count," said Patronio, "I am delighted at what you ask, and so that you can best accomplish your wishes, I want you to know what happened to a famous old philosopher."

And the count asked what had happened.

"Sir Count," said Patronio, "a great philosopher lived in a city in the kingdom of Morocco. Now this wise man suffered an illness, such that when it became necessary for him to void his bowels, he could do so only with great effort, pain, and delay. Now because of this affliction the physicians told him that as soon as he felt the need to defecate, he should immediately do so, since the longer he held back the more his stool would grow dry and harden so as to hurt him and seriously damage his health. And since the doctors had told him this, he took their advice and was healthy. And it happened one day that as he was walking along a street in the city where he lived and where he had many students, the urge to move his bowels could not be delayed. And as luck would have it, the alley he entered was inhabited by the sort of women who publicly damn their souls and dishonor their bodies. But the philosopher knew nothing of this. And so, on account of his affliction and the great length of time he lingered there; and because of the way it looked when he emerged, even though he did not realize what sort of people lived there, everybody thought that he had gone there for reasons far removed, indeed, from the life he had been living and should live. And because it looks bad when a man of good repute does something unbefitting, people gossip more and more damagingly, and it is worse for him no matter how small the thing is than it would be for a less important person or one known to be habitually careless about such things. And so the philosopher was much maligned and criticized; and the fact that that highly esteemed and venerable philosopher had entered such a place, was indeed detrimental to his soul, his body, and his reputation.

"Therefore, when he got home, his students came and with heartfelt sorrow and grief began to ask what great misfortune or sin had made him so disgrace himself and them and lose the reputation which until that moment he had protected better than anyone else. And when the philosopher heard this, he was dumbfounded and he asked them what they were talking about and what sin he had committed, and when, and where. And they told him that, since he was now talking to his dishonor and their own, there was nobody in town who wasn't gossiping about what he had done when he went into the alley where the evil women lived. And when the philosopher heard this, he was deeply grieved; but he begged them not to be greatly concerned over it, for within a week he would give them an answer.

"So he locked himself in his study and wrote a brief, excellent, and helpful essay, and among the many fine things in it, he spoke of good fortune and bad, and as though lecturing to his students he said: 'My sons, in good fortune and in bad this is what happens. Sometimes a result is sought and achieved, and sometimes it is achieved though not sought after. The sought after and found result is when a man does well, and from that good deed good fortune comes to him; likewise bad luck comes to a man for a bad deed. Now this is a good result or bad result sought after and found, because he seeks it and does the deed so that good or evil will come to him. Likewise, the found yet unsought result is when a man who does nothing to gain it, achieves some good or advantageous result, to wit, as if he went to some place and discovered a great treasure, or achieved some great advantage for which he did nothing at all; and this is especially the case when one, by doing nothing, receives harm or damage, as for example, when he goes along a street and another man aims a stone at a bird and hits the man in the head. This is an unfortunate result achieved but not sought, for in this instance the man did nothing and sought nothing from which the misfortune came.

" 'Now, my sons, you should know that in good fortune and bad, both looked for and found, two elements are required: one, a man must help himself, by doing good deeds to obtain good fortune, by doing bad ones to obtain bad; in the second place, know that God rewards a man according to his good or bad deeds. Likewise in good fortune or in bad, when achieved and sought for, two other things are necessary: first, a man should make every effort to avoid doing evil, or making himself suspect, or placing himself in a position to suffer bad repute; second, one should pray to God and ask His grace. So let each man protect himself as best he can, so that no misfortune will overtake him as it did to me the other day when I went along the street to do what I could not avoid doing for my health and my body's sake. Now what I did was without any sin or bad repute, yet to my misfortune such people dwelt there, that although I was blameless, I lost my reputation.'

"And you, Sir Count, if you want to increase and make evident your reputation, you must do three things: first do good works, pleasing to God, and once this is accomplished, then do what you can to please men, guarding your honor and status, and do not think that the fine reputation you have may not be lost should you do things contrary to those good deeds you are duty bound to do, because many men do good works once, and because they do not pursue them, they lose the good which they have done and in the end are remembered only for the evil deeds they have committed; the second is to pray God to let you live until you accomplish the kind of deeds that will increase your reputation, to let you always go forward and keep you from doing or saying anything which can hurt you; the third is to do nothing by deed, word, or appearance of which people can be suspicious. Thus your reputation will remain as it should be, for often men do good works and because of evil appearances people become suspicious, and by this fact one is harmed only a little less in the eyes of the world and its rumors than if he had actually sinned. And you should know that in matters touching reputation, what people believe and say is true helps or hinders as much as what is really true; and of all that is done for the sake of God and the soul, only what a man does and only his good intentions are advantageous or harmful."

And the count thought this a good story and he prayed God to enable him to do such works as He considered effective for his salvation, his reputation, his honor, and his estate.

And because Don Juan thought this a good exemplary tale he had it written in his book and wrote these verses:

Do good and avoid the appearance of evil,
Or fame will repute you a friend of the devil.

The story might be Eastern or Western in origin, since analogies exist in the writing and the lore of both areas; but no definite source has yet been suggested. Thompson-Keller: K. 2150; Devoto: p. 452.

47. What Befell a Moor and His Sister Who Pretended That She Was Timid

Count Lucanor talked again with Patronio, his counselor, tot wit: "Patronio, remember that I have an elder brother, and that we had the same father and the same mother. Because he is older than I, I feel that I must regard him as a father and must obey him. His reputation is excellent, for he is a good Christian and a prudent man.

"However, God has willed that I am richer than he and more powerful, and even though he never reveals it, I am certain that he is envious on account of it. Now whenever I am in need of his assistance, when he can do something for me, he gives me to understand that it would be wrong for him to do it. This so surprises me that I tell him not to do it. Sometimes when he needs my help, he says that even though I should lose everything, I must not fail to risk my life and all my possessions to do what he wants me to do. Because I am placed in this position as regards him, I beg you to advise me as to what you think I should do in this matter, and what will be most suitable for me to do."

"Lord Count," said Patronio, "it appears to me that the way your brother treats you resembles what a Moor said to one of his sisters."

The count inquired as to how that was.

"Sir Count," said Patronio, "a Moor had a sister who was so timid that she pretended to be frightened and fearful. So far did she carry this, that when she drank water from the clay vessels used by the Moors, and when the water gurgled as it was drunk, the Moorish girl pretended that the sound so terrified her that she nearly fainted.

"Her brother was a stout fellow, but very poor. Now because extreme needs cause a man to do what he does not wish to do, he could not refrain from earning a living in a shameful manner. He earned it thus: whenever someone died, he went by night and carried off the shroud and whatever they had buried with it. In this way he maintained his sister and his family.

"His sister was aware of this. Now it happened that a very wealthy man died, and they buried him with fine garments and other valuable objects. When the sister heard about it, she told her brother that she would go with him that night to carry off what they had buried with him.

"When night fell the young man and his sister went to the dead man's grave and broke into it; but when they tried to remove the priceless wrappings which clothed the body, they couldn't do so without tearing the cloth or by breaking the corpse's neck. As soon as the sister realized that unless they broke the dead man's neck they would have to tear the clothes, which would thus lose much of their value, with her own hands she grasped the dead body's head and pitilessly broke the neck, removed the garments which were on the body, gathered up whatever was there, and carried it off.

"The next day when they sat down to eat, they had scarcely started to drink, when the water in the clay jug gurgled, and she seemed faint with fright at the sound coming from the jug.

"When her brother noticed this and recalled how she fearlessly had snapped the corpse's neck, he said in Arabic: 'Aha ya ohti, tafza min bocu, bocu, va liz tafza min fotuh encu,' which means: 'Aha, sister, you seem frightened at the sound of an earthen vessel which goes *butu, butu,* but you do not shrink from breaking the neck of a dead man!' And this proverbial saying is very common among the Moslems.

"And you, Sir Count Lucanor, must realize that that elder brother of yours who excuses himself from doing what he ought to do for you in the way you mention and who says that you should do what profits him, is like the Moorish girl who feared the gurgle of water from an earthen jug and did not shrink from breaking a dead man's neck. Since he wants you to do for him things that would be damaging to you, do to him as he does to you; speak kindly to him, be of good will toward him, and do whatever you can for him, so long as it does not harm you. As for things that could harm you, avoid them as best you can, and however it may be arranged, see that you do not hurt yourself."

The count held this to be good advice, and followed it and profited thereby.

And because Don Juan understood that this was a good exemplary tale he caused it to be set down in this book, and he composed these verses:

Be slow to heed the solemn plea
Of one who'll take no risk for thee.

. . .

The source is unknown. The characters are Moors. The story might be from a literary source, but it has the ring of an actual happening about which Don Juan Manuel had heard. Devoto: pp. 452-54.

48. What Happened to a Man
Who Tested His Friends

Once again Count Lucanor was talking to Patronio, his counselor, in the usual way: "Patronio, in my opinion I have many friends who assure me that they would not fail to do for me what was needful, even in the face of the fear of death or hurt to their bodies, nor would they desert me. Now through the great knowledge you have I urge you to tell me how to ascertain whether these friends would do as much for me as they say."

"Sir Count Lucanor," said Patronio, "good friends are the best thing on earth, but certainly when great need comes, or great trouble, one finds far fewer friends than he expects; and likewise, even when the need is not great, it is difficult to tell who would be a true friend when disaster strikes; but if you are to know who your true friends are, I should like you to hear what happened to a good man and his son who claimed to have many friends.

"Sir Count Lucanor," said Patronio, "a good man had a son, and among the things he taught him and counseled him about was that he always should try to have many good friends. And the son did so and he began to share what he had with many men so as to keep them as friends. And they all said that they were his friends and would do for him all that was necessary, and that they would risk their lives and estates for him if need be.

"Now one day when the young man was with his father, the latter asked him if he had done what he had asked and had made many friends. And the son said that he had, for he had many friends, and that especially there were ten among all the others who he was certain would not, through fear of death or caution, fail him in trouble or need or in any accident which could befall him. When the father heard this he said he was astonished that in such a short time he could have made so many friends of that degree, since he himself, who was a great deal older, had never been able during his whole lifetime to acquire more than a friend and a half-friend.

"And the son began to insist, maintaining that what he said about his friends was true. And since the father saw him so determined, he asked him to test them in this way: he should kill a pig, put it in a sack and go to the home of each of his friends and tell each that his sack contained a murdered man and that surely, if this were known, nothing could save him from death nor save those who knew about the deed; and he begged them, since they were his friends, to conceal the corpse and, if need be, to be strong in his defense.

"So the young man did as he was bid and set out to test his friends according to the plan suggested by his father. Now when he went to their house and told them about the awful deed, they all told him that they would help him in other ways; but in this, because they might lose their own lives and estates, they dared not help him, and for God's sake to make sure that no one found out that he had come to their houses. And some of the friends told him that they did not dare do anything else for him, but they would go and pray for him; and others said that when he was led off to be executed, they would not desert him until justice had been carried out and then they would go to his funeral.

"Now when the young man had tested all his friends and had found shelter with none, he returned to his father and told him what had happened. And when the father saw him coming, he said that now he could see the difference between those who were experienced and those who were not. And so he told him that he himself had only a friend and a half-friend and that they should test the latter. So the son went to test the man whom his father called a half-friend, and he came to his house at night carrying the dead pig on his back; and he knocked at the door and told the half-friend that a misfortune had befallen him and what had happened with all his own friends; and he begged him, for the love of his father, to help him in his time of trouble.

"Now when his father's half-friend learned this, he replied that he did not have enough love and closeness with his father to risk that much for him, but for the love he did have he would hide the body. Then he took the sack with the pig in it, believing it to be a man, and he carried it on his back to his vegetable garden and buried it under a row of cabbages, and then replaced the cabbages just as they were before. And he sent the young man off with his blessing. And when the lad was back with his father, he told him all that had taken place with his half-friend. And his father said that on the next day, when they were in public, he should start an argument with the half-friend and in the midst of the argument strike him in the face with his fist as hard as he could. So the youth did so, and when he hit him, the good man faced him and said: 'Really, son, you have acted badly, but even so, rest assured that I will not, on this account or for any other wrong, dig up the cabbages in my garden.'

"When the young man told his father this, he ordered him to go and test his whole-friend. And when he arrived at the friend's house, telling him everything that had happened to him, he asked the good man, the friend of his father, to protect him from death and harm. Now it happened by chance that at that time a man had been murdered in the town and they did not know who had done it. And because some people had seen the young man carrying a sack on his back at night, they believed he had done the deed. But why do I spin it out? The young man was sentenced to die. Now his father's friend had done all he could to free him, and when he saw that he could not remove the blame in any way, he told the judges not to consider the young man guilty as he had not killed the man, but that his only son had done so. And he told his son about it, and he agreed to it. And they put him to death, and the son of the good man escaped death.

"And now, Count Lucanor, I have told you how friends are tested, and I believe that this is an excellent story for teaching people which friends to test before they risk great danger through trust and to teach them how much such friends will do if need be; for many friends, even most, are fair-weather friends, and as long as good fortune lasts they are friends. And also this tale can be understood spiritually in this way: all men believe they have friends, and when death comes, they must be tested in time of trouble; and they go to laymen, and they tell them to do thus and so; and they go to the clergy, and they tell them that they will pray to God for them; and they go to their wives and children, and they tell them that they will go to the grave with them and will honor them at their funerals; and thus men test those whom they think to be their friends. And when they find in them no shelter for an escape from death, just as the good man's son returned when he found no help in any of those who he thought were his friends, they turn to God, their father, and He tells them to test the saints who are half-friends, and they do so. And so great is the goodness of the saints, and especially Saint Mary, that they do not cease from praying to God for sinners; and Saint Mary shows all men what their own mothers were like and how hard they worked to keep them and rear them; and the saints show people all the misery and pain and torment they bear for their sake, in order to conceal the mistakes of sinners. And even though the saints have borne much grief because of them, they do not reveal it, just as the half-friend did not reveal the first blow which his friend's son gave him.

"Now since the sinner realizes spiritually that he cannot escape his soul's death in any way, he turns back to God, just as the son returned to his father when he found no one who could save him from death. And our Lord God, like a father and true friend, remembering His love for man, His creation, acted as a good friend, for He sent His Son Jesus Christ to die, blameless and without sin, to take away the sins and blame which man deserves. And Jesus Christ, like a good son, was obedient to His Father, and since He was true God and true man, He desired to receive death and redeem sinners with His blood.

"And now, Sir Count, note well which of these friends are best and most reliable and which are those a man ought to do the most to win."

And the count was pleased with these teachings and considered them good.

And Don Juan realized that this was an excellent story, and he had it written in his book and wrote the following verses:

> *Trust the friends whom thou dost try,*
> *Upon the rest do not rely.*

The source of this story is the *Disciplina Clericalis* of the Aragonese Jew, Pedro Alfonso, although the prince's version wanders considerably from that of the *Disciplina*. He has combined two stories of Pedro Alfonso, numbers I and II, adding new details and touches. Many authors in the Middle Ages utilized Pedro Alfonso's work, but since Don Juan had Pedro Alfonso available, there is little need here to list books that also utilized it. Thompson-Keller: H. 1558.1, R. 169.6; Devoto: pp. 454-59; Ayerbe-Chaux: pp. 161-69.

49. What Happened to the Man Whom They Cast out Naked on an Island When They Took away from Him the Kingdom He Ruled

Again Count Lucanor was talking with Patronio, his counselor, and he said to him: "Patronio, many men tell me, since I am so highly regarded and so powerful, that I can do anything I please to acquire much money, great authority, and high honor; and that this is what is proper for me and what is most relevant. And because I know that you always advise me best and that you will always continue to do so, I beg you to advise me, as you see it, what is most advantageous for me."

"Sir Count," said Patronio, "this counsel you require of me is a serious thing to give, and for two reasons: the first is that in this advice you ask of me I shall have to speak against your wishes; and the second is that it is awfully difficult to speak against the counsel given for one's master's advantage. And because there are these two things about this advice, it is hard for me to talk about it; but because every counselor, if he is loyal, should think of nothing but giving the best advice and not of looking out for his own interests nor his losses, or whether his advice pleases his master or pains him, he should think only to advise him the best that he can; therefore, in this counseling I will not fail to tell you what I consider is best and most advantageous for you. And so I say to you that the men who advise you in part are counseling you well, but it is not the best advice for you; but that I might give you the best and most fitting advice, it would be a good thing and it would please me much for you to know what happened to a man who was made lord of a great realm."

And the count asked him about it.

"Sir Count Lucanor," said Patronio, "it was the custom in a certain land each year to create a ruler. And as long as the year lasted they did all that he commanded. But once the year ran out, they took all he had away from him, stripped him bare, and cast him away on an island, and no one was left there with him. Now it happened that at one time a man arrived in that land and he was of greater wisdom and more alert than those there were before. And because he knew that once the year had passed they would do to him what they had done to others, before the year of his reign was over he secretly commanded to be made on that island where he knew they would place him a fine and well-out-fitted dwelling in which they placed all the things necessary for his entire life. And he built the dwelling place in a spot so hidden that those of that land who had given him its lordship could not find it. And he left in that island some friends well supplied and trained, so that if perchance something should be needed of the sort that might have been forgotten earlier, they should send it, so that nothing would be wanting.

"Now when the year had run its course and the people of that land took the realm away from him and placed him naked on the island, just as they had done to the others before him, because he had been shrewd and had built the dwelling place where he could live in luxury and pleasure, he went to it and lived in it most happily.

"And you, Sir Count Lucanor, if you want to be advised, take note that in the time you have to live in this world, be certain that you must abandon it, and depart naked from it, and you will not have to take from the world anything but the deeds that you have done here; and see to it that you do them in such a way that when you leave this world, you have made such a dwelling in the other world, so that when they cast you out of this world naked, you will find a good home for your eternal life. And be aware that the soul's life is not counted in years, but it endures forever and ever; for the soul is a spiritual thing and cannot decay, for it endures and remains always. And know that the good works or the evil ones that a man does in this world, God keeps them stored away so as to give from them a reward in the world to come according to one's merits.

"Now for these reasons I advise you to do such works in this world that when you must leave it you will find a fine lodging in the world where you are to live forever, and that in exchange for the holdings and the honors of this world, which are empty and perishable, you will not want to lose that which is certain and must endure forever without end. And do these good works without pride and vainglory, for even though your good works are known, they will always be hidden, so do not do them for the sake of pride and vainglory. And likewise leave here such friends, so that what you cannot carry out in your lifetime may be carried out for your life's advantage. But with these works treasured up, I consider that you ought to do all that you can do to increase your honor and your estate, and it is well for you to do it."

The count considered this a good story and as good advice and he begged God to guide him to be able to do just as Patronio said.

And Don Juan, realizing that this was a good story, had it written in this book, and composed these verses which say:

Do not exchange God's endless day
For this brief one, however gay.

. . .

This tale appeared in *Barlaam and Josaphat*, a book much utilized by Don Juan Manuel, not only in his *Conde Lucanor*, but also in the *Libro de los estados*. Most probably Don Juan simply used one of the Spanish versions. Thompson-Keller: J. 711.3; Devoto: pp. 459-61; Ayerbe-Chaux: pp. 169-71.

50. What Happened to Saladin and a Lady, the Wife of a Knight Who Was His Vassal

Count Lucanor was talking one day with Patronio in this way: "Patronio, I know of a certainty that you have such wisdom that no one, of all men now on earth, could give so good a reply to anything asked as you. Therefore, I beg you to tell me what is the best quality a man may have. And I ask you this because I clearly understand that a man needs many things to enable him to do what is best and to know how to do it, since for a man to understand something and not perform it well, will not, I think, add to his reputation. And since there are so many things, I should like to know at least one which I may remember in order to carry it out."

"Sir Count," said Patronio, "on account of your politeness, you praise me highly, and you say especially that I have great knowledge. And, Sir Count, I fear you are deceived in this. You may well believe that there is nothing on earth in which a man may be so quickly and so badly deceived as in knowing men's ways and what knowledge they have. And to understand what a man has in him, he must show by good works what he does for God and the world, for many appear to do good works and yet are not good, since their sole interest is in what people will think of them. Believe me, this kindness costs them dear because, for a single good work which lasts a day, they will suffer much and endlessly. And others do good works in God's service and do not consider the world's service, and although these have chosen the better part, which can never be taken from them, neither they nor the others keep to the paths which are God's and the world's. And to keep to both, great works as well as great understanding are needful, for it is as difficult to do as to thrust one's hand into fire and not feel its heat; but with God's help, and helping oneself, a man can do anything, for there have been many good kings and other saintly men, because they served God and the world.

"Likewise, in order to know which men have good understanding, much is required, since many men speak of good words of wisdom yet do not accomplish the good works expected of them, while others manage their deeds quite well and do not know, or do not wish to know, or cannot know, how to utter three words correctly; still others speak well enough and do very good works, but they have bad intentions, and no matter if they do good works for themselves, they do evil ones for other people. And of such as these, the Scripture says that they are like the madman who grasps a sword in his hand, or like the wicked prince who has great power. But for you and all men to understand who is good in God's sight and the world's, and who is of good understanding, and who speaks well, and who has good intentions, and to make a proper choice, you should judge no one save through the works he accomplishes over a long period of time, and not over a short period; you can also see whether he improves his affairs or damages them, for in these two ways one can observe everything that has been said above. And all these teachings I have now given you, so that you will praise me and my wit, and you may be certain that, once you have considered them all, you will praise me less. And as for what you asked, as to what is the best thing that one can have in his character, so that you may know the truth, I should like you to know what happened to Saladin with a very noble lady, the wife of one of his vassal knights."

And the count asked him what had happened.

"Sir Count," said Patronio, "Saladin was sultan of Babylon and always had a vast multitude of followers in his company. And one day, because not everyone could lodge with him, he took lodgings in a knight's house. Now when the knight saw his great master lodged with him, he did all he could to please him, and his wife and sons and daughters waited upon him in every way. And the devil, who always labors to cause men to do the most reprehensible deeds, put the idea into Saladin's head to forget all about his duty and to have an illicit love affair with that lady.

"Now his love was so great that he even took counsel with an evil adviser as to how to accomplish his desire. And you must know that we all should beg God to keep our masters from the desire to do evil, for if the master desires it, you may be certain that there will never be lacking someone to advise him and help him to do it. And so it happened to Saladin; for immediately he found someone to advise him and to help him to carry out his wishes. And the evil counselor advised him to summon the husband and to do fine things for him, to make him the leader of a large company, and to send him off in his service without delay to a distant land, and while he was away Saladin would be able to carry out his desire.

"Now once the knight had departed, believing himself to be a most fortunate man and very close to his sovereign, Saladin went to his house. And when the good lady realized that he was there, because he had so highly favored her husband, she received him well and honored him. And she and her household did everything they could to please him. And after the table was cleared and Saladin had gone to his room, he sent for the lady. And she, thinking he had sent for her for another purpose, went to him. Then Saladin told her that he loved her deeply. And when she heard this she understood it perfectly, but she pretended that she did not; and she expressed the hope that God would give him a good life and would make him very happy, as God well knew that she valued his life and would always pray that he receive what was fitting, since he was her master, and especially on account of all that he had done for her and her husband.

"Then Saladin said that, all that aside, he loved her more than any other woman. And she thanked him, still pretending that she did not understand his intentions. But why should I make a long story of it? Saladin insisted that he loved her, and when the good lady heard it, because she was very chaste and very intelligent, she replied as follows: 'Sire, even though I am just an ordinary woman, I know that love is not in man's control, but man is under its control. And well do I know that if you love me as much as you say, you mean what you say, but even though I understand this perfectly, I understand something else too: when men, and especially rulers, take a fancy to some woman, they tell her they will do anything she wishes. But once she is undone and scorned they esteem her little, as is only right, and she is left in a predicament. And I, Sire, am afraid this will happen to me.'

"And Saladin began to deny it, promising her that he would do everything to keep her in high esteem. But when Saladin said this the good lady answered that if he would promise to do as she asked, rather than to take her by force or deceit, then once he had done so, she would let him do with her as he wished. But Saladin said he was afraid that she would require him to say no more about the matter. But then she told him that she would not require that nor anything else that he could not reasonably do. So Saladin promised. And the good lady kissed his hand and foot and told him that what she wanted was for him to tell her what was the finest quality a man could have, the mother and chief of all virtues. And when Saladin heard this he began to have qualms that he might not be able to find an answer for the lady. But because he had promised not to use force nor seduction until he had kept his promise, he told her that he wanted to think about it. And she agreed that at any time, whatever his answer, she would fulfill his desires. And there their pact stood.

"Now Saladin went about among his people, and as though he were dealing with something else entirely, he asked all his advisers about it. And some said that the best thing that a man could have was a noble soul. Others told him that that was well enough for the world to come, but that merely to be a noble soul was not enough for this world. Others told him the best thing was loyalty. Others said that although being loyal was a fine quality, one could be loyal and still be a coward, or stingy, or dull, or ill-mannered, and therefore more was needed than just loyalty. And so they talked about all the qualities, but they could not find the answer that Saladin needed.

"When Saladin found that no one in all the land could answer his question, he took two bards with him, and in order to travel more easily he went incognito. He crossed the sea and went to the papal court where all the Christians gather. And though he asked his question throughout that land, he never found an answer. Then he went to the residence of the king of France and to all the other kings, yet he got no answer from them. And he tarried so long about the matter that he regretted what he had undertaken. But by then he was not seeking, on the lady's account, so much as because as a good man he believed it would be a fault on his part if he failed to find out what he started to; for doubtless a great man commits a grave error if he abandons what he has once begun, unless the matter be evil or sinful. But if on account of fear or hardship he abandons it, the fault is inexcusable. And therefore, Saladin did not wish to leave off seeking what he had left his realm to learn.

"Now it came about that one day, as he was traveling along with his bards, he ran into a squire returning from the hunt, and he had killed a stag. And the squire had only recently gotten married. And he had an old father who had been the finest knight in the kingdom. And because of his great age he could not see and could not leave home, but he had so good and so knowledgeable a mind that old age denied him no understanding. And the squire, returning so happily from hunting, asked the men who they were. And they told him they were bards. And when he heard this he was delighted, and said that he was going home happy from the hunt and to make his joy complete, as they were good bards, they should spend the night at his home.

"They told him they were in a great hurry, since they had left home a long time ago in search of an answer that they had been unable to find, and they were anxious to get home, and for this reason they could not stay with him that night. Now the squire was so insistent that perforce they told what it was they needed to know. When the squire heard this he said that if his father could not give the answer no one could, and he told them what manner of man his father was. And when Saladin, whom the squire thought was a bard, heard this, he was overjoyed. And they went home with the squire. And when they arrived at his father's house, the squire told him how pleased he was with the hunt and that he was even more joyful because he had brought the bards home. And he told his father what they were asking about, and begged him to tell them what he knew about it, because he had told them that since they had not found anyone to give them satisfaction, if his father could not do so, no one could.

"Now when the old knight heard this, he knew that the man asking the question was no mere bard, so he told his son that after they had dined he would answer the question. And the squire told Saladin, whom he still regarded as a bard, and Saladin was pleased. But time passed slowly because he had to wait until after dinner. Then after the tablecloth had been removed and the bards had performed, the old knight, who had been told that they were asking a question, and had found no one to answer it, said to ask him the question and then he would tell them what he thought.

"Then Saladin, dressed as a bard, put his question: what was the best quality a man could possess, the mother and chief of all virtues? And when the old knight heard the words he understood them exactly, and also from the question he recognized Saladin, for he had been a long time in his house and had received much favor and honor from him. So he said: 'Friend, my first answer to you is that surely no bards like you have ever entered my house before today. And you must know that if I were to behave properly, I should acknowledge the many kindnesses I have had from you; but of this I shall say nothing until I talk with you privately, so that no one may know your affairs. But as to the question you ask, I say that the best quality a man can have, the one which is the mother and chief of all virtues, is shame, for because of shame a man endures death, which is the most serious thing there is, and through shame a man avoids doing anything which does not seem right, no matter how much he desires to do it. And so in shame all virtues have their beginning and end, and shamelessness is the source of all evil acts.'

"Now when Saladin heard this he knew that it was just as the knight had said. And since he knew he had found the answer to his question, he was overjoyed, and they took their leave of the knight and the squire whose guests they had been. But before he left the house he talked with the old knight and asked him how he knew that he was Saladin, and he told him how many kindnesses he had received from him. Then he and his son did what they could for him, but in such a way that it would not be noticed. And when they had finished, Saladin made ready to go home as quickly as possible.

"Now when he reached his own country the people were happy and celebrated his return. And when the celebration was over, Saladin went to the home of the noble lady who had asked the question.

"As soon as she learned that Saladin had come, she received him well and was courteous as could be. And when he had eaten and gone to his room, he sent for the lady and she came to him. Then Saladin told her how hard he had tried to find the true answer to her question and that he had found it, and since he could answer, as he had promised, that she should carry out her promise. And she asked him to please keep his promise and to tell her the answer to her question, but that if it was as complete an answer as he thought, then she would willingly fulfill her promise. Saladin told her that he was pleased with what she said, and he told her the answer to her question, to wit, what was the best quality a man could have, the mother and chief of all virtues, and that quality was shame.

"When the good lady heard this reply she was joyful and said: 'Sire, now I know that you are speaking the truth and you have done all that you promised. Now I beseech you for mercy's sake to tell me, since a good king should tell the truth, whether you believe that there is a better man than you on earth.'

"And Saladin told her, even though it embarrassed him to say it, since he had to be truthful as a king should be, that he believed himself to be the best man of all and that no one was better than he. And when the good lady heard this, she fell to the floor at his feet and said as she wept bitterly: 'Sire, you have spoken two very profound truths: one, that you are the best man on earth; the other, that shame is the best quality a man can have. And, Sire, since you know this, and since you are the best man on earth, I beseech you to display the best quality in the world, which is shame, and be ashamed of what you have asked of me.'

"Now when Saladin heard all that she said and understood how the good lady, through her virtue and intelligence, had known how to keep him from such a great sin, he thanked God for it. And though he had loved her more than any other love, he loved her even more henceforth with the pure and true love of the kind that a good and loyal ruler should have for all his people. And especially because of his love for her, he sent for her husband and showered such honors and benefits upon them and all their people that they were the happiest of all their neighbors. And all this good came about through the virtue of that good lady, because she had gotten Saladin to discover that a man's best quality is shame, and that it is the mother and chief of all virtues.

"And since you, Sir Count Lucanor, ask me what is the best virtue that a man may have, I tell you that it is shame; for shame makes a man strong and generous and loyal and well mannered and of good habits, and makes him do whatever good things he does. For well you may believe that a man does more things out of shame than out of the desire he has to do them; and likewise through shame a man refrains from doing all the untoward things which his will urges him to do. Therefore, how good it is for one to feel shame at doing what he should not, and at refraining from doing what he ought to do! What a wicked, harmful, and ugly thing it is when one loses his sense of shame!

"You must know that a man errs greatly who commits a shameful act and believes that since he does it secretly, he need feel no shame. For rest assured that there is nothing, however secret, that will not be known sooner or later. And even though there may be no shame at the moment the act is committed, a man should understand that it will be shameful once it is known. And even if one is not ashamed of it, one should be ashamed of himself when he understands the shameful thing that he does. And although he does not consider all this, he should realize how devoid of virtue he is, since he knows that if a young man were to see what he was doing he would stop it for shame's sake. And if he does not stop, and is not ashamed, and not afraid, God, who sees and knows all, will surely mete out to him the punishment that he deserves.

"And now, Sir Count Lucanor, I have answered for you the question which you asked me, and with this reply I have answered all fifty of the questions that you have asked. And you have been so long here that I am sure your companions are annoyed by it, especially those who have no desire to hear or learn what can be of great profit to them. For it is with them as with pack animals loaded with gold, which feel the weight they carry on their backs, yet do not profit from its value. And they take umbrage at what they hear and do not take advantage of the profitable and good things they hear. Therefore, I tell you that for these reasons on the one hand, and on the other, for the effort I have made in the other answers which I have given, I do not wish to answer any further questions which you may ask, for with this exemplary tale, and with the one that is to follow, I want to end this book."

And the count regarded this as a good exemplary tale, and in view of what Patronio had said about not wanting the count to ask any more questions, it was agreed that this should depend on how matters developed.

And because Don Juan considered this tale very good he had it written down in this book and composed the following verses:

> *Shame fights evil, as it should,*
> *And makes it easy to do good.*

. . .

Saladin, like his noble enemy Richard Coeur de Lion, fascinated medieval man. Many legends circulated about him, as did tales which had no true relationship with him or his life. The motif assembled by Don Juan Manuel for this long story could have come from many sources, although it is possible that he found the entire account in some Arabic, Latin, or Spanish chronicle; but it is more likely that he had the story from the Moors. Thompson-Keller: J. 81, T. 320.4, K. 1388, J. 152; Devoto: pp. 461-62; Ayerbe-Chaux: pp. 124-37.

51. Untitled [What Happened to a Christian King Who Was Very Powerful and Haughty]

Again Count Lucanor talked with Patronio, his counselor, as follows: "Patronio, many people tell me that one of the ways that a man gains favor with God is by being humble; others say the humble are little esteemed by others and are regarded as weak and of little courage, and that it is fitting and profitable for a great lord to be haughty. And because I know that no one understands better than you what a great lord ought to do, I ask you to advise me which of these two manners is better for me or which way I must act at first."

"Sir Count," said Patronio, "for you to understand what in this matter is best and most fitting to do, I would very much like you to know what happened to a Christian king who was most powerful and haughty."

The count asked him to tell him how it had been.

"Sir Count," said Patronio, "in a land whose name I forget lived a very youthful, very wealthy, and very powerful king, haughty to a remarkable degree. Indeed, to such a point did his haughtiness go that once when he was listening to the canticle of Holy Mary which runs *Magnificat anima mea dominum*, he heard a verse which goes *Deposuit potentes de sede et exaltavit humiles*, which means 'Our Lord God removed and humiliated the haughty rulers from their high station and elevated the humble.'

"Now when he heard this it greatly upset him, and he commanded that throughout his realm this verse be expunged from books. In its place they were to write: *Et exaltavit potentes in sede et humiles posuit in tierra*, which means 'God elevated the thrones of the haughty rulers and cast down the humble.'

"This greatly displeased God, for it was very much the opposite of what Holy Mary had said in the canticle; for when she saw that she was the mother of the Son of God whom she had conceived and would bring forth, remaining ever-virgin and free from sin, and that she was Queen of Heaven and of Earth, she said about herself, praising above all her virtues, *Quia respexit humilitatem ancille sue, ecce enim ex hoc benedictam me dicent omnes generaciones*, which means 'Because my Lord God beheld humility in me, His handmaiden, therefore all people will call me blessed.'

"And so it was that never before or afterward could any other woman be blessed, for through her virtues, and especially through her exceeding humility, she deserved to be Mother of God and Queen of Heaven and Earth and the Lady set above the choirs of angels. But something quite the opposite of this befell the haughty king, for one day he took a notion to go to the bath, and he went there proudly with his retinue. And while he was bathing our Lord God sent an angel to the bath, who through the power and the will of God was the likeness of this king. And he came out of the bath and clothed himself in the king's raiment, and all the people accompanied him to the palace. And he left at the bathhouse door some vile and very ragged garments, like those of the beggars who cry at gateways for alms.

"Now the king, who was in the bath, knew nothing of this, and when he thought it was time to get out of the bath, he called for his chamberlains and his retinue. But no matter how much he called, no one responded, since all had gone away, believing that they were with the king.

"When he saw that no one was answering him, he flew into an appalling rage and began to swear that he would have a cruel death meted out to all of them. And considering himself badly mocked, he came out of the bath naked, thinking to find some of his people, but he found no one. He began to look all through the bathhouse and found not a soul with whom he could speak.

"And wandering about thus, much disturbed and not knowing what to do, he saw some wretched and ragged garments in a corner, and he thought he would put them on and go disguised to his house, where he would exact a cruel vengeance upon all those who had heaped mockery upon him. Therefore, he donned the garments and walked unrecognized to the palace. And when he arrived he saw one of the gatekeepers whom he knew very well, and he was the private doorkeeper and one of those who had been with him at the bath; and he called to him under his breath and told him quietly to open the door and let him in very secretly, so that no one would realize how embarrassed he was.

"The doorkeeper had a very fine sword hanging from his neck and a great mace in his hand, and he asked him who he was to say such things. And the king said: 'Ah, traitor! Isn't the shame great enough which you and the others heaped upon me, leaving me by myself in the bath to come here as embarrassed as I am? Aren't you So-and-So, and don't you recognize me, since I am the king, your master, whom you abandoned in the bath? Open the door before someone who knows me comes along, for if you don't, rest assured that I shall put you to death most cruelly!'

"And the doorkeeper replied: 'Madman! Wretch! What are you talking about? Get out of here while you can and say no more crazy things, for if you don't, I will beat you for the madman you are! The king returned from the bath only a short while ago and we all returned with him, and he has dined and gone to bed. So be careful to make no noise and wake him up!'

"When the king heard this, believing that the man was saying it to mock him, he began to rant and rave with fury and hatred, and he rushed at the doorkeeper and tried to pull his hair. When the gatekeeper saw this he did not want to strike him with the mace, but he hit him hard with its handle so that blood ran from several places. And when the king saw that he was hurt and that the gatekeeper had a good sword and mace and that he himself had nothing to wound him with nor even with which to defend himself, thinking that the gatekeeper had gone mad and that if he said anything else to him he would kill him, he thought he would go to the house of the majordomo to hide until he was properly dressed. And he thought that he would avenge himself on the traitors who had so shamed him.

"Now when he reached the majordomo's house, if harm had come to him from the gatekeeper, worse befell him there. Then he went as secretly as possible to the dwelling of the queen, his wife, believing that surely all this misfortune had come upon him because people did not recognize him. And he believed that doubtless, even though everyone else failed to recognize him, the queen, his wife, would not fail to do so.

"Now as soon as he came before her and told her what they had done to him and that he was the king, the queen was fearful that if the man in the house whom she thought was king should discover another man in the house, he would be very angry. Therefore, she ordered the madman, who was speaking so wildly, beaten badly and thrown out of the house. The unfortunate king, when he considered how unhappy he was, did not know what to do and he went, beaten and broken, to a hostel and stayed there many days. And when he got hungry, he went begging from door to door, and people mocked him, since he was, as king of that land, going about so miserably. And so many said it so many times, and in so many places, that he himself decided he was crazy and that because he was mad he believed himself to be king.

"Now in this way a long time passed, with all the people who had known him believing him ill of a madness which befell many people who believe themselves to be something which they are not. And while the king was in such a dire plight, the goodness and holiness of God, which always desires the good of sinners and leads them along paths on which they can be saved no matter how great their sins, worked in such a way that that wretch of a king, who had fallen into such great destitution and disgrace through pride, began to think that the evil which had befallen him was due to his sinfulness and to the great haughtiness which he had; and he believed specifically that it was on account of the verses which he had changed in the canticle of Holy Mary through pride and madness. And once he believed this he began to feel deep sorrow and such great repentance in his heart that no one could describe it; and he was in such a state that he grieved more, indeed, about the sins he had committed against our Lord than about the realm he had lost; and he saw how bad off his body was, and therefore he did nothing except weep and mistreat himself and ask mercy from our Lord God to pardon his sins, so that his soul might be pardoned. And his grief over his sins was so great that it did not even occur to him to ask God in his mercy to return him to his kingdom or to his honor; but he saw little worth in that and asked nothing except to be pardoned for his sins and to be able to save his soul.

"And well may you believe, Sir Count, that I do not say that all those do wrong who make pilgrimages and fast, give alms, and offer prayers, and do other good works, so that God will protect them or improve their health, their honor, or their earthly goods. But I do say that if they do all these things with hypocrisy or pretense to be pardoned for their sins or to have God's grace, which is earned through good works, without hypocrisy and without pretense, it would be better; and doubtless they would have their sins pardoned and would have God's grace, for what God most desires from a sinner is a contrite and humble heart and a good and righteous intention.

"Then, by the grace of God, the king repented of his sin, and God recognized his deep repentance and his good intention and pardoned him. And because God's will is so strong that it cannot be measured, He pardoned not only all the sins of that sinful king, but He even gave him back his kingdom and his honor in a fashion more complete than before, and he did so in this way. The angel who occupied the king's place and had his form, called to a gatekeeper and said: 'They tell me that a madman, who says that he is king of this land, is wandering about and saying quite mad things. In God's name, who is he and what is he saying?'

"Now it so came about that this gatekeeper was the very one who had hit the king on the day that he came naked from the bath. And since the angel, whom he thought was king, asked him about all the things that had transpired with that madman, he told him how people were laughing and teasing him to hear the mad things he would say. And when the gatekeeper told the angel this, he ordered him to call the madman and fetch him. And when the king who seemed mad came before the angel who was in his place, he took him aside and said: 'Friend, they tell me that you say you were the king of this land and that you lost it, I do not know by what bad luck or from what cause. I beg you, in the name of the faith you have in God, to tell me how you think it all stands. Conceal nothing from me, and I promise you, in good faith, that no harm will come to you.'

"When the wretched king, who was held as a madman and a wretch, heard these things said by the one whom he now thought was the king, he knew not what to reply. On the one hand he feared they would interrogate him and trick an answer from him, and then if he said he was king they would hurt him and make him more unhappy than he was; and therefore he began to weep bitterly and he spoke like a man very disturbed.

" 'Sire, I do not know how to answer, but since I see how that death would be as good as life—and God knows I have no desire for wealth or the honors of this world—I do not wish to hide anything of what I think in my own heart. I say to you, Sire, that I see that I am mad, and all men so consider me, and such deeds do they do to me that for a long time I have been in this condition. And though some may err, it cannot be unless I am crazy that all people, the good and the bad, the great and the small, those of little or great understanding, consider me as a madman; but even though I see this and understand that it is so, certainly my understanding and my belief is that I used to be king of this land and that I lost the kingdom and God's grace, and very justly on account of my sins, and especially on account of the great pride I had within me.'

"And then he related with deep sorrow and tears all that had happened to him, including the verses which he had had changed and his other sins. And since the angel, whom God had sent to assume his form and to act as king, understood that he was grieved more for the sins into which he had fallen than for the realm and the honor he had lost, he spoke to him thus by God's command:

" 'Friend, I see that you are telling the truth in everything, for you *were* the king of this land. And our Lord God took it from you for the very reasons you have given, and He sent me, who am His angel, to take your form and your place. And since God's pity is complete and wants nothing from the sinner except genuine repentance, this fact has truly revealed two reasons for true repentance: the first is to repent so as never to return to that sin; and the other to repent without pretense. And because our Lord God has understood that your repentance is such, He has pardoned you and has commanded me to return you to your own form and leave the kingdom to you. And I beg you and counsel you among all sins to guard yourself from the sin of pride, for know that of all the sins into which men fall by nature, this is the one which God abhors the most, for it is truly against God and His authority, and it is always ready to ruin the soul. And be certain that there never was a land, or a family, or an estate, or a person where this sin ruled which was not destroyed and cast down.'

"When the mad king heard the angel say these words, he fell down before him weeping violently, believed all that he said, and adored him out of reverence for God, whose messenger the angel was; and he besought him not to leave him until all the people were assembled, in order to make known this great miracle which our Lord had wrought. And the angel did so.

"Now when all were gathered together, the king spoke and told how the entire matter had taken place. And the angel, by God's will, made himself manifest to all and told everything. Then the king made all the amends he could to our Lord God, and among other things he commanded in memory of this that throughout his realm forever that verse should be inscribed in letters of gold. And I have heard it said that it is perpetuated in that land.

"And when all was carried out the angel sent by God departed, and the king remained happy and blessed with his people. And from that time forward the king was virtuous in God's service and in the service of his people, and he did many good deeds through which he had great fame in this world, and he deserved the glory in paradise which God pleases to give us through His grace.

"And you, Sir Count Lucanor, if you wish to have God's grace and great repute in the world, do good works and let them be well done and free from pretense and hypocrisy; and among all other things avoid pride and be humble without deceit and guile; but let humility always protect your state of being so that you may remain humble, but not humiliated. And let the proud and haughty never find mock humility in you, but let them always find in you the humility of the life that is good and filled with pious acts."

This advice greatly pleased the count and he prayed God to help him to carry out his obligations.

And because Don Juan was exceedingly pleased with this exemplary tale he had it put in his book and wrote these verses:

> *God uplifts the humble crowd,*
> *And humbles soon the great and proud.*

.   .   .

The origin may be the *Gesta Romanorum*, Number 59, although since Eastern sources are also likely, Don Juan might have found his source in Arabic texts. Thompson-Keller: L. 411; Devoto: pp. 462-64.

Bibliographical Essay

What follows is a brief working bibliography. If one wishes to find most of what has been written about Don Juan Manuel and his works—that is, most editions, translations, articles, reviews, motif studies, etc.—he should consult two basic books: the remarkably complete *Introducción al estudio de Don Juan Manuel y en particular 'El Conde Lucanor,'* by Daniel Devoto (Madrid: Editorial Castalia, 1952) which contains 505 pages of valuable information and is a critical bibliography; and the lengthy work of Reinaldo Ayerbe-Chaux, *El Conde Lucanor—Materia tradicional y originalidad creadora* (Madrid: José Porrúa, 1975), which studies sources, parallels, structure of the fables, and other literary matters.

H. Tracy Sturcken in his *Don Juan* (New York: Twayne Publishers, Inc., 1974) mentions that over forty school editions of *El Conde Lucanor* have been published in this century. His brief bibliography is up-to-date, containing listings of the best editions.

Since so many editions of *El Conde Lucanor* have been printed, only a few can be listed here, along with a few of the editions of Don Juan Manuel's other works. The edition of Pascual de Gayangos in *Escritores en prosa antes del siglo XV* in the always-in-print *Biblioteca de Autores Españoles*, while not a critical edition and often inaccurate, is nonetheless a valuable text. Included in it are the texts of *El Conde Lucanor*, listed as *El libro de Patronio;* the *Libro del caballero et del escudero;* the *Libro de las armas;* the *Libro infinido* and its continuation, the *Libro de las maneras del amor*, not generally considered as a separate book; the *Libro de los estados* and what is generally regarded as a part of it, the *Libro de los fraires predicadores;* the *Tractado en que se pruebe por razon que Santa Maria esta en cuerpo et en alma en Paraiso.* Some valuable editions of *El Conde Lucanor* are *El libro de Patronio por otro nombre El Conde Lucanor*, edited by Eugenio Krapf (Vigo:

Librería de E. Krapf, 1898), which is based upon not only the 1642 text of Argote de Molina, but also, and to a greater extent, upon the text of Gayangos; Krapf's *El libro de Patronio o El Conde Lucanor* (Vigo: Librería de E. Krapf, 1902) which is based upon the manuscript in the library of Count Puñonrostro; *El libro de los enxienplos del Conde Lucanor et de Patronio*, edited in 1900 by Adolf Birch-Hirschfeld after the death of Hermann Knust, is still considered a valuable text with excellent notes; *El Conde Lucanor*, edited by Eduardo Juliá (Madrid: V. Suárez, 1933), contains a long and scholarly introduction; *El Conde Lucanor*, edited by Pedro Enríquez Ureña (Buenos Aires: Editorial Losada, 1939), though a standard classroom text, is nonetheless sound; one modernized edition is worthy of mention—*El Conde Lucanor*, edited by Juan Loveluck (Santiago, Chile: Editorial Universitaria, 1956), which contains a fair amount of critical study; the best critical edition is that of José Manuel Blecua, *El Conde Lucanor* (Madrid: Editorial Castalia, 1969, and in subsequent editions) which is apparently to be kept in print by Editorial Castalia.

Some of Don Juan Manuel's other works have appeared in other editions than the anthology of Gayangos in the *Biblioteca de Autores Españole:* for example, *Obras de Don Juan Manuel*, edited by José María Castro y Calvo and Martín de Riquer (Barcelona: Consejo Superior de Investigaciones Científicas, 1955); but so far only one volume has appeared which contains the *Prologo General*, the *Libro del cavallero et del escudero*, the *Libro de las armas*, and the *Libro infinido*. The *Crónica abreviada* has been edited by Raymond L. and Mildred B. Grismer (Minneapolis: Burgess, 1958) and published in mimeographed form; as far back as 1880 Gottfried Baist (Halle) published an edition of *El libro de la caza* with a most excellent and clear introduction. It is no wonder that José María Castro y Calvo based his own edition, *Libro de la caza* (Barcelona: Consejo Superior de Investigaciones Científicas, 1947) upon that of Baist. Castro y Calvo published an edition of *El libro de los estados* (Barcelona: Consejo Superior de Investigaciones Científicas, 1968).

Barlaam e Josafat. Lauchert, Friederich, ed. "La estoria del rey Anemur e de Iosaphat e de Barlaam." *Romanische Forschungen* 7 (1893): 33-402. This old edition is to date the most reliable.

Caballero Cifar. Wagner, Charles Philip, ed. *El libro del Cauallero Zifar*. Ann Arbor, Mich.: University of Michigan Press, 1929.

Calila e Digna. Gayangos, Pascual de, ed. *Calila e Dymna* in *Biblioteca de Autores Españoles*, vol. 51. Madrid: Real Academia Española, 1952. Keller, John E. and Linker, Robert W., eds. *El libro de Calila e Digna*. Madrid: Consejo Superior de Investigaciones Científicas, 1957.

Castigos e documentos. Rey, Agapito, ed. *Castigos e documentos para bien vivir del rey don Sancho*, vol. 4. Bloomington, Ind.: Indiana University Press, 1952. Gayangos, Pascual de, ed. *Castigos e documentos del rey don Sancho* in *Biblioteca de Autores Españoles*, vol. 5. Madrid: Real Academia Española, 1952.

Corbacho. Simpson, Lesley Byrd, ed. *El Arcipreste de Talavera o sea el Corbacho*. Berkeley, Cal.: University of California Press, 1939. González Muela, J., ed. *Alfonso Martínez de Toledo, Arcipreste de Talavera o Corbacho*. Madrid: Editorial Castalia, 1970. Translation: Simpson, Lesley Byrd, trans. *Little Sermons on Sin, the Archpriest of Talavera*. Berkeley, Cal.: University of California Press, 1959.

Disciplina Clericalis. Hilka, Alfons and Söderjelm, eds. *Petri Alfonsi Disciplina Clericalis* in *Actas Societatis Fennicae*, no. 28. Helsinki: Carl Winter, 1911. Translation: Jones, Joseph R. and Keller, John E., trans. *The Scholar's Guide, A Translation of the Twelfth-Century Disciplina Clericalis of Pedro Alfonso*. Toronto: Pontifical Institute of Mediaeval Studies, 1969.

Engaños. Bonilla y San Martin, Adolfo, ed. *Libro de los engaños e los asayamientos de las mugeres*. Madrid: Librería de M. Murillo, 1904. Keller, John E., ed. *El libro de los engaños* in *University of North Carolina Studies in the Romance Languages and Literatures*, vol. 20. Chapel Hill: University of North Carolina Press, 1959.

Exenplos por a.b.c. Gayangos, Pascual de, ed. *El libro de los enxemplos* in *Biblioteca de Autores Españoles*, vol. 51. Madrid: Real Academia Española, 1952, pp. 443-542. Morel-Fatio, F., ed. *El libro de los exenplos por a.b.c.*, *Romania* 7 (1878): 481-526. Keller, John E., ed. *El libro de los exenplos por a.b.c.* Madrid: Consejo Superior de Investigaciones Científicas, 1961.

Gatos. Northup, George Tyler, ed. *"El libro de los gatos*, a Text with Introduction and Notes," *Modern Philology* 5 (1908): 477-554. Keller, John E., ed. *El libro de los gatos*. Madrid: Consejo Superior de Investigaciones Científicas, 1958.

BOOKS AND ARTICLES PERTINENT TO THE STUDY OF DON JUAN MANUEL

Baibros de Ballesteros, Mercedes. *El Príncipe Don Juan Manuel y su condición de escritor*. Madrid: Publicaciones del Instituto España, 1945.

Burke, James F. *History and Vision: the Figural Structure of the "Libro del Cavallero Zifar."* London: Tamesis Books Limited, 1972.

Doddis Miranda, Antonio and Sepúlveda Durán, Germán, eds. *Estudios sobre don Juan Manuel*. 2 vols. Santiago, Chile: Edición Universitaria, 1957.

Giménez Soler, Andrés. *Don Juan Manuel. Bibliografía y estudio crítico*. Saragossa: Academia Española, 1932.

Huerta Tejadas, Felix. "Gramática y vocabulario de las obras de Don Juan Manuel." Ph.D. dissertation, University of Madrid, 1957.

Keller, John E. *Motif-Index of Mediaeval Spanish Exempla*. Knoxville: University of Tennessee Press, 1949.

———. "A Re-examination of Don Juan Manuel's Narrative Technique: *La mujer brava*," *Hispania* 58, no. 1 (March, 1975): 45-51.

———. "From Masterpiece to Résumé: Don Juan Manuel's Misuse of a Source." In *Estudios literarios de Hispanistas norteamericanos dedicados a Helmut Hatzfeld con motivo de su 80 aniversario*, edited by Criado de Val. Madrid: Ediciones HISPAM, 1975, pp. 41-50.

Kinkade, Richard P. *Los lucidarios españoles*. Madrid: Editorial Gredos, 1968.

———. "Sancho IV: Puente literario entre Alfonso el Sabio y Juan Manuel." *PMLA* 87 (1972): 1039-51.

Lida de Malkiel, María Rosa. "Tres notas sobre Don Juan Manuel," *Romance Philology* 4 (1950-51): 155-94.

Macpherson, Ian. "Dios y el mundo—the Didacticism of *El Conde Lucanor*," *Romanca Philology* 24 (1970): 26-38.

Marín, Diego. "El elemento oriental en Don Juan Manuel: síntesis y revaluación," *Comparative Literature* 7 (1955): 1-14.

Nykl, Aloisius R. "Arabic Phrases in El Conde Lucanor," *Hispanic Review* 10 (1942): 12-17.

Ruffini, Mario. "Les Sources de Don Juan Manuel." Translated by Mlle. Mund. *Les Lettres Romaines* 7 (1953): 27-49.

Scholberg, Kenneth R. "Sobre el estilo del *Conde Lucanor*," *Kentucky Romance Quarterly* 10 (1963): 198-203.

Steiger, Arnold. "El Conde Lucanor," *Clavileño* 4 (1953): 1-8.

Sturm, Harlan G. "The *Conde Lucanor*: the First *Exemplo*," *Modern Language Notes* 84 (1969): 286-92.

———. "Author and Authority in *El Conde Lucanor*," *Hispanófila* 52 (1974): 1-9.

Thompson, Stith. *Motif-Index of Folk Literature*. Enl. and rev. ed. 6 vols. Bloomington: Indiana University Press, 1955-58.

Only two translations of *El Conde Lucanor* into English exist previous to our own. The first is that of James York entitled *Count Lucanor, or Fifty Pleasant Stories of Patronio* (Westminister: B. M. Pickering, 1868). York did not translate from the Spanish, which he did not know well, but from the French translation of Puybusque; this occasioned certain concepts not found in the original work. The second translation, an adaptation of York's destined for children and reviewed in the *New York Times Book Review* for November 8, 1970, obviously had to suppress certain of the more violent and unrefined concepts found in the medieval work.

CPSIA information can be obtained at www.ICGtesting.com
Printed in the USA
BVOW04s0025100816

458488BV00001B/6/P